CW01648846

£1.29

CITRON
PRESS

SAM **NORTH**

Sam North M.A. is a lecturer in Creative Writing at the University of Lincolnshire and Humberside's HND in Media Production at the Grimsby Campus. He has had four novels published previously.

CITRON
PRESS

Fresh ideas from

NEW AUTHORS
CO-OPERATIVE

Published by Citron Press
Connors Corp. Ltd., Suite 155, Business Design Centre,
52 Upper Street, Islington Green, London N1 0QH, Great Britain
www.citronpress.co.uk

This Book is a Work of Fiction. Names Characters, Places and Incidents are either products of the author's imagination or are used fictitiously. Any resemblance to actual events or locales or persons, living or dead, is entirely coincidental.

ISBN 0754400042

Printed and bound in Great Britain by Esparto Digital Ltd, Slack Lane, Derby.

A copy of this book is held at the British Library.

GOING INDIGO

SAM **NORTH**

CHAPTER ONE

LEAVING NOWHERE

If he shut his eyes for thirty seconds more and counted them out, squeezed his eyes tight, really tight, so he could see shapes of stars floating past his eyelids, absolutely, really concentrated, maybe, just maybe, the man sat opposite him would disappear. It clearly said 'No Smoking' on the sign stuck to the window, but no one seemed to care that this horrible, shabby man, sat opposite with his cracked black leather boots and stained overcoat was poisoning the air. Oliver counted the last ten seconds out – nine, eight, seven... God, wasn't the train ever going to get there? Six...five...the man at the hospital had promised him it would be a high-speed train, not this old diesel thing that moved at the pace of a dead sheep, four, three, two...Oh God, please make the man curl up and die...one...

The Sprinter train let escape a low-throbbing snarl, then began to slow, the brakes emitting a shriek of pain. Oliver opened his eyes; the man opposite him was standing, looking for his hat. He dropped his still burning cigarette on the filthy floor where it rolled next to a paper bag and began to smoulder. Oliver watched the smoke begin to rise and the edge of the paper bag glow, fed by the breeze coming from the badly fitting door. An elbow nudged him.

'Everyone off here, Duck, it's Newark, you change here,' the woman sat next to him instructed, her voice friendly, concerned. 'Children shouldn't travel alone, didn't when I was a bairn. Too many perverts out there.' She clamped a foot on the smouldering paper bag and pointedly looked at the man who had been smoking, but he was busy pulling on his hat and missed the implied insult. Oliver looked at him more carefully. Was this what a pervert looked like? The nicotine stained fingers and nails, the cloth on his trousers worn to a shine. The man suddenly met his eyes and unexpectedly smiled at him, revealing huge brown streaked teeth. Oliver looked away, trying to hide the horror on his face. How could anyone bear to live with such teeth in their heads? It was so gross he felt like puking up on the spot. Then, for no reason at all he remembered his own teeth, the three that had unexpectedly fallen out six months before and how he'd nearly choked when he swallowed them. Double yuk. He'd cried for days. Three second-teeth and another loose. It was just luck they weren't his front teeth. The dentist told him the radiation treatment had affected his gums, the rest would be OK, he was sure of it, but nevertheless, one thing Oliver had successfully learned in hospital was...trust no one.

The diesel train came to a gradual halt at Newark station and almost immediately another train rocketed through the station on another set of tracks, buffeting the Sprinter train, almost knocking Oliver to the ground as he stood in the open doorway. From Oliver's perspective, it looked to have been doing 200 miles an hour at least. He'd felt the power, the incredible rush of air; that was a train! Not the pathetic wheezing junk he'd been sat on for the last hour. Oliver felt a surge of optimism, he was going to get on a train like that, going so fast you could hardly see it when it flashed by, and it was going to London. He knew right away that he was going to an important place, someplace where you had to get to real fast. That was what was wrong with where he'd been living all his life. It was just too slow, the bus was even slower, the trains didn't even go there, you had to catch a bus to the bloody train, it was so remote. He remembered his father complaining about living in a town that was hardly on the map. 'No one comes here, no one knows how to leave, it's a dead town for people who are too scared to be alive.'

Abruptly Oliver was jolted from behind; people were wanting to get off. This was no time to be missing his father. 'Oi, move it,' someone shouted at him. 'Get off you silly bugger.' Oliver grabbed his shoulder bag and jumped down to the platform, slipping on the wet surface and almost falling. It was only then he remembered Flop. 'Flop,' he shouted and instantly scrambled to get back on board the train again. 'Move out, mind out,' he was shouting as passengers tried to get off and weren't too keen on letting him by.

'This yours?' someone was asking him as Oliver managed to squeeze back onto the carriage. 'Is it dead?'

Oliver came up abruptly as the train guard stood before him with a large box in his hands, Oliver's cat box.

'You won't be able to take this onto the passenger compartment, y'know. It'll have to go into the baggage car. What do you want to carry a dead cat around for anyway?'

Oliver's heart had already stopped. Flop was dead? How could this be? Flop dead? His only friend. Flop had seen him through everything. He seized the cat box from the guard and although he nearly dropped it, he struggled with the box through the doorway and onto the platform below. Oliver ignored everyone as he set down the cat box and squatted down beside it to peer at his cat. Flop wasn't dead, couldn't be. He studied the ginger tom very intently, calling his name softly, 'Flop, Flop, it's me, you're alright aren't you?' Flop said nothing, but after a while of staring hard, Oliver could see his little stomach rise and fall in a regular rhythm. He could make out his little pink tongue slightly protruding out of his mouth. Flop was really zonked out. The nurse had said he'd sleep, she'd given him something in his milk that morning. She'd liked Flop; she couldn't have done anything bad to his cat, not her. There were people who had hated Flop and wanted to get rid of him, but not her. 'It's OK Flop, we're going to London, you'll wake up and you'll have a whole new life.'

A bitter chill wind swept over the whole platform. Oliver looked up and saw people picking up their cases and bags, he guessed another train was approaching. 'We have to go Flop,' he announced as he scrambled to his feet, noticing for the first time that his knees were wet now. He shouldn't have knelt on the wet ground. He hated having cold wet knees.

'Baggage car's usually in the middle,' the guard told him as he stood looking down the track, then he reached back into the train and pressed a buzzer, simultaneously closing the door after him shouting 'That cat's dead.' The Sprinter train began to pull out of the station. Oliver didn't look up, didn't wonder why it didn't wait for the other train. He swung his bag over one shoulder then bent down to pick up the cat box again. He was used to being teased; it was something he knew you had to put up with in life.

The London train was pulling in and somehow Oliver got the impression that it was impatient, as if it didn't really want to stop at such a pokey place as Newark, it only really liked to stop at big cities, but he didn't know where he got that impression from.

He lugged his cat box towards the train, his shoulder bag swaying annoyingly at his hips where something sharp was digging in at his hips. He couldn't see any sign of a baggage car. He turned to a man waiting beside him for the train to come to a complete rest. 'Is there a baggage car?' The man glanced at him and pulled a face at Oliver, making the grey moustache look something like a mouse resting above his lips. 'Other end, this is first class. Can't you read?' Oliver sighed, he didn't exactly comprehend what first class meant, but somehow he sensed that he wasn't, and the man was.

'Over here.' another passenger called out to him. Oliver saw it was the woman who'd sat next to him on the train. 'You have to get on here, it won't wait for you y'know.'

Oliver ran over towards her as she waited by the door for him. The cat box seemed to be heavier than he remembered and it didn't smell so good, obviously Flop had peed when he was put in there, he'd been so scared.

'You'll have to find the baggage car,' the woman told him. 'Leave your cat here, I'll mind the box whilst you look for it.'

Oliver was about to politely refuse the offer when someone told him it was two carriages down and Oliver nodded at the man and lugged the cat box in the direction he'd indicated. A sea of hostile faces stared at him as he struggled down the aisle, noticing that the train was already pulling out of the station. He saw no vacant seats, just a hundred eyes fixed upon him. He felt his hands and armpits getting sweaty, so many people... he kept his eyes firmly fixed on the sliding door ahead, aware that someone with a large suitcase was coming towards him. Oliver was just about to stop and start walking backwards when the man swung the suitcase up in the air, trying to place it on the overhead rack. He swore loudly when he discovered the rack was obviously too small. Oliver quickly moved past him before he lowered the case and blocked the aisle.

'Bloody animals now, they'll let anything on these trains,' he heard someone remark as he reached the sliding door. One more carriage to go. He felt his legs shaking, why were all these people so angry?

The baggage car was better, there wasn't anywhere to sit except the floor, but at least there was no one here to say where to go or what to do. He was happier now he was with Flop, even if he was a bit cold. He studied his surroundings. There were several misshapen boxes bound for France. Nancy. He didn't know where it was, but his Pa would have known, he'd been everywhere. Flop stirred, a faint bleat came from his dry mouth, whatever the Nurse had given him, it had worked almost too well. Flop was probably having nightmares Oliver leaned in, and pressed his lips to the metal cage. 'We'll be in London soon Flop, I promise. We'll have a new life. Grandma will love you, there'll be new fields, everything will be new, you'll see, we'll have a great time.'

Oliver felt the train slow down for Peterborough. He wondered if anyone would come and see him, check his ticket, but no one did. He wondered what Peterborough looked like, wondered why there wasn't a window in the baggage car, then, quite without warning, he began to think about his mother and school.

He remembered having this stabbing headache in old Stonesy's class, the Maths teacher, who had at least noticed when he'd slid unconscious under the desk. Mr Stones had quickly grabbed him and taken him to hospital himself because Oliver had looked so bad, especially when he'd begun to cough up blood. Back came the stench of the hospital, the surgeon who'd come in wearing a rugby shirt and made terrible jokes about all the blood pouring out of Oliver's nose, how later he'd shown Oliver the picture of the hole he'd made in his head and the tumour he'd cut out of it, the size of a tennis ball. Then they made him have chemotherapy and told him his hair would grow back, that he'd never have headaches again. They'd lied to him of course. They'd lied a lot. Didn't tell him about his Ma. Didn't tell him anything. He'd lain in bed, bored, unable to read because of the headaches and often having to put the pillow over his head 'cause he couldn't bear the noise of the other kids laughter and their constant talking. Then their jeers when no one came to visit him.

At first he'd thought no one had told his Ma where he was, that somehow she'd not noticed he hadn't come home, that perhaps she'd gone looking for him and there had been some sort of mix-up, they'd gotten his name wrong at the hospital desk, or confused him with someone else. After a week had passed and no one showed up and his Ma hadn't appeared, he began to fear the worst. He began having dreams about his mother lying dead at home, and his father in some prison somewhere. He awoke from sweaty nightmares, a dead scream on his lips. The other kids complained about him. But still no one told him what was going on. His Ma was weird, he knew that. He knew she got hysterical at the slightest thing, she'd just freak out if he said or did something she didn't like, then be all friendly and cuddly to try and make him forget her shrieking at him, or throwing things at him. Once she'd thrown him against a wall and he'd been bruised for a month. She hated Louth, she hated being trapped in a tiny market town where nothing ever happened.

She was always cursing his absent father, Stephan, perhaps as much as ten, twenty times a day. His Dad had been working on the local newspaper as a photographer, then, suddenly, he'd decided to go to Bosnia, become a war photographer. He'd always wanted to put together a book on the aftermath of a war, and given that his grandfather was a Croat by birth, he felt that it was his duty. This had been two years ago. The war was coming to an end then, there was supposed to be peace, even though the Serbs still were talking of burning Sarajevo down. Oliver had been ten years old. Stephan didn't really think the war would end, there would be too much bitterness. He wanted glory; he had a publisher interested in his book 'Ruins'. He was determined to bring a poet's eye to the conflict. Oliver remembered him leaving; it had been sudden, just after he'd gotten back from school one afternoon. Charlotte, his Ma had thundered at them both and locked herself in her bedroom, thrown a lot of things at the door. He remembered watching a silver alarm clock sailing through the air, towards the taxi, that had come for his father. He recalled being hugged, his father's rasping day old beard on his face, the pain of a father's kiss, wiping his mouth with embarrassment, but that's all, try as he might, he couldn't conjure up his father's face, not a single detail of his face. His mother had destroyed almost all the photographs of him that night, burned them in the garden and, most of his clothes. Oliver had managed to hide one photo, but liven in fear she would ever find it.

No one came to see him ever. Hospital was like a prison. The summer was hot and the double-glazed windows wouldn't open. As soon as he made a friend, they'd go and they wouldn't come back. Everyone said his mother had taken his illness badly, but they never said exactly what this meant, even when he asked to see her, they just ignored him and said 'You can see her soon. when she's better.' That was the only clue he'd had that she was ill.

He wrote to the address his father had given them in Bosnia, but mostly his letters arrived back covered in international postmarks marked 'return to sender', but never any actual words about the whereabouts of his father. He knew it was stupid to imagine some stranger in a foreign post-office would know, but sometimes he wished they'd write something else on the letter, 'Try this city or this place,' but they never did.

Oliver began to hate the hospital; he was worried about Flop. Who was feeding him? A month had gone by since he'd entered the hospital. He missed

Flop, had dreams about him. It took some persuading, but he made Nurse Swaine go to his house and look for Flop. She'd brought back this emaciated ginger rag with big green eyes. Flop had been locked in the empty house for a month, lived on flies and drinking water from a dripping tap. Oliver had cried for a day when he'd seen how thin and sick Flop looked, but Flop came right to him and clung on. He wasn't ever going to let Oliver leave him alone again in a hurry.

The hospital had rules, but Oliver had determination. Nurse Swaine helped him find a hiding place for Flop in the old shed in the grounds, and although Flop wasn't keen, they fed him on hospital food. Neither one of them got fat on it. Neither one of them could abide the smell of the plastic warmers they put over the food that seemed to permeate everything.

The Doctor noticed how quickly Oliver began to recover once he knew his cat was found and, sensibly, he began to encourage Oliver to play with Flop in the hospital gardens, as long as he kept his head covered. Nothing would have persuaded Oliver to remove his woolly hat, not even when one freaky day the temperature reached 90 degrees. It was his personal horror that he would be bald forever, with this big red scar on his head. He didn't appreciate it when the Doctor kept calling him 'lucky'. He didn't feel lucky. His Pa never wrote, his Ma had disappeared, his cat nearly died, they'd taken all his hair...

He remembered the day they said he could finally see his mother. She was having a 'good day', they told him. Standing in the doorway of the psychiatric ward he'd seen his mother, sat on a chair in the sun on the stoop. She was wearing a white dress and looked as beautiful as he could ever remember. At first he thought she was just lost in thought. He crossed the room and went out through the French doors to the jasmine scented stoop. He particularly recalled the heat, and how his mother was sat with her hands holding onto the chair very tightly, as if she thought she might fly away at any moment and wanted to be sure she had anchored herself. 'Ma, it's me, Oliver. Ma, it's me.' Then he saw her eyes, her blue empty eyes, and he knew she'd gone, long gone. This is what they hadn't wanted to tell him; this woman, his mother, wasn't going to visit anyone, ever again.

Oliver realised that he was crying. He hadn't cried once, not since Flop had been found. Not even when he felt the dent in his head after the operation, or he got the letter from the newspaper his father had worked for, saying they'd heard from the Red Cross. No one had seen his father for almost eighteen months now, but not to despair, he wasn't on any of the P.O.W. lists. He hadn't even cried when he'd taken hold of his mother's hand and she hadn't even tried to squeeze it back, but now, in the freezing cold baggage car on the London train he was bawling his eyes out. Life had to get better, it just had to.

Lena Thomas stood anxiously at the barrier entrance watching the passengers streaming off the Leeds to Kings Cross train. She felt overheated in her Burberry coat, but too lazy to remove or loosen it. The station was dense with people at 5pm and she was concerned that she might miss Oliver. She felt a tad delicate, perhaps just one too many sherries in the station bar. She swayed a little as people brushed by her. Her eyes were momentarily diverted from the scene by a sign that read 'Beware of Pickpockets' and she clutched her little Ralph Lauren leather strap purse closer to her, her bloodless knuckles revealing a clue to the vaguely anorexic frame under the coat. At forty-two, Lena still had the traces of the 'unusual beauty' she'd once been considered when young and beginning her career on the stage. For a brief while she'd been in demand enough to feature in 'Harpers' and 'Cosmo' as an up-and-coming star of the future, but somehow the breaks had never come. She'd ended up playing murder victims in Michael Winner films, or briefly, for a year had been the 'Lux Girl' in a series of commercials. She might have made more, done more, but sadly the bottle intervened. Whether it was the sherry that finished her looks or that they simply went out of vogue, at thirty she found she couldn't get a decent part in TV and at thirty-five even theatre didn't want her, or her agent (who'd publicly dumped her at the Brasserie on the Fulham Road when she'd insulted his manhood rather too loudly). Somehow, after that she'd ended up as housekeeper to Grandma Otis, unmarried and resigned to a less than thrilling future. She kept telling herself that an opportunity would knock soon. Grandma Otis was always promising something would happen to her, but she knew in her heart that it would be hard to leave Grandma Otis and the strange life they led, very hard.

The train had been in the station ten minutes now and although the passengers were still approaching her from the furthest reaches of the platform, it was thinning out, there was no sign of a bald young boy. Lena had been surprised that Grandma Otis hadn't mentioned Oliver before, never mind contemplated taking him in. Certainly there was no photograph of the boy, (unusual for a Grandmother to have no photo of her only daughters child). She had photographs of kids from all over the world in the house, kids who'd grown up now and still sent her letters and flowers- and even though they weren't related to her, all called her Grandma Otis; but of her own kith and kin, hardly anything. All Lena knew was that Oliver was fresh out of hospital, bald from the chemotherapy and sickly. Lena was irritated at the thought of having to look after a child and the old woman, even though she was going to get an extra ten quid a week for it. A boy was bound to cause a lot of trouble, they always did. She had always been confident in her choice of being childless. She'd once had a choice, but she couldn't go through with it, too much bother, too many heartaches. She hadn't wanted to be like her mother, shouting all the time, wheedling, begging, crying, trying to restore order in a house where no one actually gave a shit. Lena sighed, a bloody child, a sick child at that, did Grandma Otis know what she was taking on? At sixty-three she was too old to take on kids, it was sheer folly, and she knew it.

Where was the child? Did he even get on the train? She approached a child lugging a big plastic bag with 'Asda' printed on it, but he passed by her into the arms of a man who lifted him up and swung him around, both their faces full of smiles. Lena studied them, making a judgement, divorced husband, weekend child, the usual.

Where the hell was that boy? It had been twenty minutes now. The last passengers were approaching, two old women in button down coats accompanied by a porter trundling their huge suitcases. Lena didn't think people still travelled like that anymore. That was it. The train was empty. The boy had vanished, missed the train, or run off, with a bit of luck, embarrassing, awkward. Oh hell, where was he?

She began to walk down alongside the train. Perhaps the boy had fallen asleep, and no one had thought to wake him.

Oliver was far from asleep. He'd gotten off the train only moments after it had arrived, carried the cat box to the platform and, although Flop was now awake and desperate for a pee, he hadn't quite known what to do about it. He didn't want Flop to stink up his box anymore than he had to and create a bad impression at Grandma's. Flop was hungry, angry and desperate to bite his way out of the cage. A woman stopped to watch the scene. Oliver shrugged.

'He's pretty pissed off. Flop's never been in a cat-box before.'

The woman frowned. 'He looks distraught. He needs water'.

'I know,' Oliver replied, 'I'll get some, I've got a dish in my bag.'

'You do that, remember this animal loves you, he's relying on you to look after him.'

The woman sped away then, leaving Oliver feeling pretty guilty about his cat. He spotted some string on the platform and got a good idea. 'It's OK Flop, we can get you some water together.'

When Lena reached the baggage car she found Oliver stood at the edge of the platform with a skinny ginger tomcat, a string tied around its neck, a dish of water before it as it peed generously up against the baggage car wheels. No one had mentioned a cat, not once. The boy looked small for his age, the woolly hat was nothing but a rag with the wool ends trailing down his neck.

'Oliver?'

Oliver looked around at this tall woman who had approached him and he studied her, her eyes, the grey streaks in her hair. Her clothes looked expensive and she was wearing black suede boots, 'Cats', no less, weird.

'Flop had to pee again, he's been twice since we got here. He's starving, he didn't get any breakfast.'

Lena's lips curled, unfortunately this was the boy, how disappointing. He wasn't even cute. So pale, looked like he might die. They'd said he was better, he didn't look better, he was pale and thin and they'd no business sending him to them. That's what was so disgusting about the National Health Service, not taking care of the really sick, they'd no business foisting the undead on Grandma, how could they?

'Your Grandma doesn't like cats.'

Oliver immediately felt a shiver of apprehension. The idea of anyone not liking cats, especially his own Grandma, wasn't conceivable. 'She'll like Flop, he's a terrific climber and he catches rats and eats them.'

Oliver saw Lena momentarily shudder, the imaginary image of a cat tearing a rat to pieces lay between them like undigested lunch. Flop broke the spell as he began to miaow again and tug against the string which immediately began to choke him.

'You're going to strangle that cat,' Lena informed him. Oliver quickly grabbed Flop and loosened the string, simultaneously shoving him back into the box, a move much resisted by the dazed animal. Flop placed his paws either side of the box and dug in. Oliver bundled him in anyway, getting a scratch for his trouble. Flop growled inside as the door shut on him.

'We haven't got any rats.' Lena told him. 'She won't have any cat in the house, I'm telling you. I'm Lena, your Grandma's housekeeper.'

'I know.' Oliver replied, picking up his bag and swinging it over his shoulder.

Lena walked back up the platform leaving Oliver to struggle with the cat box alone. She didn't look back, not once. Oliver didn't mind, he was used to people ignoring him. Even before his Ma was sick, she'd often not speak to him for week at a time. He'd have to cook some days 'cause she'd forget to, or she'd been shopping at Somerfield and just bought tuna. She often just ate tuna, almost everyday. Oliver used to gag at the sight of a can, but Flop didn't mind.

Lena paused in the main hall, irritated that the kid was taking so long. She looked back, finally, and saw him struggling with the cat box. She was doubly irritated; no one had mentioned a bloody cat, not once. 'Hurry up,' she insisted, but Oliver didn't hear, the Tannoy was announcing delays to trains from Newcastle due to crew shortages.

It was with some relief that Oliver approached the taxi and climbed in, wedging the cat box between himself and a horrified Lena. She pulled a disgusted face and clasped a handkerchief to her face. 'Oh it stinks, it stinks, your cat stinks.'

Oliver looked at the city, in a constant state of astonishment, even if they were hardly moving in the rush hour traffic. He'd never seen so many cars or such tall buildings. He'd no idea that there could be so many people in one place at one time. You could see a city on TV, but it never conveyed the noise, the all-enveloping sound of a city, or the smell. He looked at Lena in wonder. 'It's so huge. You can walk around Louth in ten minutes. How many people live here?'

Lena allowed herself a smile. She too recalled arriving in London for the first time from Lyme Regis. She'd thought Lyme Regis big enough, busy enough in summer, but nothing had prepared her the city, the sheer volume and size of it.

'Millions', she replied, 'eight or nine, I forget.'

Oliver nodded his head. 'I knew it, millions. Do we live near a park? Do we live near a forest? Flop loves trees, he's always hunting in the trees, brought home a crow once.'

'Do you see any forests?' Lena asked him, her voice spiked with sarcasm.

Oliver had to admit he didn't see any forests, just four lanes deep of cars going nowhere.

Five minutes later he was looking up at a huge tower when he saw a road sign that said 'Tower Bridge, car traffic only.' Immediately he was excited all over again. 'Tower Bridge, will we see it? Will there be a ship waiting to go under it? You hear that, Flop, we're going to cross the Thames.' Oliver looked back at Lena and smiled. 'Thanks, I've always wanted to see Tower Bridge.'

Lena shrugged, she had no idea which way the taxi was going, but if he thought she'd planned it, so be it. Kids- nothing but trouble and pain. It was a familiar refrain echoing through her brain: nothing but trouble and pain. Grandma Otis was going to throw a fit when she saw this urchin and his cat. She'd throw the cat out, she hated cats.

'Oh my God,' Oliver shouted suddenly, 'did you ever see anything so beautiful.' Lena looked, but all she could see was yet another glass building with 'To Let: 190,000 square feet' emblazoned across it. 'I can see the bridge,' Oliver exclaimed, unable to contain his excitement.

Oliver was stunned into silence as the taxi rumbled over Tower Bridge. He just couldn't believe all the places he'd seen pictures of and really desperately wanted to see, were all in one area; the Tower where Raleigh had been prisoner, as well as the two murdered little Princes; the river, even a Navy ship moored alongside illuminated wharf buildings. Seeing it all, at night, for the first time, it was just so stunning, so beautiful, everything glistened and everywhere Japanese tourists photographed everything. Oliver still had stars in his eyes from the Japanese girl who had rushed over to the taxi and flashed her camera at them. This was London all right, this was the place trains went to, this was a huge city and it was his home now, and Flop's. He wasn't ever going back to Lincolnshire. He was going to live in the city where people used the streets at night and shone lights on buildings just because they wanted to, not because they had to keep things bright to stop the kids breaking all the glass windows.

'Do we live here?' Oliver asked, thinking they'd gone far enough now. Flop was making distress noises again; he didn't like the swaying motion of the taxi.

Lena took out a cigarette and lit up, using an elegant gold lighter that went 'clunk' when she closed it. She blew smoke over Oliver, enjoying watching him wince and cough. 'No, we live in Greenwich,' she informed him, pointedly, 'you might as well get used to it.'

Oliver didn't pick up on the sour tone in her voice; he was much too much in love with London and everything he saw. So many people, so many buildings, so many lives. Suddenly he remembered his head, his bald head. Would people laugh at him here? Would kids pick on him, call him 'Baldy', throw stones at him? He vividly remembered Jason Bennett when he'd contracted something, a muscle problem in his leg and he'd limped for a term. Everyone had called him a spacker and shunned him. Would kids here call him names? Would there be gangs? Would he have to join one?

Lena noticed the change in mood, but misunderstood. 'Greenwich isn't so bad, it's by the river. You like boats don't you?'

Oliver wasn't listening anymore, his head was filled with a rash of doubts and imagined terrors. Just how would kids in Greenwich treat a bald boy? Would they kick the shit out of him? What were Greenwich kids like? Oliver began to register his surroundings and began to worry as they sped through Deptford. The tower blocks looked ugly, the metal shuttered shops shabby, as were the people crowding the pavements. Skinhead kids were gathered in knots doing nothing in particular. Litter was everywhere, and graffiti. He'd built a fantasy about his Grandma's house. His mother had always talked about this big house with a view of the city from her bedroom. He'd never seen a picture, but he remembered her tale of the huge rooms and the open fire in the living room and the kitchen garden where a huge old grapevine grew. Had Grandma moved? Worse had his mother made it all up like Sara Nix's mother who pretended they lived in a house, when they lived in a caravan in a farmer's field and Sara was always having to take baths when she visited other people's homes 'cause she never got a wash at home. Just where was Greenwich anyway? Just how far from London was it?

The cab plunged into even more depressing territory, the road widened momentarily. A small bridge caused a small rise in the road and as Oliver looked out he glimpsed a huge scrap yard, an empty muddy narrow river and even more blocks of flats, with burned out cars lying at the side of the road. The cab slowed by a pub where a crowd of dread-locked Jamaicans was shouting at someone who was carrying a baseball bat. Oliver had a distinct uneasy feeling, who were these people? Everyone looked so different to the people in Louth.

'Are we there yet?' Oliver asked, his voice betraying his anxiety.

'Not far now,' came the worrying reply, 'never seen a black face before? You look scared.'

Oliver chewed on his bottom lip. 'Yes, of course,' he answered, but he nearly said, 'Never so many'. He heard his mother's voice in his head. 'They're the same as us, only better, at least they like each other. I wish I'd been born black.' Oliver never knew what she'd meant by it. But he'd grown up listening to Whitney Houston, Janet Jackson and Terence Trent D'Arby records; it was all she'd listen to, all she'd let him listen to.

The cab turned a sharp corner and the transformation was immediate. Greenwich. Oliver immediately glimpsed the Cutty Sark and he shouted enthusiastically. 'A sailing ship.'

'This place is nothing but a museum,' Lena drawled. 'Feels like one too.'

Oliver was reviving now. Gone were the tower blocks, here were old buildings, on a low scale. It looked like a small town, a lot like the town he'd just left, decay mixed with neon. Here were things to see. The cab swung right, then left again. The National Maritime museum came into view. Oliver had read about this. Nelson, 'Queen Elizabeth the First' had lived here, history was made here. He felt giddy; this was where they lived? It wasn't going to be so bad after all.

'I know this place,' Oliver told Flop, who was making noises again. 'It's right by the river. This is where the Royal Observatory is. We studied this in school.'

'Well I hope they told you how damp it is.' Lena muttered as she rooted in her bag for her purse. 'We're nearly there. Don't go shouting, your Grandma gets headaches, you go in quietly and I'll show you to your room.'

'But where is it?' Oliver asked as the cab turned yet another corner and entered a narrow cobbled street, its tyres rumbling on the uneven surface. It was getting misty now, a strange fog that seemed to concentrate only in one area, the place they were heading. Out of the gloom another scrap yard appeared on the left and opposite poor, one-up and one down brick homes. This is where his Grandma lived? She was poor? These houses didn't look big enough for two people, never mind him too. He felt the bitter, heartfelt disappointment that only a child knows. His mother had lied to him. 'Ma said she lived by the river.'

'This is the river, can't you smell it?' Lena answered, proffering the cab driver a twenty pound note. Oliver noticed he didn't give her any change. They had stopped by a corrugated metal fence. 'Price and Fahd Scrap', a sign read. Another sign, dark blue and hard to see in the mist read 'The Lord Nelson – Freehouse'. A pub and a scrap yard. Oliver began to steel himself for the worst. He had read a Charles Dickens novel and this place had all the hallmarks of the worst in them. Scary people lived here. Smugglers, murderers and...his Grandma. It didn't seem right somehow.

The cab had gone. Oliver was standing in the bitter cold, damp mist carrying his cat-box, Flop still protesting inside it. Lena pulled up her coat collar and took in a deep breath. 'Always stinks like this when the river mist comes up,' she told him. 'Follow me.'

Oliver watched her go towards an opening in the metal fence and he had to force his legs into action. The mist was creepy. It almost felt like it was coating him in some alien fluid, the smell of diesel was quite distinct now. He went after her, nearly stumbling over the uneven bricks that made up the road.

Lena led him through a heavily barbed wired alleyway, which seemed to pass right through the scrap yard. A ship was moored at the riverside, its mooring lights shining dimly through the river fog, more dense here. There seemed to a kind of overhead crane, and he could hear the sound of a train in the distance, and from the river, the sound of a low mournful foghorn. Grandma lived here? It just didn't seem possible.

'Here,' Lena called out, pausing by a gate. 'In here.'

Lena saw Oliver hesitate. 'It looks better in the day.' She tried to reassure him, not that Oliver believed her. Not that she believed it herself. Then Flop began to cry out loudly from his box. He was hungry, Oliver knew that miaow. Once started there was no stopping him, 'till he was fed.

Lena looked at the cat box and pursed her lips before saying, 'She won't have that smelly thing in the house y'know.'

Oliver clutched the box more fiercely. 'I'm not going in without him.'

'Suit yourself,' she answered, opening the gate with a nudge of her skinny hips. 'Bitch of a fog tonight, always wrecks my throat.'

Oliver watched her go up the pathway, swallowed up by the mist. He looked down at the cat box and made soothing noises to Flop, who at least stopped biting the wire grill to listen for a moment. 'If she says you can't stay, we're going, we'll find a forest to live in, a big forest where no one can find us, no one.'

With that promise made, he walked up the uneven path towards Grandma Otis's house. The mist pretty well hid most of it. One single porch light pointed the way, but was quite dazzling as it lit up the moisture-laden air. Oliver couldn't tell if the house was big or small, all he knew so far was that it was next to a scrap yard. Behind it, looming in the dark like a huge shadow within a shadow was another building. Oliver could dimly make out a red light at the top of it blinking. What was it? A tower block? Whenever Oliver had envisioned London and the river he'd always imagined this big house with lots of trees. Not this, a home squeezed in between scrapyards and tower blocks.

'Come on, you're letting the heat out,' Lena complained, the knife-edge in her voice cutting precisely through the mist and chilling his heart. Even Flop stopped miaowing.

Oliver emerged from the darkness. It seemed to him that Lena had almost reeled him indoors, closing the door after him with a swoosh and a click, almost as if closing a jar or sealing a lid.

'We're finally back,' Lena remarked, hanging up her coat and sitting down to remove her boots. 'I hate going up town now. All those crowds.' She looked at Oliver. 'Remove your coat, set that cat box down and get washed up, the downstairs loo is just over there. Make sure you look clean for Grandma Otis, she's upset enough without wanting to see you looking like a scruff.'

Oliver did as he was instructed. He noted that the passageway was narrow, but warm at least. Still, this appeared to be an odd way to come into a house. Lena could see he was puzzled.

'This is the back way. Grandma only uses the front for her visitors.'

Oliver did sort of think he was a visitor, but he didn't say anything. He just sat on the floor beside Flop and took off his boots. Flop looked at him from inside the cat-box confused and anxious.

'We didn't get Flop anything to eat,' Oliver remembered.

'Does he eat pilchards? I've got some pilchards.'

This reassured Oliver, at least they were contemplating feeding his cat. He'd hate for Flop to have to run away to the forest without eating first.

'You wash and I'll go and see to Grandma Otis, don't let that cat out, you hear? I don't want it getting used to this place.'

Lena left them and walked up the stairs in her stocking feet.

Oliver immediately opened the cat-box door. Flop sniffed the air and surprisingly elected to stay in his box, scared and unsure of where he was.

'It's OK,' Oliver reassured him, but this gesture probably didn't sound convincing, besides he was far from sure everything was OK. He found the bathroom and dutifully peed and washed his face and hands, genuinely amazed at the amount of dirt in the bowl. He sniffed the Pears soap and memories of his father flooded in. He had always used Pears. He wondered if Grandma knew where he was, or if she even cared.

'You can come up now.' he heard Lena call from upstairs. Oliver hesitated, he'd never met his Grandma before. What if she didn't like him? What if she really wouldn't let Flop stay? He'd have to leave, he'd promised Flop. A promise had to be kept, even ones you made to yourself.

Oliver walked towards the stairs, noticing for the first time the red carpet held in place by brass stair rods, the lip of each stair threadbare, so that you could see the wood beneath. As he mounted the stairs he heard each one creak, each in a different way. He stepped back a moment to the previous stair and experimented with his weight on it...yes, one could almost detect a tune, a stairway of tunes – ridiculous.

'Oliver?' A voice enquired, imperiously.

Oliver remembered that he was supposed to be going upstairs, simultaneously he recalled that when he was younger he'd once found his bear on the stairs at home with a broken arm, and the memory of that and 'that voice' at the top of the stairs had totally transfixed him.

'Oliver!' The same voice commanded.

'Oliver,' Lena's voice added to the confusion, 'don't keep her waiting.'

Lena came to the top of the stairs and looked down. She could see him poised mid-way, as if trapped by some unseen force.

'She won't eat you,' Lena told him, her tone softer now. 'She's as scared to meet you as you are her. Come on.'

Oliver ordered his legs to move and they did make some effort, but it was awfully slow, one step at a time, both socks in line, toes to the edge, then one more step, socks in line, toes to the edge.

'In my lifetime, please' Lena sighed, an edge of desperation in her voice. 'The sooner you get up here, the sooner I can go down and make your supper.'

Oliver registered nothing. He was an automaton now, he was going to meet his Grandma and she was going to hate him. He knew it. It was just a matter of making the inevitable happen as slowly as possible. 'She'll hate me and I'll be unhappy for the rest of my life.' was one of the thoughts that passed through his head.

Lena reappeared at the top of the stairs wearing a lime green dressing gown and fluffy carpet slippers. She was holding a newly lit cigarette in one hand and narrowed her eyes at him. 'I don't think you appreciate just what a lucky thing it is for you that your Grandma's taking you in, Oliver. She could have let you go to the orphanage; you could have been fostered to serial killers. Who knows what could have happened to you if your Grandma hadn't intervened.'

Oliver continued to stare at Lena, the still burning cigarette in her hand and her thin drawn out face, he thought of something to say, something rude, but decided against it. He did wonder if perhaps Lena might be a secret serial killer herself, she certainly looked scary enough.

He mounted another step and sighed. Yes perhaps being adopted by your Grandma was probably better than being taken in by killers, but would they live next to a scrapyard? Did Grandma's house have to be so spooky?

'I'm coming now,' he said, making the last four steps in quick succession.

'That's better. You go in, you talk to her. I'll make your supper.'

Lena gave him a little push towards the furthest door on the landing and Oliver immediately slid on the Persian rug situated on the highly polished floor. 'Arrggh!' Oliver yelled, falling hard on his backside. He heard Lena's cruel laugh as she descended the stairs.

Oliver finally got the message. Lena didn't want him here.

'Oliver? Is that you?' He heard his Grandma call. 'Come on, I've got some chocolate for you.'

One thing Grandmas can be relied upon is to have a plentiful supply of chocolate. Oliver picked himself up and moved towards her room. Chocolate sounded OK to him.

The first thing he noticed was that Grandma Otis had double doors opening out into her bedroom, with thick crystal-cut glass panes. The room was huge and warm, lit by many lamps covered with silk scarves to diffuse the light. There, sat in a large bed, was Grandma Otis, smiling at him from behind pearl-framed glasses. A real flame gas fire was burning in a genuine marble fireplace and everywhere there were photographs of people and children and views of places from all over the world. The whole room was filled with books and knickknacks. Three burning candles stood on a bureau, in front of a mirror, and flickering shadows. jumped across the walls. Oliver noticed a collection of dolls and bears in one corner of the room and he couldn't help but instantly fall in love with this room. The thick carpet, the mixture of reds and maroons and some flowering fuchsias in front of the window, the whole room was bigger than the house he'd left behind. How was it possible such a grand room, in such a small house, and all this next to a scrap yard? It was so strange.

Grandma Otis was examining Oliver critically, pulling her shawl closer around her shoulders. She was thinking that her grandson was so small and sickly, her initial reaction was one of disappointment and then pity as she saw the holes in his socks and just how neglected he looked. Oliver was standing at the end of the bed now, looking anxious, chewing on his bottom lip, just like his mother had when she was expecting a hiding. He even clenched and unclenched his fists like Charlotte. She hoped this wasn't a bad sign.

'You don't look a bit like Charlotte. You must look like him. We don't wear our hats indoors here.'

Oliver wasn't about to remove his hat and was about to try and stare his Grandma out when he felt something soft brush against his legs. Flop. He looked down and simultaneously Flop and Grandma caught sight of one another.

'A cat! A cat in my house!' She shrieked.

Flop arched, hissed and dashed from the room, just as if he'd been shot at. Oliver was astonished. He'd never seen Flop do that before.

Grandma sat up in bed, her face quite ashen. 'What is that? Whose cat is that? Lena? Lena. Come up here now.'

Oliver began to back away from the bed, obviously Grandma Otis was not exactly a cat lover.

'It's my cat, Flop. He's never done that before.'

'I don't like cats,' came the reply. 'Lena. There's a cat in my house.' She looked at Oliver with glaring eyes and raised a finger to him. 'It can't stay.'

Oliver felt his own anger rising. Flop not welcome? His only friend? 'Then I'm leaving.'

Oliver turned on the spot and ran from the room, almost flying as he reached the stairs, all the while calling out Flop's name. He barely registered Grandma Otis's shrill, 'Suit yourself, but I'm not having a cat in my house, you hear me?'

Oliver almost collided with Lena at the bottom of the stairs. She tried to grab him, her fingers closing around his thin arms. 'What did you do to her, what did you do?'

Oliver shook himself free and dived into another room where sheets were draped over much of the furniture. 'Flop, we've got to go, we've got to go now.'

Lena rushed upstairs, convinced that Grandma Otis had been attacked, at the very least.

Oliver was busy looking for Flop however, and rushed in to every room, becoming increasingly desperate, calling out Flop's name. 'Flop, come on, we've got to go!' He caught sight of his tail under an old oak cabinet and he crawled under it to join him, knowing he risked being mauled by a very angry animal. Flop was hunched up, staring at him, panting, all his hair fluffed out, his mouth was slightly open, his tongue moving in and out as if he was finding it hard to breathe.

'What scared you, Flop, what scared you? You can tell me.'

Thirty minutes later Oliver was once again wrapped in his coat, his bag packed and standing outside the house in the cold fog. It was eerie out there with foghorns sounding on the river. The cat box was at his feet, Flop stood beside it licking his paws and although Oliver was determined to leave, he was a bit unsure about where to go, or how. He didn't have a penny to his name and both he and Flop would need to eat.

'We could find a forest Flop. We could live there, you could chase squirrels, I could build a home in a tree or something.'

Flop continued to wash his paws, seemingly quite unconcerned now. This was puzzling, his cat was behaving in a very strange manner, also it was bloody cold and the fog seemed to penetrate every piece of his clothing.

The front door opened and Lena appeared, clutching her dressing gown around her. She stepped out a little way to see more clearly. Flop pricked up his ears, but didn't run.

'Your suppers ready. That cat of yours can eat. Two cans of pilchards! Didn't you ever feed it?'

'Flop's very particular,' Oliver answered, rather regretting his rash decision to leave. He badly needed to eat something.

'He's neglected, that is what he is. You're neglected. You get your skinny bones in here Oliver and eat. Then we can talk about the cat.'

Lena saw he was not moving. She sighed again, stepping out further, to see him better. 'It's spaghetti and meatballs, I've never known a boy to refuse it.'

Oliver tried to be resolute, tried to persuade himself that taking Flop to a forest was the right thing to do, but it was cold and damp and he was very tired. He sighed and picked up his bag again, moving towards Lena. Flop didn't hesitate, he dashed for the front door, he wasn't going to be left outside in the cold fog, no way.

'That's one hungry cat,' Lena remarked as Oliver moved past her back inside. 'Get those boots off and go into the kitchen, you need a hot meal inside you.'

The click of the lock in the door behind Oliver felt like the shutting of a cage. This was to be his new home, an old, cat-hating woman upstairs and a very scary woman down. He thought... 'Daddy, where are you, come home, come and get me now!'

Later, Lena was watching him eat, the boy lost in thought as he chewed his food (at least he chewed his food). She felt her eyes being drawn to his head and couldn't help herself.

'Does it hurt?'

Oliver looked up at her, confused by her remark.

'Hurt?'

'Your head, does it hurt?'

Oliver took some bread and dipped it into the tomato sauce, thinking about the question as he did so. Then, almost as if a switch had been thrown he turned back to Lena and smiled, running a hand over his head as if he had a full head of hair, then suddenly groaning, as if in real pain. He watched Lena's astonished reaction with delight, then laughed.

'Doesn't hurt now, did when they first cut me open,' he grinned at her. 'You should have seen the growth. Doctor Vanich gave it to me. It's the size of a tennis ball. Really! I'm not kidding, right inside my brain.'

Lena screwed up her face, she felt a touch queasy, then, deciding upon decisive action she leant forward and snatched the decrepit wool mess off his head.

'This hat is going,' she declared firmly, standing up.

Oliver couldn't believe it, he was in shock, no one had ever touched his hat before. He was instantly devastated and very bald. He hated anyone looking at his head. Lena grimaced at the red weals on his head and the white scar tissue. It looked nasty. 'Are you going to be bald forever?'

Oliver found it difficult to speak. Almost as if she'd stolen his voice. 'It might grow back.' he muttered.

Lena felt sorry for him now, and even a little guilty that she'd snatched his precious hat, and although she was tempted to let him have it, she looked down at it and it was so disgusting she could hardly bear to touch it. It had to be burned.

'I'll be back, don't forget there's pudding.'

'But...my hat...' Oliver was stammering as she quickly sped out of the kitchen. Oliver looked at the door with total disbelief. He knew she was going to burn it, he just knew it. He looked back at his plate and angrily pushed the remainder of his food away; hatless, he had no appetite. He reached over the table and grabbed a paper napkin quickly unravelling it and plonking it on top of his head. He sighed, he knew it looked stupid, but it was his head, she had no right to take his cap, no right at all.

Lena was watching the old hat burning in the living room fireplace, taking some satisfaction in how brightly it burned on the hot coals. She imagined a million mites dying and drew some pleasure from it. It was obvious to her that no one had been looking after that boy for a long time.

Ten minutes later, Oliver was washing his dish in the sink when Lena returned, one hand hidden behind her back. 'I'll wash up,' she said, acting all friendly now, so that he was immediately suspicious. 'You go back to the table Oliver and I'll bring you your pudding.'

Oliver was about to say he didn't feel like pudding now, when Lena came up really close to him and snatched the paper napkin from the top of his head 'This should suit you better,' she said, placing a black wool American cap on his head. 'This cap has been waiting for you, a kid from Chicago left this behind.'

Oliver felt the hat, the leather ear flaps, furry and comfortable inside, against his skin. It felt good, but he didn't really want to say so. He was still upset she'd snatched his old one. He turned to see himself in a reflection, anywhere, and had to be content with his dim reflection in the window. He liked what he saw, even if it did look something like Jim Carrey would wear to get a laugh, the ear flaps were really warm; he'd always hated his ears getting cold in winter.

'I can keep this?'

'Can't have kids laughing at you. I suppose that worries you a bit.'

Oliver shrugged. 'They'll laugh anyway.' Then, as if he remembered something positive he moved over to his bag and removed a plastic jar and smiled at her. 'But I can really make them sick when I go to school and show them this.'

Lena looked at the pickled tumour in a jar and a wave of nausea washed over her. It was huge. He hadn't made it up. 'Oh put it away, it's horrible. Didn't you have massive headaches?'

Oliver nodded, then put the jar away, moving back to the sink to wipe his hands. Lena went over to the fridge and opened it up, taking out some green jelly in a white porcelain bowl. Oliver studied her as he went back to his seat.

'You think my Dad is dead?'

Lena paused momentarily, then continued to spoon out the jelly into a Thai wooden bowl. She could see Oliver was waiting for an answer, but what could she say? 'Yes'? For that is what she thought. Instead she put the bowl in front of him and smiled.

'I'm sure he'd be very proud of you if he knew you'd been so sick and survived. Do you think he is dead?'

Oliver lifted his spoon and slid it into the jelly, quite thoughtful now. 'I think he's trapped somewhere. Maybe in a secret Serbian prison camp. I wrote to lots of people. My Doctor posted the letters.'

'Did you get any replies?'

I got two letters. One from a French General and another from the UN. They told me they'd put Dad on a list, but that was a year ago. I know he would have written to me if he were able to. He wrote to me when we had to leave him behind before.'

'You lost him before?' Lena sat down. To lose a father twice was pretty careless. What kind of man goes missing twice?

'We had to come back from Libya. My Dad was working on putting together some book about the water pipeline they were building. He's done books on other projects too. A dam in Brazil,' Oliver tried to think of some more but couldn't. 'Anyway, this pipeline, it's hundreds of miles long y'know and they flew in all these people to work on it and if they tried to run away they'd shoot them. I used to hear them shooting at night, honest. Anyway Ma hated the desert and made us go home. I didn't want to go, but Ma said we had to. Dad used to send me letters all the time after that, but mostly they'd all arrive at once with most of the words crossed out.'

Lena was curious as to how matter of fact Oliver was about his life. So much had happened to him and yet he was so untouched by it all. Libya – how did one even begin to get a job there, let alone drag along a wife and child? She watched Oliver eat his jelly.

'I'm sure you'll hear from your father when he's able to write. I think you should speak to Grandma about him. She wants to see you now. Your cat won't disturb her, I don't think he's going to leave that boiler, do you?'

Oliver grinned. Flop must have known they were talking about him because his ears were twitching. He stretched one arm out to touch the boiler with his little pink pads. Oliver frowned. 'Is Grandma my mother's mother?'

Lena cocked her head to one side; the concept of the question even seemed strange. 'Of course. Don't be scared. She won't bite, I promise.'

Oliver wasn't so sure. He tended to trust Flop's instincts better than his own and if Flop thought she was scary, then she was scary.

'No one is like your Grandma Otis. You'll discover she's almost famous. People come from all over to see her. She's strange, but she'll always tell you the truth. That's rare.'

Oliver took one last look at Flop and sighed. He had to do it.

Lena watched him go and quickly she went to the door and shut it after him, noticing Flop had already woken and was keenly aware that Oliver had left the room. Lena already understood just how close these two were. She was beginning to accept the situation now. The question was 'Why'? Why had his family disintegrated? Why hadn't his father written (assuming he was alive)? It was cruelty for the sake of it in her opinion.

Grandma Otis sat up in her bed totally rigid; her eyes were open, but unseeing. There was a hint of a green glow in the room, but Oliver couldn't see where it was coming from exactly. All he did know was that this was the spookiest situation he'd ever been in. Grandma Otis seemed to be in some kind of trance. He'd come into the room and she'd told him to stand still. Oliver could see himself reflected in a mirror, his big toe protruding from his left sock. Grandma Otis suddenly seemed to take in a deep breath and she began to speak, but her voice was now entirely different, almost as if she was pretending to be a man.

Oliver felt the skin on his head crawl and the green light seemed to spread all over the room.

'You want to know if your father has passed over to the other side?' the strange voice asked him.

Oliver began to shake. Grandma was possessed. He'd seen this movie! Any minute now something utterly gross was going to crawl out of his Grandma's mouth and try to attack him. Or worse her head was going to spin all the way around! Some part of him was hoping it was just a trick, something to scare him, see what he would do.

'You OK, Grandma?' he asked weakly.

'Be quiet, boy.' came the immediate response. 'Your father is still alive.

He cannot write to you. He wants to, but he cannot. He is suffering, he is not ready for death.'

Oliver realised that he had seen this kind of thing before, on TV. Someone was speaking through Grandma Otis. It was like 'Ghost', the movie. Somehow this reassured Oliver. Yes, Grandma was doing the same thing Whoopi Goldberg did. Rationalising this, he was able to deal with the situation. He decided he wouldn't be scared. This was his Grandma; nothing was going to hurt him. They wouldn't do that, not on his first night. Would they?

'Who are you? How do you know this? Where's Grandma?'

'My name is Quon, be a good boy Oliver and I will tell you many secrets. There is no need to be scared, I am your Grandmother's friend.'

Oliver was still shaking, but curious now, almost enjoying the sensation and the green light that seemed to make everything sparkle in the room. 'Where's Grandma? What have you done with her?'

'She is here. She says 'be calm'. I am her guide, I am here to help you as well. I know the question you want to ask me. It is...'Will my hair grow again?'

Oliver began to feel weak at the knees. That was the exact question he'd wanted to ask. He was seriously spooked now.

'The answer is 'Yes' Oliver, but not the same as before and not yet.'

Oliver began to shake. His voice was reduced to a whisper. 'My mother, what will happen to her?'

'That is something that only time can answer, Oliver. Some things are beyond knowing. I can promise nothing.'

Oliver stared at his Grandma and although he was scared, he was kind of reassured that whoever was really speaking didn't know the answer to that. Then he saw his Grandma let out an enormous sigh and the green light began to dim as Grandma Otis's eyes and breathing seemed to return to normal. They slowly began to focus on Oliver who was now squashed up against the far wall staring at her with complete astonishment on his face. She could quickly see that he had been scared and she smiled at him.

'So, you had a talk with Quon? Don't be scared, he tells the truth. You can be sure of that. You weren't actually afraid were you?'

Oliver discovered that he forgotten to breathe and he sucked in a huge amount of air, trying to re-adjust to the new situation. His Grandma was watching him, a genuine look of concern in her face. 'He said...' Oliver took another breath. ' He said my father was still alive, that he couldn't write to me. He said Ma might not get better, not for a while.'

Grandma Otis sighed, then reached back to her bedside table and grabbed a little packet of something. She held it out for Oliver, beckoning for him to come closer.

Oliver did not feel like going closer, but he could recognise a packet of M&Ms from a hundred yards away and he was seriously tempted.

'Come on, I know you like them. Quon told me they were your favourites.'

'How could he know that?' Oliver asked, puzzled. 'How could he know?'

Grandma Otis shrugged. 'I never ask how he knows, he just does. He's been telling me for a long time that your mother, my Charlotte, was going under, but she wouldn't answer my letters. Y'know how many years I have waited to see you? Not seen you since you were a child. She wouldn't visit, not once. And that father of yours, him going off like that, leaving you with her. Stupid man, fancy going back to Croatia, why do you he think his Grandfather left? It wasn't so his children could go back and fight yet more stupid wars.'

Oliver advanced a little closer and she pressed the M&Ms in his hands.

He opened the packet with his teeth, remembering something his mother had told him about this woman.

'Ma told me you threw her out when she was pregnant with me.'

Grandma Otis immediately looked pained; she reached under her pillow and withdrew some photographs. She laid them out before her for Oliver to see and he took his first bite of some M&Ms, letting the chocolate melt slowly in his mouth. He saw his mother as a young woman, she was so pretty. He laughed with surprise and delight. 'That's Ma, and there's you. Is the baby me?'

Grandma Otis settled back against her pillow and smiled. 'Aye, see the hair? You were born with such a fine head of hair. You were born right here, on the kitchen table. You squawked night and day young man. Wouldn't sleep, worried us to death. You and your mother lived here for two years. I cried for a week when you left, but she had to go. Your father came for her.'

'You didn't throw her out?'

'Oh yes. He wanted her back and she didn't want to go. She was content to let me cook and clean for her, but your father loved her and wanted her. I should have known then that Charlotte wasn't right.' She sighed, helping herself to a couple of Oliver's M&Ms. He rather resented that, but she had given them to him. 'God knows how to test a mother, he really does. He can test, test, test. And then laugh when you come back for more. I threw her out, made her go and live with the man who loved her and she never forgave me for it.'

Oliver took another look at one of the photographs. He had never seen a photograph of his mother laughing before. Never seen his mother laugh, she'd looked so pretty then. He frowned and looked at Grandma Otis. 'Who is Quon, exactly?'

Lena stood at the bottom of the stairs listening, but not hearing. She looked happier, there were no shouts, they were getting on. She was pleased about that. She took a sip from her sherry glass and headed on back towards the kitchen.

Grandma Otis had more photographs on the bed, showing her dressed in safari clothes and holding a fly swatter. Oliver examined the shots with interest, impressed when he saw elephants or lions in any of the pictures.

'How long were you in Africa?' Oliver asked.

'Oh, nearly thirty years, went out there just after the war. It was still an adventure then. I was teaching. My husband was teaching also. We lived out in the bush. Nicolas, that's my husband, your grandfather, he took sick and died. It was so sudden; I hardly had time to register it before I also fell ill. Such a fever it was too. I was burning up. The village natives were quite ready for me to die and I was waiting for the moment, when quite suddenly I felt a cool hand stroking my face and a voice saying, 'Everything is fine, I'm here now, I'll take care of you.' That was the first time Quon came to me. He died a long time ago y'know, but he found me and told me I would be saved.'

Oliver looked at her with a new-found fascination. Africa, voices, saved from death. He knew these things happened on television, but in real life, to his own Grandma? It was great.

'Quon had always wanted to travel, you see. He knew I'd be travelling.'

Oliver ate some more M&Ms as he filtered this information through his brain. 'But how can he know anything if he's dead? How can he know about my father? Even the UN couldn't find him.'

Grandma Otis sighed and clasped her old slightly puffy hand over Oliver's. 'Quon would know if he was dead Oliver. He wants to help you, you'll see, you'll see.'

A while later Oliver sat in his own bedroom, formerly his mothers, and pondered the change in his life. On the wall, yellowing with age, was pinned a Rod Stewart poster and all around him were records and tapes and magazines from his mother's past. It was so weird. It was as if Grandma Otis had never once set foot in this room since his mother had left all those years before. On his bed lay hairy gonks, and an abandoned teddy bear with just one eye. He listened to his mother's old vinyl LPs that crackled, but he was quite impressed by David Bowie singing about 'Spiders from Mars'. His mother must have been such a different person when she was young. He turned over and stared at the row of shoes on a rack. Then laughed out loud when he saw the huge heels and six-inch soles attached to bright yellow plastic shoes. Grandma Otis nudged open the door and smiled, happy to see him laughing. She looked at the rack of shoes and laughed herself. 'You mother always suffered from an excess of bad taste.'

'I never knew she was a David Bowie fan. She used to dance too. See the picture on the wall? Look, that's Ma getting an autograph from Bowie. She was a space cadet, Grandma, she never told me she was a groupie.'

Grandma Otis shook her head in the sad memory of it all. A rash of ugly memories crowing through her brain, the drugs, the arguments, the attempted suicides, the screaming and slamming of doors. She shut her eyes.

'I wonder why she stopped listening to music,' Oliver was saying, but Grandma Otis was leaving, she couldn't bear to look into this, the memories just never went away. Never.

Downstairs a few minutes later Grandma Otis sat with Lena in the living room. They stared at the dying coal fire in the grate. Grandma Otis was wearing a huge quilted silk dressing gown and she sipped a mug of hot Horlicks. Lena topped her mug up with a dash of brandy. Upstairs the sound of Davie Bowie was coming through loud and clear from Oliver's room.

'It's funny.' Grandma Otis said, after a while, 'I used to hate Charlotte's music, but now it doesn't seem so bad.'

Lena smiled and huddled her dressing gown closer to her neck.

'I met William at a Bowie concert in Reading. Gives me goosebumps to hear it now.'

Past midnight, Oliver lay asleep in his bed, the music long since ended. His door began to creak a little, opening an inch, then two inches, finally four. Flop slinked in and jumped up on his bed, purring and settling down beside Oliver. Although asleep, Oliver instinctively put out a hand to cuddle the cat and Flop licked his fingers. Flop had decided. They'd stay. It was warm, they had food, they'd stay.

In Grandma Otis's room, she lay awake, troubled, watching the moon through her window. She was worried. Something about the boy. Something strange about the boy.

CHAPTER TWO

Everything smelled like porridge. That was the one thing Oliver's Pa had liked in the morning, and although Oliver had been entirely sceptical about eating it at first, once he had smothered it in milk and honey, it was edible. Flop had gone, but the indentation of the missing cat was clear to see on the bed cover. Oliver swung his legs out of the bed and examined his mother's bedroom again. It was so strange to be in a room full of old posters and faded hippy clothes, but he had mixed feelings about his new situation. He knew his mother wouldn't ever again appreciate what she had, probably didn't care, but the scariest thing was the unspoken fear he had about whether he too might go crazy one day. Add that to the list of things he was scared of. Eating rissoles, AIDS, aliens, mushrooms, spiders, frogs (or was that toads?), cheese, monkeys – but only because they smelled bad – and then there was the Dentist. He'd just looked scary, right from the beginning. His toxic breath that smothered Oliver when he lay, squirming in his slippery red chair, with a stupid picture of a pig on the ceiling. Yes, going mad really was scary, there was a lot of it in the family, he could see that now. Grandma was clearly crazy, but kind of nice with it, like it was OK she was mad, at least she smiled and talked, unlike his Ma. But it was always going to be there; his Grandma was mad, his mother had gone over the edge completely and his father had never really had much sense (according to his Ma and she should know)...there was no hope for him, none at all, it was all just a matter of time, he'd start dribbling one day and they'd come and get him, he just knew it.

The scent of porridge wafted into his room again and reminded him that he was hungry and needed to pee. Time to get up, start his new life. His eye caught a poster he hadn't noticed before; half-curled up on the rear wall, partially faded from where the sun had touched it over the years. Oliver stood up and placed the palm of his hand on it to flatten it out so he could read it. 'We are not alone,' it proclaimed... 'Close Encounters of the Third Kind'.

'Wow, Ma was a science fiction freak!' Oliver exclaimed aloud. He grinned, for some reason really pleased about this latest discovery. He'd seen the movie on TV and been scared to death - OK, confession - he'd watched most of it from behind the sofa. It was strange, but somehow just the existence of this poster, brought him closer to his Mother than all the other things in the room.

Lena was making coffee in the kitchen, stirring boiling water into the cafetière. Harriet was reading her stars in the Daily Mail as she nibbled on a piece of brown toast. 'It says 'Big decisions today. The eclipse of the new moon will alter everything, but ask yourself, are you ready for such changes?'

Lena smiled. 'The last big change in my life was when my hair turned grey.'

Harriet looked surprised, frowning as she examined Lena's hair. 'You're grey?'

'Not since my date last night with Harmony. Grey is social death. I mean, a man goes grey and we're all supposed to say how distinguished he looks. I go grey and they ask me if I would play Miss Marple in "Murder at the Gallop" or something dire, it's like you died overnight.'

Harriet brushed back her own genuine ash blonde L'Oreal hair and tossed it to one side, giving it the once over, as if to make sure it was still there. 'I'm never going grey, I'm going to stay blonde until they arrest me for bringing old age into disrepute.'

Lena brought the cafetière to the table and set it down, noticing Flop the cat patiently sitting by the door, 'I've got to get that boy up.'

'Does Grandma Otis know there's a cat in her kitchen? Doesn't she have a 'thing' about cats?'

Lena smiled, sitting down at the table and pulling the sugar towards her. 'She and the cat met, I don't know who was the most frightened, you should have been here last night, quite some scenes. But it's a nice cat, I could do with the company. You think I should let it out?'

Harriet shook her head most emphatically. 'First day? Is it safe to let a cat out here? I wouldn't let my cat out in this neighbourhood – correction – I wouldn't let my cat live in this neighbourhood. Every time I come here I'm surprised I still have wheels on my car when I get back.'

Lena pulled a face to let Harriet know that she was exaggerating. 'No one steals anything around here, everyone knows Grandma Otis. It looks bad, but I think it's one of the safest places in London, it's a real community.'

'That's because there's nothing worth stealing around here, except scrap metal. She's not poor, why doesn't she move? She could live up on Maze Hill by the park.'

Lena pushed the plunger down on the cafetière and shrugged. 'She's been here all her life, it was a her father's place, he was the power station manager. Her father was God around here in the war and after. He got a medal from the King for his services to the nation. Made a pile on the black market too, from what other folk tell me, but Grandma Otis told me that he was the straightest man in London and he never profited once, but then, she does tend to idolise him.'

Harriet frowned. 'Growing up here in all those sulphur fumes – yuk – it must have been disgusting. Coal fires, smog, London must have been ghastly.'

Lena nodded in agreement. 'Yes, but everyone had a job back then. You couldn't breathe, but everyone had a bit of pride.'

The kitchen door opened and Oliver appeared dressed in jeans and a faded red sweatshirt, his head covered with his new wool cap. He seemed to Lena to look more pale and woefully undernourished than the night before, if that was at all possible. Flop immediately began to wail to be let out, stretching his body up towards the door handle. Lena stood up, flustered, not exactly sure what to do or say, she just wasn't used to having someone else living in the house.

'I can smell porridge,' Oliver said, matter-of-factly, walking to the door and squatting down beside Flop, who immediately placed his nose to Oliver's, miaowing loudly, clearly communicating with the boy.

'You can go out,' Oliver told him sternly, 'but don't go far, you don't know where you are, OK?' Oliver looked over at Lena. 'Did he eat anything yet?'

Lena shook her head. 'Not yet. Got nothing for him until I get to Sainsburys.'

'Good,' Oliver said, pleased. 'He won't go far if he's hungry.' He returned his gaze to the cat. 'I'm going to have some porridge, you can have some milk when you finish, OK? Better go, can't have you messing Grandma's house.' Oliver opened the back door from his squatting position and Flop shot out, perhaps more desperate to go than he was letting on. Harriet had been watching all this with total fascination. 'You were really talking to that cat weren't you?'

Lena was at the stove pouring out the porridge into a large ceramic bowl, adding milk and treacle to it. Oliver and Harriet watched as she scooped the treacle out of a glass jar and held it suspended over the bowl from two feet, letting the thick treacle fall in slow motion from the spoon to the waiting grey matter below. She suddenly remembered Harriet. 'Oliver, this is Harriet, she's a regular with your Grandma, she's going to take you out today – to look around.'

Oliver looked at Harriet with narrowed eyes, as if making a decision as to whether he approved of this scheme, or Harriet. He got up off the floor and went to sit at the table where Lena slapped down the bowl of porridge before him. Oliver continued to stare at Harriet, taking in her blonde shoulder-length hair and her meticulously made-up face, her heavy gold bangles wrapped around her slim wrists and he wondered what type of woman she was. She was pretty, but looked tightly wound up; she reminded him of someone's mother at school who'd once been a model and couldn't forget it. He ate his porridge, savouring the rush as the sweet treacle slid down the back of his throat.

'Not going to say anything?' Lena asked him as both she and Harriet watched Oliver eat his porridge with the etiquette of a starved refugee.

'Is there anymore?'

Harriet laughed. 'Didn't anyone ever take care of you at home?'

Oliver regarded her with a frown, but then quickly realised that she didn't know anything about him. 'You ever have to eat hospital food for four months?'

Harriet was genuinely appalled. 'Four months and you're still alive? You poor kid! Lena get this boy some more porridge, he's starved.'

Oliver laughed and finished what he had in the bowl.

'Four months and six days, some people died, they got poisoned, but I couldn't eat the meat, it smelled like plastic. I used to visit the old people and eat their fruit.'

Lena laughed. 'Kids know how to survive.'

Harriet put out a hand towards Oliver's head but he instinctively shrank back. 'Don't you worry Oliver, we're going to take good care of you here. Did it hurt? The operation, I mean.'

Oliver shrugged, leaning back to allow Lena to place another steaming bowl of porridge before him, the milk slopping about over the top of it, revealing a black treacle hole just visible beneath.

'Eat it slowly, it's hot. Your stomach might explode.'

Oliver just grinned and ate his porridge just as quickly as before, a frown on his face as he considered of how to reply to Harriet's question. 'The chemo didn't hurt, but it makes you sick, a lot. I used to puke every time I ran and when I had to climb the stairs.' Oliver grinned remembering something. 'One time I puked, stood up and slipped in it and rolled the whole way down the stairs and when the nurse ran after me, she slipped in it too and she fell the whole way down. She was really pissed off with me. Doctor Anderson said that they'd given me too big a dose and that's why I was sick. I didn't have to have any more treatment then, except for when they did something to the burns on my skin.'

Harriet stared at Oliver with a mixture of disgust and respect. She recognised that this boy had been through Hell. It was remarkable he was so cheerful, so calm about his experience.

'Did you ever think you were going to die?' Harriet asked. Lena gave her a sharp look and Harriet realised too late that this was a dumb question to ask a boy who'd been through so much. 'I'm sorry, I didn't mean to ask that Oliver, it was stupid of me, I'm...'

Oliver shrugged; he was used to this question. It was something he'd discussed with all the kids on the cancer ward. Death was like a lottery ticket. That was what Dr Campbell had told him. He was as likely to die as winning a million on the lottery and that was really difficult. 'I knew I could die, but...' He frowned again, putting his spoon down and looking at Lena and Harriet very carefully, as if making his mind up about whether to tell them something important. 'Promise you won't tell Grandma this...?'

Harriet looked at Lena and both of them exchanged worried glances. It was good to feel he trusted them, but what was he going to say? It was worrying.

'Your secret is safe with us,' Lena reassured him.

Oliver pushed his half-finished bowl of porridge towards the centre of the table as he considered how to express what he had to say.

'Is it about your operation?' Harriet asked. 'Because if it is too gross, don't tell me. I'm scared enough of catching something. I mean I've stopped using my mobile phone in case it's going to fry my brain.'

Oliver looked at her with a puzzled look. Harriet was forced to explain.

'They use the same frequencies as microwave ovens, so if you spend too long talking on one, your brain gets cooked.'

Oliver pulled a face. 'Eeue...that's gross!'

'Harriet's brains were cooked a long time ago – and not by any phone,' Lena remarked dryly. 'What were you about to tell us, Oliver?'

Oliver watched her cross the kitchen to a pile of washing in a basket and proceed to fold the bundled clothes and towels. 'When they were operating on me,' he began, 'I could see everything. I could see them cut open my head and the Doctor lean right over and look into my head. At first I thought it was strange because his face was all blue, then I realised that the blue light was shining out of my head. The Doctor was pointing at it and I remember a nurse looked away, as if she was scared. Then the Doctor got a pair of things, I mean tongs and he went right into my head and pulled out this blue box. The Doctor was really surprised; he showed it to everyone. Everyone was looking at it as he held it up to the light, it was really pretty. The light shone out of it and it was a brilliant blue, you could see the blue light touch everything in the room.'

Lena and Harriet exchanged worried glances again. A blue box in his head? How weird, how extraordinarily weird.

'Then they closed me up again,' Oliver continued. 'It was amazing. They didn't give me the box later. I asked for it. But they never told me what happened to it.' He sighed. 'I never told anyone about that box before.'

'A blue box, you say?' Harriet asked, looking at Lena again, uncertainty in her face.

'How did you see this? Didn't they put you out?' Lena asked.

'Put me out?' Oliver asked, confused.

'Put you to sleep,' Harriet explained.

'Yes, but I still saw everything.'

Lena shook her head. He had imagined it, of course, but still, what did it mean? She looked at Harriet who seemed to nod with her, agree with her unspoken thoughts that Oliver was a lot more strange and complex than your normal young boy.

'Got to go to the bathroom.' Oliver announced abruptly, a note of alarm in his voice.

Lena laughed. 'I told you not to eat your porridge too quickly.'

Oliver got up from the table and ran from the room, embarrassed as well as desperate.

Harriet smiled, 'Poor kid.'

'Weird kid...a blue box, in his head? He actually saw it?' Lena retorted.

Harriet poured herself some coffee and added milk. 'Not so mad. Perhaps it is just his way of dealing with it, y'know. It's his way of explaining what went on. He had something bad in his head and they cut it out. He thinks it was a blue box. It's cute. I think it's kind of special.'

Lena thought about that. 'Why brilliant blue? I mean, how did he see it? I suppose it could have been a vivid dream he had under the anaesthetic. That would explain it.'

Harriet sipped her coffee. 'Let him believe it was a box. Don't try to disillusion him Lena. Let him keep the box.'

Lena looked at Harriet and saw that she was serious. She shrugged. It was none of her business anyway.

'What happened to that bloke you were seeing?' Harriet asked suddenly.

'What happened to yours? Steve wasn't it?'

Harriet pretended to stick her fingers down her throat and gag. 'That bastard? Don't even mention his name!'

Oliver sat on the loo and sighed. On one hand he was happy to take a dump, but on the other, the hot porridge was still sitting in his stomach like he'd swallowed a hot-water bottle. He wished he hadn't been so greedy. He had been hungry, but not that hungry. He got up and did the business, washing his hands, noticing a picture on the wall of Grandma Otis and his mother when she was just a kid. She was smiling out of the picture and looked happy, she had a big bandage on her leg. Oliver wondered what had happened to her. He flushed and left the toilet, walking back downstairs. He could hear Harriet talking, her voice was much higher than Lena's. He didn't know what to make of Harriet. She was different to anyone else he had ever met. She was going to take him out – why? She looked friendly, but it was too soon, he was still a bit nervous about being in London. He stopped outside the kitchen door. He could hear Harriet getting worked up about something.

'I'm not kidding Lena, he grabbed me by my hair and threw me out. I mean, shit, you'd figure a normal man would want you to spend the night once he's shagged you, but no, he just threw me out and tossed my clothes out of the window. My green Versace tube, for God's sake! £400 that cost me! Doesn't he know you just don't do that to a Versace dress?'

Oliver pushed open the kitchen door and entered. Harriet immediately realised that he'd heard her and pulled a face. Lena shook her head, hoping Oliver hadn't heard. 'The boy's only twelve, Harriet, watch that mouth of yours.'

'Twelve? He looks older.'

'But not old enough for you, thank God,' Lena remarked, narrowing her eyes at her.

Harriet giggled as Oliver did his best to ignore both of them and strolled to the back door to open it and call Flop back in. He didn't have to say a word. The moment the door was wide enough Flop shot back in and practically hugged the boiler, plonking himself down beside it with a brief half-cry, as if to say, 'It's bloody cold out there, where were you?'

'That cat's never going to leave this place, ' Harriet remarked.

'He needs some milk.' Oliver declared, closing the back door and walking towards the fridge.

'I've got some warm milk for him here,' Lena told him. ' You sit down. Do you have to take any pills? I forgot to ask.'

Oliver looked back at her and nodded. 'Just one at night.' He rejoined the table and poured himself some milk as he watched Lena take the milk saucer to his cat. Flop ignored it and just licked his paws.

'Probably likes cream.' Harriet suggested.

'He only likes me to feed him, usually.' Oliver told her.

'Well, I fed him last night and he nearly ate my hand off,' Lena told him, returning to fold her laundry.

Oliver drank some milk, then placed his eyes on Harriet, asking, 'Did he really throw you out on the street, naked?'

Harriet swallowed hard. She looked at Lena but Lena just mouthed at her, 'You are on your own' and fixed a mean stare on Oliver, perhaps noticing for the first time just how piercing, how brilliant blue, his eyes were.

'He was a real pig, Oliver. Don't you ever get like that. Of course, I go for the pigs every time. If there is a choice between the Devil and a Saint, I pick the Devil. I can show you the bruises, they're huge.'

'Harriet,' Lena drawled, a distinct warning note in her voice.

Oliver was still curious however. 'But why? Why pick someone who'd do that to you?'

'Because Harriet is doomed Oliver.' Lena intervened. 'You'll find out, some women are just born victims. Harriet is a prize specimen, an Olympic champion victim. Bad men can sniff her out, they probably swap her phone number on the Internet or talk about her at Abuse Anonymous meetings.'

Harriet glared at Lena a moment and thought of something really bitchy to say but Oliver got in his question first.

'But why don't you just say no?'

The concept of this approach was just so startling Harriet and Lena both instantly broke out with laughter, that built with every moment, a hysterical wave of astonishment.

'No?' Harriet repeated, coming up for air. 'You want me to start saying 'No'? Sweetie, you start saying 'No' in this town, you might as well be dead.'

Lena steadied herself and tried to regain her former composure. 'You're giving him the wrong idea about things, Harriet. I don't think he's safe in your hands.'

Harriet made an attempt to look innocent. 'Me? Rubbish. Right, we have to go. Are you ready? You better have a coat on, it's chilly today.'

Oliver looked out of the window and saw the wind bending the tops of the trees. It did look cold. 'I'll get my jacket. Where are we going?'

Harriet stood up, finished her coffee and smiled. 'My shop first, then Mr McTeal.'

Lena looked very interested all of a sudden. 'McTeal, the psychic? You've got bored with Grandma Otis?'

'He's supposed to be the best. The Royals use him all the time. Anyway, Grandma Otis never says anything different; she's always seeing disaster around me. I want a second opinion.'

'Is he a Doctor?' Oliver asked.

'He's a fortune teller,' Lena remarked. 'He only pretends to be a psychic. He won't tell you anything different to what Grandma Otis says, and if he does you know he's making it up.'

Harriet stuck her tongue out. 'Well, I'm still going. He's expensive and Dorothy Minner says he's brilliant. He did total immersion with her and told her she had to get a divorce and exactly who her husband was cheating with. She swears by him.'

Lena just snorted. She didn't think much of McTeal at all.

'What's immersion?' Oliver asked as he went to get his jacket from the corridor.

'It's when you go naked into the hot tub with him and he pours all kinds of herbs into the water to make you relaxed and he taps into your inner senses.'

Lena smirked. 'He should be paying you for that. He's a perv, Harriet, just a bloody perv!'

Oliver returned with his jacket on and looked embarrassed. 'Are you going to get into the hot tub with him today?'

Harriet grinned at his embarrassment. 'Don't panic. We're just going for the reading. The hot-tub treatment costs a fortune. Besides, I wrinkle easily.'

Oliver looked pensive for a moment. 'A gypsy came to our door once and read Ma's hand. Ma was really angry with her, I don't know what she said. She cried for hours after it. Why do you go? I'd be scared to know what's going to happen to me.'

Harriet shrugged as she put on her thin orange cotton coat. 'Look, Oliver, all I want is just one decent man in my life. It shouldn't be so hard. Actually, preferably hard, he should definitely be hard.'

Lena laughed, but it was stopped short when a bell rang out surprising them all. Lena reacted instantly by switching on the electric kettle. 'That's your Grandma. Come on, let's get you out of here before she thinks of something for you to do.'

Oliver looked at Flop and quickly went over to his cat, squatting down to hug him. 'Be good, drink your milk. I'll bring back something to eat, I promise.'

He stood up again and Flop looked up at him, perhaps uncertain as to whether Oliver was coming back. Oliver picked up the uncertainty in Flop's eyes. 'I'll be back, I promise.'

'Enrol him at the library, Harriet. I think a boy should read.'

'Boys only read dirty books or computer magazines,' Harriet remarked cynically. 'Did you ever read a book, a real story, Oliver?'

Oliver knew she was just trying to provoke him. 'I read 'A Tale of Two Cities', then I read 'Neuromancer', I liked that. But I read some old science fiction in hospital by Philip K. Dick and he's my favourite writer now. He wrote the original story for 'Bladerunner', y'know'.

Lena looked surprised. 'Oh, I used to read his stuff when I was young. I loved it. It was all so depressing. Everything turned out just as bad as he predicted it would.'

Harriet wasn't impressed. 'Just typical of you, anything with a 'Dick' in the title.'

With that Harriet was out of the door dragging Oliver with her, leaving Lena to prepare Grandma Otis's breakfast, a lingering smile upon her lips. Harriet would sort Oliver out. Let him know what was right, what was not. Harriet would sort him out.

Oliver emerged into his Grandma's walled garden and was impressed. He'd not really seen anything the night before what with the fog and everything, but this was an amazing place. The trees and bushes went right up to a huge brick wall and beyond that loomed the power station with it's four huge brick chimneys he'd mistaken for Tower blocks the night before. There was a door in the wall covered by overgrown roses and a cobbled car parking area where a double garage stood, also covered by climbing wild roses.

'It's like the secret garden,' Harriet explained. 'God knows why she lives here. Scrapyard one side, the river the other. The house needs at least fifty thousand spending on it. When she's gone they'll knock it down for sure.'

'I love it!' Oliver exclaimed, looking back at the old brick house and its blue slate roof. He was astonished to see a crane moving at the back of the house with a big black car clutched in its jaws. Suddenly there was the sound of scrunching as something grabbed the car and began to crush it. Scrap yards, cranes, walls, a river and a Secret Garden, it was weird, but great. He was sure he was going to like it, so would Flop.

'Do you like Flop? My cat?' he asked Harriet as she came to a halt by her ice blue Renault Megane Coupe. 'He's really good at catching rats.'

Harriet smiled as she unlocked her car. 'He is? Then maybe I should take him on my next date.' She grinned at Oliver and indicated he should get into the car. Oliver laughed, thinking that perhaps Harriet would be OK after all.

Grandma Otis was standing at her window watching Oliver with Harriet, wondering how it was he was so at ease with her, but grateful for it nevertheless. Having a boy around would be a handful and Harriet would be useful to be his 'aunt', give him advice when he needed it.

Lena entered the room with breakfast and Grandma Otis shuffled back to her bed. Lena brought the breakfast to her bed, set it down, then plumped up the pillows behind her.

'Of course, he's got the gift, y'know,' Grandma Otis said as she reached for her tea. 'He doesn't know it yet, but he's going to be a magnet for trouble.'

Lena sat with her own mug of coffee and thought about it, thought about that story he'd told about the blue box. 'He's very sweet, very trusting. You don't think he'll be a problem surely?'

Grandma Otis dipped a piece of toast into her tea and turned to face Lena, her face stern now, as if she'd seen the future and it was all bad. 'Harriet can sense it. She's got the most developed nose for trouble I know. She can find it where none ever existed. Believe me, Oliver is going to change our lives.'

Lena nodded and stuck her face close in to her coffee mug so that the steam covered her face and made her sweat. 'Did Quon tell you that? He's a good boy, I hope you haven't taken against him.'

'No, I like him. I'm just saying he's got a trusting nature and that'll invite trouble. You have to take him shopping. He needs new clothes. He looks like a gypsy tyke.'

'Tomorrow. Let him have some time with Harriet and she'll tell me what suits him. Though God knows he'll want what all the other kids have and it will cost a fortune.'

'Well, he can have what he likes. That boy hasn't been spoiled for a long time. It's not as if I'm short.'

'I just hope his hair grows back, the kids will give him a hard time around here if it doesn't.'

Grandma Otis sighed. 'You can't grow grass on barren rock. Now...have you got the book? How many today?'

Lena set down her coffee and flipped open a large diary. 'Got someone from Eltham first, new woman, never been before. Then Mrs Gothard, she's bringing a VIP, she says, someone in the Government. He's a bit nervous, we've already had someone to look the place over to make sure it's safe.'

Grandma Otis shook her head. 'I don't like these sort of people, they've always got so many problems and they never believe you if it isn't what they want to hear. Sometimes, Lena, I think I should just give up. We could sell, move to Bournemouth.'

'Bournemouth? Things are depressing enough without you going there. Couldn't we go somewhere more exotic, say Seville or Florence? Or Deauville? I know you like Deauville.'

Grandma Otis just smiled as she sipped her tea. 'I've told you before Lena, you'd miss England...sooner than you think.'

CHAPTER THREE

Harriet swore as she noticed the time on her dashboard clock. 'Stay here,' she instructed Oliver, as she immediately got out of the car, ran around in front of it and dashed across the road, narrowly being missed by an annoyed van driver. Oliver watched her disappear through an archway, into Greenwich marketplace. He noticed the shop she had run by sold maps and paintings. One huge print seemed to show the river and how it ran in a horseshoe. Oliver itched to examine the map and the old sailing ship models in the windows. He made a mental note to return to this place.

The traffic was the worst he had ever seen. Greenwich was choked with cars and trucks and he was sure Harriet had parked illegally on these double yellow lines because people would blast him with their horns as they went by. He wondered what Harriet was doing. He knew she was going to be late for her appointment. Oliver was fascinated by how busy this area was, quite different to Louth, even busier than his town on a Saturday morning. He spotted Harriet again. She'd changed her coat to a bright yellow one with a black velvet collar. She waved to Oliver, but then, quite without warning it began to rain and he saw Harriet dash back through the archway again. Oliver was puzzled. Where had she gone? The rain bucketed down, making everything virtually disappear. The sound of the rain on the car roof was deafening and traffic almost came to a stop all around him. It was darker and the rain was bouncing high off the road forming little pools around the drains that couldn't cope with the sudden rush of water. Oliver was just getting worried (he'd seen a traffic warden hurriedly crossing the road further down) when Harriet reappeared at the driver's side of the car frantically opening the door as fast as she could and climbing in, slamming the door after her. Oliver noticed she was now wearing a sensible black waterproof coat with an enormous hood inlaid with some tartan material. Harriet said nothing. Just started the engine and almost without a glance at the traffic surrounding them, drove out into it, blasting her horn, weaving her way around dithering motorists.

'Bloody rain, they said it would be sunny today.'

'I met Michael Fish once,' Oliver told her. 'He said it would be sunny and it rained.'

Harriet glanced at him. 'Michael Fish? The weather man? You met him?'

'He was in Grimsby, talking about the weather, and he told me that he didn't believe in country ways.'

Harriet was puzzled now. 'You lived near Grimsby? You poor kid. What did you say to him, exactly?'

'Well, Nick – he's the gardener at the hospital, he said that he could tell what the weather would be like from month to month just by looking at the animals and birds in the gardens.'

'And Michael Fish said he didn't believe it.'

'Yes. I told him Nick predicted the hot summer and the surprise snow in November last year, and he even said it would rain for the fete, two months before it happened. He watches the rabbits. If they jump and bite the tree bark, that's how high the snow will be.'

Harriet smiled. 'Well, no one likes amateurs, especially good ones. It's like my Doctor. He thinks there's no such thing as seeing the future and he thinks your Grandma is making it all up. When she told me four years ago that I have to have an operation, my Doctor said no. But Grandma Otis insisted. So I went to another Doctor and he had me in hospital the next week and fixed the problem. Doctors don't like amateurs, y'see.'

Oliver was sure he thought he saw, but not really. He pondered this as Harriet negotiated the traffic, ducking down a side road and then sharp right, going between two brick gateposts. 'We'll go through the park,' Harriet said, 'you'll love the park. There's some deer up by the far wall. I don't know why they don't let them wander, it would be much prettier. They do in Richmond. This is where the Royal Observatory is. Y'know? Greenwich Mean Time and all that.'

Oliver knew 'all that' and was keen to see it, but Harriet just drove on up the hill, sweeping around behind the Observatory and then down the long drive away from it towards the gates at the far end. Oliver longed to walk in the park, discover what was here. He looked back, but the sweeping rain obscured his view.

'Do you live near here?'

'Of course. I've got a little place in Blackheath. You'll see. You'll like the village. It's cute. Really cute.'

Oliver was puzzled now. Somehow, all his life he'd thought of London as one huge city, but so far all he'd seen were 'villages'. It was so much like home, but just so much more of it. He didn't know if he was disappointed or pleased. Both, he supposed. He wondered where Richmond was, and whether he'd ever get to see the deer.

Harriet's car turned off the main road into the Cator Estate, passing two gateposts on the way that seemed to signify that they were entering a special, more exclusive area. They passed expensive, mansion-style homes and although Oliver didn't much care for the speed bumps, he thought the homes and the wide avenues would be a pretty good place for his Grandma to live in. One could rollerblade on these avenues in safety.

'We're here,' Harriet suddenly announced, slowing down and looking for parking space. The only clue that Oliver had that Mr McTeal's grand house was different to any other in the estate, was a not so discrete sign in the basement of a large human hand hung up by two chains. It was sort of creepy, like a disembodied giant's hand. Harriet must have sensed Oliver's nervousness and she put out a hand to his head and rested it on his new woolly cap. 'It's OK, he's just going to tell me how wonderful the rest of my life is going to be and then we'll go for an ice-cream, or something.'

Oliver looked at her, wondering if she was thinking he was five and could be so easily reassured with a bribe of an ice-cream, but then, when he looked at her face he realised that it was she who was nervous and wanted him to say something to reassure her.

'I bet he'll tell you you'll meet a handsome prince.' Oliver told her.

Harriet laughed and made to get out of her car. 'I hope so, I've been through enough frogs already.'

Walking to the house Oliver noticed there was a large, silver Celtic cross in one of the bedroom windows. He took this as a good sign. Harriet stood at the basement door as Oliver waited at the top of the steps, looking at the giant's hand. Harriet was looking at it too.

'If you look at the lines, they all have names-love-lines, life-lines. That's how he reads the hands. He can tell what kind of person you are and what kind of life you'll lead.' She saw Oliver's sceptical look and smiled. 'You'll see.'

'I believe you. My mother said it was just a Gypsy trick, but the Gypsy scared her, so I know what she said was true.'

'Gypsy?' Harriet asked, but the door was being unlocked inside and the question died on her lips.

Oliver was watching Harriet nervously adjusting her clothes and licking her fingers to smooth down her eye make-up. She sighed. 'This rain makes my hair go crazy,' she said, but to no one in particular.

The door opened at last, and there stood a young girl, no more than seventeen or eighteen and astonishingly thin. She was dressed completely in black, from her glossy braided raven hair to her opened black painted toenails. Oliver just stared at her with wonderment as he walked down the steps and into the reception room. Harriet seemed all smiles and was talking to her as if she knew the girl.

'Nice dress, is it Moschino? Thought so. Black makes you look so mysterious, but I'd add a blue contrast or a shade of purple in your eye make-up, give you a lift, y'know.'

The girl looked at Harriet as if she were going to say something rude, then smiled, revealing perfect white teeth. The spell was cast. Oliver was in complete awe of her, her smile had him charmed completely. He knew she was just out to shock with what she wore, but he immediately wished he was older and she would notice him.

'I tried white, but my father sort of freaked out about it,' she was telling Harriet.

'White is for the theatre. You need a warmer tone to compliment the black.' Harriet reaffirmed. 'I'm sure I've seen you before.'

The girl went to the corner of the room and opened a fridge. 'Would you like some Coke? I'm afraid I've run out of everything else.'

Oliver nodded, but Harriet declined and the girl threw him a cold can which he only just caught. Harriet was still looking at the girl. 'Ophelia. You were Ophelia at Rose Bruford last term. I came to the end of semester production. It was a disaster, but you were excellent.'

The girl seemed completely astonished. 'You saw that? I was supposed to be the understudy. Oh shit, you actually saw that?' Clearly the girl had not been as impressed with her performance as Harriet. 'I was terrible. I nearly quit college after that.'

Oliver opened his Coke and watched Harriet and the girl. They seemed so at ease, yet they didn't know each other. He wondered if he'd ever be able to do that, just talk to people, not worry about asking their names or anything.

'I remember you forgot your lines at one time, but I thought you covered it so well by crying and running off stage. It was quite dramatic.'

The girl smiled. 'It was fright. I really was crying. They spun me around and sent me back. All I needed was one word, but it just wouldn't come and blocked everything else. God, I'll never be an actress unless I can learn lines. Denis tried hypnosis on me, but I still can't remember a whole play. Well I can, but not necessarily in the right order.'

Harriet smiled. 'It will come. You should definitely continue, everyone was so taken with you. I had no idea you were Mr McTeal's daughter.'

'No one does, thank God. I'd have people plaguing me to read their fortunes all day. Denis can do it, but I'd go crazy.' She smiled at Harriet, then shrugged. 'I hope he tells you what you want to know. 'Bye.'

Oliver watched her go, caught a glimpse of her long thin hands. Somehow he knew she was the one who had the silver Celtic cross in her window.

Harriet turned to smile at him as the girl left the room. 'You were scared of her when we came in, weren't you?'

Oliver was about to protest, but Harriet cut him off. 'Anyway, I think she's going to be very famous one day. She's someone you can just watch and they have a kind of magic. You'll see. She'll be famous.'

Oliver thought about that, about how everyone he knew now were always talking about the 'future', making predictions. Just about everyone was different to the people he knew back in Louth. 'Why do you want to know the future anyway?' he asked.

Harriet stole a sip of his Coke to freshen her mouth and then looked at him with surprise on her face. 'Don't be foolish. Don't you want to know if your hair will grow back? Or if you meet a beautiful girl one day who will love you? Or if you'll write a piece of software that'll make you rich?'

Oliver was about to reply that computers gave him headaches and he already knew that the chances of his hair coming back were near zero, when a door at the end of the room opened. Both he and Harriet stared with mouths agape as a huge fat man exited the inner room sideways to get through the doorway. The very floor shook as he lumbered past them to the outer-door with an audible asthmatic wheeze. Harriet caught Oliver's eye and they both shook their heads in wonder that anyone so large could walk, let alone want to see a fortune-teller.

'What do you think he wanted to know?' Oliver whispered as the door closed again.

Harriet shrugged. 'The usual, probably. Y'know, will he ever find the right diet or the right girl?'

Oliver pulled a face. 'A girl? Yuk. He'd want a girl?'

Harriet gave him a piteous look. 'People never give up hope. You'll see.'

But Oliver was still reeling from the possibility that any man, so large, could want a girlfriend. Perhaps all he really wanted to know was about the diet, that had to be it.

'Stop pulling those faces. Try to act civilised. You don't know what kind of problems the poor man has.'

Oliver buried his face into his Coke can and sighed. Everyone was so strange. He looked up again and saw a man staring at him. Mr McTeal was standing in the inner doorway mopping his brow. He was short, only five feet or so, and wearing a flamboyant blue silk shirt opened at the top revealing a gold chain. He wore red rimmed glasses and a small toupee which sat on his head like a dead squirrel and made him look like a TV presenter of some quiz show where they gave away really stupid prizes.

'Oh my God!' he heard Harriet whisper under her breath as she caught sight of him. Oliver sensed this wasn't necessarily a good sign. He couldn't take his eyes off the man's toupee. He wondered how much further it could slip before it would leap off his head and run for cover. He found himself having to bite his bottom lip to stop himself from laughing.

'You must be Harriet.' McTeal said, smiling, his voice softly Irish. 'You met my daughter? She looked after you, I hope. Is this your boy? You didn't tell me you were bringing your son.'

Harriet regarded McTeal with some surprise. Oliver looked at her and realised that she was quite flummoxed. He smiled, thinking about how he could tease her about this later.

'This is my Aunt Harriet. I'm afraid she's stuck with me today.'

McTeal nodded, accepting this reasonable explanation, although Oliver sensed that he didn't entirely like the situation.

Harriet stood up and dragged Oliver up with her, squeezing his shoulder, thankful for Oliver's common sense. 'This is Oliver, my nephew, Mr McTeal, he's here to make sure you don't drug me and pack me off to whiteslavers.'

McTeal allowed himself a momentary smile, revealing pure white, elegant but very false teeth, which made Oliver feel quite queasy.

'I only supply slavers on Thursdays, so I'm afraid you're out of luck, Oliver.'

Oliver wasn't absolutely sure what slavers were (perhaps he was confusing them with pirates) so he kept his mouth shut and did his best to avert his eyes from the toupee that now seemed to have slipped another inch or two and wriggle when McTeal spoke. Harriet was walking towards McTeal as he backed himself into his inner room.

'I saw your daughter play Ophelia.' Harriet informed him, 'it was very moving.'

McTeal shrugged. 'She died well, but I'm afraid she was utterly traumatised by the event, it will be difficult to get her back on the boards now.'

Oliver followed Harriet into the room and sniffed the air. Incense. He recognised it instantly. His mother had burned incense for as long as he could remember and he felt almost comforted by the cinnamon scent. He was too scared to say anything. The room was moody, made moodier by the blue grey walls. There was a long, maple-wood floor and a Japanese-style low slung table centred within it surrounded by large silk over stuffed cushions. He could hear his shoes squeak on the wooden floor and he saw that Harriet was removing hers, so he followed suit, almost falling over in the process. As he kicked off his first shoe, it landed by a large electric machine parked near a wall. He saw that McTeal was frowning at him.

'Careful, that machine is very sensitive. It charges the air with positive ions and lifts the atmosphere. Can you sense it? It should make you feel more energetic.'

Harriet made some kind of noise that indicated that she agreed with him, but Oliver didn't really comprehend. How could an electric machine change the atmosphere? Well actually, he did feel like he was standing on the edge of a steep cliff with a whoosh of wind coming up at him from the sea below, but he often felt like that when he felt nervous.

Harriet was examining the masks on the wall, huge Japanese face masks with lurid paintings on them. McTeal sat beside the table and squatted on one of the cushions, indicating to Harriet to join him. He saw she was looking at his masks.

'Japanese Noh theatre masks. I collect them. I have eighty upstairs. It's my only indulgence'.

Harriet was impressed. 'I had no idea fortune telling was so profitable.'

McTeal smiled. 'My financial astrology column is syndicated in hundreds of magazines world-wide. You would be surprised just how closely one can predict the stock market using astrology. A lot of people rely of Denis McTeal's stock tips.'

Harriet sat down before him and regarded the little man with his crooked toupee with a little more respect. He had built himself quite an empire, but as a specimen of manhood he was a big disappointment. She sighed. Why was it that all the good-looking ones never had any money?

'You can sit here,' McTeal pointed to a spare cushion. 'Remember this is your Aunt's reading not yours, so please, just observe.'

Oliver complied. He wasn't going to say a word, this was all too spooky. What was McTeal going to say? He was keen to see how someone 'read' a hand. He looked back at the window again, his eyes catching sight of a crystal hanging by a thread, one strand of sunlight catching it and being bounced to the far wall as a streak of rainbow. Just as quickly a cloud covered the sun outside again and the rainbow vanished.

Harriet smiled at McTeal as she detected that he wasn't as comfortable on the cushion as he'd like to be. He was trying to fold his legs under him and sweating a little with pain. He noticed her look. 'I'm fifty now, take a tip from me, keep your legs supple when your young and they'll look after you when you're older. Wish someone had told me that when I was twenty.'

Harriet just thought about all her broken promises to work out and join the gym, lift weights. Sex was the only workout she got and that wasn't as regular as she liked these days.

McTeal reached for her left hand and Harriet watched him quite intently as he studied her palm. She could see him sweating under his toupee and Oliver was watching a droplet trickle down his neck under his shirt collar. Both Oliver and

Harriet made brief eye contact and quickly looked away lest they broke out into hysterical laughter. Oliver only just held it in.

McTeal was oblivious to their observations and concentrated hard upon Harriet's palm.

'There is much pain in your hands, such trauma. I can understand why you came to see me, my dear. Your love-life... (He momentarily shook his head as if he'd seen real trouble)...it must be Hell...a real emotional roller coaster. Such passion one moment, such coolness the next...such terrible risks...such miscalculations...so many foolish decisions...'

McTeal shrugged and arched his back as if in pain, all the time searching for the appropriate words.

'To be frank, my dear, I can't see anything that might make you happy. There have been betrayals, there is violence... someone you trusted has betrayed you... someone you like will betray you...' McTeal let go of her hand and stared hard at Harriet. 'Tell me, didn't you ever consider becoming a nun?'

Harriet swallowed hard and looked back at him with a mixture of horror and despair. She involuntarily crossed herself, breaking into hysterical laughter, water welling up in her eyes.

Oliver watched this with absolute fascination. Harriet didn't seem to be taking it very well so far. McTeal reached out and grabbed her other hand, quickly upturning it and tracing her love line with a sharp pencil. 'Let me look at your right hand, my dear, perhaps there is some hope.'

Harriet winced as the pencil tickled her palm, but she already had that sinking feeling, the man didn't even have the grace to lie to her. She snatched a look at Oliver who was now examining his own hands and trying to compare them a wall-chart hanging behind him.

McTeal continued to shake his head as he traced her lifeline. Harriet began to bite her bottom lip, rather regretting the £200 this was costing her.

'Let's face it,' McTeal told her at last, 'I'm afraid you'll never be lucky in love. Your mound of Venus is all wrong. Your love-line is so feint and pitted. You know that it has been one tragedy after another, or else you wouldn't have come to see me. You just can't choose men and somehow they know you can't commit and take advantage of you. You have been engaged more than once, I guess.'

'Six times,' Harriet admitted guiltily.

McTeal nodded. He knew this. 'And each time you broke it off...each time you convinced yourself there was a good reason.'

Harriet looked at him with rising anger. 'If you call breaking my arm the night before the wedding a "good reason", if you call finding another girl in bed with my fiance a "good reason". Actually I didn't break off the last one, he broke off with me when I wrote off his new Alfa Spider.' She shrugged. 'Hell, it was only a car, but he thought more of that car than me. I swear.'

McTeal sighed and clutched at both her hands again. 'On the upside you are going to live a long life and there's money...not a fortune...but enough and ...I'm sorry...but...'

Harriet frowned. 'What? What now? Any children?' As soon as she said it she realised that she'd said it with more passion than she'd intended. McTeal heard the anxiety in her voice and made a note to tread carefully.

'I think that perhaps this would be unwise. My dear, it is rare to see such an unlucky hand, truly. Tell me honestly, are men that important to you?'

Oliver rolled his eyes, he couldn't believe he'd ask that! Harriet let loose a sudden loud snort of derision. McTeal was taken aback. He let go of Harriet's hand and watched impatiently as Harriet tried to compose herself, perhaps thinking of the money she was paying him. Harriet sobered up and took a deep breath as she considered for a moment what she might say, snatching a look at Oliver who was all wide-eyed, also nervously wondering what she was going to say next.

'So, let me get this right,' Harriet began, holding up one hand and looking at it with an exaggerated impression of McTeal's manner, 'the bottom line is that I'm going to be an old, borderline, poverty stricken fucking spinster with no grandchildren.' She pinned her eyes to McTeal who was now sitting up straight, looking very defensive. 'Is that about right?'

McTeal smiled back at her like some salesman who'd already got your name on the contract and knew you couldn't back out. 'Well, I wouldn't put it so negatively myself. You could always take up sculpture. You might find it very soothing. Even yoga, or art might save you, help channel your energy.'

Harriet ignored him, and showed Oliver her palms, putting them up right close to his face so that he couldn't exactly avoid them. 'What do you think, Oliver?' She looked at McTeal before Oliver could answer. 'I mean, I'm paying for half an hour right? Might as well read the kid's hands as well.'

Oliver immediately sat on his hands, looking at Harriet with imploring eyes.

McTeal understood Oliver's reluctance and looked at his watch. He sighed. Perhaps he hadn't earned his £200 yet. He had only talked for ten minutes. He reached out and grabbed Oliver's cap of his head before Oliver could do anything about it. Oliver shouted 'No'!, but McTeal had already pulled him towards him and placed his fingers on his head.

'Sit still boy, this won't hurt you.'

Oliver froze, the last person to say that to him had drilled a hole six inches deep into his skull. 'Harriet my head...' he wailed.

Harriet was speechless with silent horror at the scars and contusions on Oliver's still raw head, but McTeal seemed unfazed as he felt for the bumps and traced his fingertips over Oliver's skull, seemingly covering every inch.

'This boy has suffered a great deal, but I needn't dwell on that. You are a brave boy Oliver, I can see that. You have great tenacity and strength of will. You have survived a major test and now can plan a way forward in your life. Often it is said that reading a child's hand reveals nothing, because the real tests of life have not yet been made. However, the head has already been formed and can reveal a great deal. Phrenology is much underrated in this country, but in Turkey they have a great respect for it. Feel this bump here, Oliver?'

Oliver nodded. He wasn't actually in pain, he just hated anyone looking at or touching his head, this was a very sensitive area for him.

'You may not realise this, but you are a very lucky kid, this bump is your patron saint of luck. Take good care of your head Oliver and it will take good care of you. You'll be a good reader, might even become a good writer. I see a strong artistic bent here, definitely something creative, working with people a lot, helping people shape their lives. Perhaps you will write something that reaches lots of people, a computer game or a something? Who knows? You have a strong sense of loyalty and hate to let anyone down. People like you and you will always have friends, I see an affinity for animals. They trust you.'

Oliver was about to say something when McTeal turned his head the other way.

'You have been having very vivid dreams, am I right?'

'Yes,' Oliver admitted. It was true. Sometimes they were so real it was hard to believe that they hadn't happened.

'So real you think they may be true, yes?'

Oliver nodded. He wondered how McTeal knew that. McTeal was rubbing a bump on the side of Oliver's head now. He looked up and caught McTeal's expression, much more serious than before.

'What?' Oliver asked, worried now. 'Am I going to get sick again?'

McTeal shook his head. 'No, nothing like that. Your hair might come back one day, but...there's something else. It's a feeling I get. I don't really like to say.'

'What?' Harriet asked, a concerned note in her voice. 'You can't leave him hanging in the air like that, he'll fret.'

McTeal looked at Harriet and she immediately understood that he didn't really want to say, but Harriet insisted. 'Tell him, he's been through enough, he's strong.'

McTeal shrugged. 'OK, there's a specific warning to Oliver here...a danger. You mustn't climb trees, mountains, anything high. You understand me? I want to be specific here. This particular configuration is a warning signal. It stands out. Take no risks where heights are concerned. Perhaps even flying would be a risk for you. Stay close to the ground. You need not be worried about the tumour coming back, but climbing, flying, that is out of the question.'

McTeal rested his hands and sat back on his cushion. He was done. Harriet looked at her watch. There was still fifteen minutes to go, it seemed churlish to complain too much, but she felt she had to, this man was not offering value for money.

'That's it? Two hundred pounds and we get fifteen minutes for the two of us?'

McTeal was growing annoyed now. 'You want me to tell you how bad your love life is for thirty minutes? Or would you prefer me to tell you lies?' He sighed, watching Oliver replacing his cap on his head with determined precision. 'OK...I tell you what. You send me one new client and I'll give you a free crystal reading for next time.'

Harriet made a sour face as she handed over the cash. McTeal took it and stashed it in a small wooden box without even checking to see if it was right. He began to unfurl his body and try to stand up, not without revealing some evidence of pain. 'Just don't go into relationships expecting so much, my dear, perhaps they will last longer than usual.'

Harriet stood up and staggered a little as a sudden blood-rush caught her off guard. She didn't say another word and Oliver took his cue from her, tagging along behind her.

McTeal watched them go with a frozen smile on his face.

Oliver looked for McTeal's daughter as they left, but she was nowhere to be seen. For some reason he'd wanted to say goodbye to her.

Outside in the cool, damp air, Harriet slammed the door behind her and stomped towards her Renault. Oliver could tell she was in a 'mood' that was growing blacker by the minute.

'I'm too mad to go back to work. We'll go to the river and have a drink,' she said, indicating to Oliver to get back into her car.

Oliver said nothing, he judged it wasn't safe. He'd seen his mother in moods like this and knew when to keep his mouth shut.

Harriet remained in a bad mood as she tried to join the traffic crawling through Blackheath. She squeezed back into the flow and lit a cigarette.

'What an asshole. Thank you, Cupid. Thank you, Mr "Fortune Teller to the stars", Mr McBastard-Teal. No love life, no kids,' she mimicked McTeal's limp voice... 'Have you ever thought of becoming a nun.' Hah...The cheek of it. The absolute bloody nerve!... And I paid him £200 quid.' Harriet let out a shriek that could have cracked the windscreen. Oliver sank down into his seat trying to disappear as people turned to look at their car.

'I'll show him. I'll marry the next wimp who bloody looks at me and give him poxy twins.'

Oliver was thinking that that wasn't too good an idea when Harriet took out a tape from her glove box and slammed it into the cassette player. Mozart's 'Requiem' filled the car with music so loud Oliver thought his head would explode, but at least it seemed to calm Harriet, who blasted her horn and carved herself a space out of nowhere to break out of the stalled traffic. Oliver began to suspect that perhaps not everyone was quite normal in London. That there was, perhaps, a lot to learn about the people who lived here.

CHAPTER FOUR

'Tides on the turn, smells bad. The river always seems to stink when the tide goes out.' Harriet remarked, as she led Oliver towards the riverside pathway. She pointed towards the nearest pub. 'We can get lunch there, God I need a drink.'

'Can we go down to the beach? ' Oliver pleaded.

Harriet looked down at the pebbles, stones and mud left behind by the river and was amazed to see there was a thin strip of quite respectable beach. She was surprised. She had no idea that there was a beach in Greenwich. 'Oh God, I guess. I forgot, you're a boy, you need to do these sort of things.'

'I just want to walk on it, we could skim. I'm good at skimming.'

Harriet suddenly smiled. 'Skim? You're good at skimming? You are talking to the champion skimmer of London here. My father taught me and he was taught in Scotland, lived by Loch Ness when he was a boy. Never challenge someone to a skimming contest until you know something about them, boy. My hands are hot.'

Oliver laughed and ran for the stone steps that led to the beach below.

'Watch out for the slime,' Harriet shouted out after him, but too late. Oliver was already on the steps and she heard him 'Whoo-oop', as his feet slid out from under him and sent him flying to the beach below. He fell towards the stony beach with half turn and landed solidly on his back. Ominously for Harriet, he made no sound. Her heart began to race. She had visions of Oliver dying whilst in her care and she began to panic. She ran towards the steps and almost fell herself on the green slime before checking herself on the railings. 'Oliver!' she shrieked. 'For God's sake, Oliver, say something.'

Oliver opened his eyes and looked at the sky. How quiet the world seemed. He watched with momentary astonishment as the clouds in the sky appeared to fall towards him, almost as if they were coming in to cover him, like a blanket. He began to register the sounds of seagulls and somewhere, further back, a woman shouting his name. Abruptly sound flooded in, loud, almost explosive in his ears.

'Oliver?' Harriet appeared in the sky above him, her face filled with worry. 'Say something, say something.'

Oliver took a deep breath, nothing seemed to be broken. He was fine really, he was sure of it.

Harriet knelt down beside him, staring with silent horror at the debris scattered all around him and the amount of broken glass. 'My God, another inch to the left and your head would have hit this.' Harriet removed an up-ended jagged broken wine bottle from the sand and threw it into the river. Oliver sat up and saw all the broken glass lying around him and realised that he had been lucky. 'People shouldn't throw bottles into the river, they're supposed to re-cycle them.'

'Tell that to 'them'.' Harriet remarked, helping him up. 'How's your balance?'

Oliver nodded his head from side to side. 'OK'

Harriet pulled a face as she tried to get the wet sand off her coat. 'This isn't a real beach. It's dirty too. Let's go eat.'

Oliver frowned. 'You were going to beat me at skimming.'

Harriet's worried expression melted away as quickly as it came and she shook her head. 'You'll regret this.'

Oliver laughed and began looking for flat, well-rounded stones. Harriet immediately began doing the same, amazed that a) she was actually standing on the beach and b) wearing her new Gazelles. She'd expected Oliver to cry, or something. It was clear that he had hurt himself, but he was tough. She found herself thinking that she liked him. He was different to all the other children she'd come into contact with. Unspoiled.

Oliver was standing by the water's edge, looking for stones, occasionally stooping down and clutching one, then just as quickly rejecting it, tossing it back into the river. A barge was sailing by, pulled by a ramshackle tug. Oliver looked up and stared beyond it to where Canary Wharf stood towering over everything. It looked so close from his position at the side of the river. Oliver abruptly looked back at Harriet who was closely examining a stone.

'Did you believe everything he told you?'

Harriet looked at him with surprise.

'Why? You think I should lie down here and wait for the tide to come in? That might solve my problems, don't you think?'

Oliver shook his head. 'But did you believe him?'

Harriet laughed, but Oliver could tell from the way she tossed her hair and stared out across the river, that she did believe.

'I guess part of me does...but why should I? Why is my love life so screwed up? What did I do so wrong? That's what I want to know.' Harriet shrugged, then suddenly took a firm stand in the sand, bent her knees, flipped her arm back, got her eye on the water and with a flick of her wrist sent her stone flying across the river.

'Wow.' Oliver shouted as the stone skimmed seven...eight...nine times before hitting a little wave.

Harriet grinned, suddenly remembering the pleasure to be found in skimming. 'Nine. Beat that Sonny Jim.'

Oliver drew a deep breath, hunkered his feet down in the sand and with all his force swung back and flung his stone towards the river. It plunged immediately into a wave and was lost.

'You call that skimming? You lose.'

'Wait!' Oliver demanded urgently. 'Wait.' He placed his second stone in his fingers and drew his hand back, urging himself to keep control, keep balance, keep his knees bent, keep the stance...he let go. The stone kissed the water and skipped four times before hitting a floating log.

Harriet laughed, but not as harshly as before. 'That would have been good, but you've got waves from the barge, you have to wait for the water to be flat, be patient.'

Oliver quickly hunted for more stones, Harriet likewise, enjoying herself now. Oliver was still thinking about what McTeal had said to Harriet.

'If your luck is so bad, why don't you change it?'

Harriet sighed, examining her palms with mock despair. 'How? I was born with these hands. That's it, bad karma. I've got a lousy loveline, shitty mound of

Venus. I should be a zombie. They don't have to worry about feelings.'

Oliver laughed and looked quite animated about the subject. 'They can't be killed either. You can run a sword through them and they keep on coming at you. I saw 'Evil Dead' and 'Night of the Living Dead' on TV. Zombies are real hard to kill, it's a problem.'

Harriet grinned at how serious Oliver sounded. She began looking for stones again. 'That's me. 'Harriet the Greenwich Zombie'. I get hit, I keep on going. I get hit again, sure enough I crawl back for more. It's pitiful and all because of lousy hands.'

Oliver looked at his own and then at Harriet again. 'So why don't you change them? Get new hands. People change their noses, don't they?'

Harriet was about to make a sarcastic comment, when it suddenly hit her. She shrieked and rushed over to Oliver, embracing him, lifting him off his feet and swinging him around her, whooping and laughing. Oliver joined in with the laughter, (but he wasn't sure why). Also, he was scared to death he was going to lose his hat to the river.

'That's it, that's it.' Harriet was shouting at him, real joy in her face. 'If people don't like their faces they change them. No one thinks that is crazy. I can change my hands. I can change my bloody hands!'

She set Oliver down on the sand and he looked at her askance. 'You mean you'd really cut your hands off and get new ones? That's yuk.'

Harriet laughed. 'No, stupid, I'd have surgery. Look, see my palms? They can change my love line, my life line – everything. They can cut out the bad luck and groove in good luck. God, I need to find out what a perfect lucky hand is like. I can't believe I didn't think of doing this before.'

'But isn't that cheating?'

Harriet looked at Oliver with despair. 'Don't they teach you anything at school anymore? Cheating is how you win. Besides, you weren't born with nuns' hands. I'll do anything to change my luck. Shit, I can get my palms fixed. Then let's see what that bloody fortune teller McTeal says, huh? Hah-bloody-hah!'

Oliver broke free from Harriet and was about to skim again when he spotted a pair of shoes floating in on the tide. He walked further along the water's edge to look at them as they bobbed and eddied in towards the beach, slowly coming nearer with every little ripple in the water.

Harriet was watching him, wondering how a pair of shoes could be out on the river and float together. Oliver looked back at her a moment.

'Won't it hurt to cut new lines on your hands? I mean, how will you know what a lucky love-line is?'

Harriet picked up a stone from the sand and skimmed it across the water, watching it skip the water six times. 'I could have Liv Tyler's hands, I bet she's got lucky hands. Or Michelle Pfeiffer's. Of course I could have Elizabeth Taylor's hands, but then I'd probably get fat and I don't want to marry body-builders.'

Oliver was still waiting for the shoes to come in, fascinated by them now. He could see they were black and the laces were tied together.

'Who's Elizabeth Taylor?'

Harriet pulled a face. There was a whole generation now who didn't know who anyone was anymore. 'What about Cindy Crawford? Shit no, I'd have all those people wondering if I was a dyke. Maybe Julie Delpy, she's beautiful and she's got exquisite hands. I wonder if she's happy? Maybe Claudia Schiffer's hands...nah, I couldn't stand hanging out with magicians. God, I wonder what a palm-job costs.'

Harriet mused over her hands and Oliver dipped his toes into the river a little to try and grab the pair of shoes. Quite abruptly the shoes caught a little rush of water and they surged towards him.

'Leave them be.' Harriet told him. 'They're no use to you. Don't get your feet soaked. Come on Oliver, get back on the sand.'

Oliver reluctantly stepped back, just in time too, as a small wave pushed the shoes right up towards Oliver and deposited them beside his own damp footwear. Oliver laughed and looked down at his 'catch' only to change his expression entirely and let escape a gasp...

'Harriet...shit! Look.'

Harriet heard the squeak of surprise in his voice and walked over to Oliver's side to take a look at the shoes. 'I suppose someone just left them on a rock and...' Harriet got to see the shoes up close and Oliver's pale expression. 'Oh my God, someone's feet are still in them!'

Oliver and Harriet stared at the shoes experiencing a wave of disgust, mixed with awe. Shoes with feet in them. It was truly gross.

'Wow!' Oliver declared. ' I wonder who cut his feet off?'

Harriet shook her head and looked out across the river with a wistful sigh. 'I finally get to meet a man who can afford Gucci shoes and all I meet is his feet. I tell you, Oliver, it's the story of my life.'

'Shouldn't we call the police?'

'Why, you think someone might have called in complaining someone stole their feet?'

Harriet turned away and began walking towards the steps. 'You can call them, I need a drink.'

Half an hour later, Harriet and Oliver were enjoying a drink on the river terrace of 'The Trafalgar' pub as they watched the police comb the beach for more evidence. There was an ambulance on standby and a few gawkers, but in the main it wasn't that interesting. They'd had a good laugh at the young cop whose job it was to place the shoes inside an evidence bag. He'd tried, but every time he tried to do it, he wanted to throw up and had to stagger away from the shoes. In the end a more senior cop had to pick them up and seal the bag. He didn't look amused to be having to do it. Oliver laughed, but Harriet told him the young cop would be a laughing stock back in the Greenwich police station, his life would be a misery.

Harriet knocked back her gin and tonic and grew serious for a moment.

'I wonder what his palms were like?'

'The cop?'

'What cop?'

'The one who got sick.'

'No, the man who got his feet cut off. I'd liked to have seen his life-line.'

Oliver was sipping his Coke and watching the cops on the beach when a young woman in a blue anorak approached them in the restaurant. 'Are you the young man who made the call?' She waved a badge at him.

Oliver nodded.

'Detective Kray. I'd just like to thank you for making the call. It's good to get some cooperation 'round here..'

Oliver smiled. He was surprised she'd said she was a Detective, she didn't look a bit like the TV Detectives, but she had the badge. 'How did it happen?' He asked.

The woman ran a hand through her hair and sighed. 'Who knows? It was a clean cut, so it wasn't accidental, someone had to have chopped them off. I've seen industrial accidents and they make a real mess.'

Harriet swallowed some more of her drink, glad she'd skipped lunch now. 'He wore expensive shoes. £300 a pair if I recall.'

Detective Kray looked surprised.

'I'm in the trade,' Harriet explained. 'But they might have been fakes. You can get good Gucci fakes in Thailand.'

Oliver looked down suddenly at some activity on the water and his hat slipped off. He quickly picked it up and clamped it on his head again, but Detective Kray had seen his scars.

'My cousin had chemotherapy. He was bald as a coot for a couple of years, then suddenly...'

Oliver looked at her with hope. 'He grew hair?'

Detective Kray shook her head, a sad expression on her face. 'No, he was hit by a cement lorry. Died instantly. It was a terrible waste.'

Oliver looked back at the river, a suddenly feeling of doom spreading over him. He looked back at his own palms again. 'Harriet, I think I have to get my palms changed too.'

Harriet hugged him and laughed. Detective Kray didn't understand. She rose and smiled at them both as she fished for her business card. 'I understand you're local. If you hear anything, here's my card. Anything.'

Oliver watched her go, then looked at Harriet. 'Will they look for him?'

'Look for who?'

'The man who wore the shoes?'

Harriet shrugged. 'It's probably gangland stuff Oliver. Someone sent a warning. It's the river. You read your Charles Dickens, you'll discover that this is the place where all the bodies end up. It's not new and it'll probably happen again.'

Oliver finished his Coke and digested that news. Then, suddenly a wave of sadness washed over him. He had an overwhelming urge to run off and tell his mother what he'd seen and just as quickly, a jolting reminder that she wasn't around, wouldn't be interested, would never be interested. He was on his own now.

'I'd like to go now,' he said quietly and Harriet nodded. It was time.

CHAPTER FIVE

Sometimes you are caught a little off guard. Just because you have made the biggest discovery of your life, doesn't necessarily mean that anyone else will be impressed. When he got home and told everyone about the feet being sliced off whilst still being in their shoes, Grandma Otis just fretted, and Lena was so deep into a bottle of sherry, all he'd gotten out of her when he'd told her was glazed eyes and a 'That's nice, dear.' Grandma Otis had just crossed herself many times over and gone on about 'I knew you'd bring trouble. It's written as clear as the wind.' Then she told him it was time for her afternoon nap and he was instructed 'Not to make any noise.' In short, his afternoon was turning out to be somewhat anti-climatic.

Flop was out, hunting mice and not in the least interested in hearing about the river, or Harriet. So Oliver decided it was time to explore the outer limits of Grandma's house. The garden was self-evident. Full of trees and shrubs and lupins, but what was behind the house? There was something peculiar about the whole house. The way the door was positioned and how everything seemed to be at the back. Of course, having a scrap yard on one side probably would have something to do with it, and the huge wall that led to the old power station. Oliver found a side passage filled with overgrown weeds and a doll's pram, rusting, covered with ivy. When Oliver finally threaded his way to the back of the house, he realised that his bedroom actually overlooked the neighbours' house, and this house - (it was more of a shack, really) - came between Grandma's place and the actual scrapyard.

Now he was at the back he realised something else. Grandma's house was the wrong way around. Or more precisely, the front door was at the back as were the bay windows. There was even a short driveway that stopped where a metal fence had been built across it, and the neighbours' shack was sort of occupying the front lawn. It was very strange. On the other hand, living in a house that overlooked the scrapyard and cut off the view of the river couldn't be so good either. It was no wonder Grandma had sort of turned it around to face the garden at the back.

A shower of sparks arose from behind an overgrown lilac bush. Oliver pushed his way through and found himself at the back of a makeshift garage alongside the shack and, through a broken wooden door he could make out a small man in goggles and a pair of oily, overalls welding some metal bits together. There was another shower of sparks and the snap of electrical power. The man suddenly looked up and started as he laid eyes on Oliver.

'Hey...private property. This is private property. You go.'

Oliver immediately realised that the man was Chinese, or at least from the Far East.

'What are you doing?' Oliver asked, ignoring the man's aggressive manner. 'What is that?'

The man was still angry that Oliver was standing there. 'This place not yours, go! I call the police.'

Oliver decided to stand his ground. 'This is my place. My Grandma's place. I can stand here if I want.'

This did not seem to pacify the man in goggles at all. 'You live there? With the witches? Go away. You evil. You witch too.' He seemed very serious about this and quite agitated that Oliver was standing his ground. For his part, Oliver found the idea of him being a witch funny.

The man was waving his acetylene torch in the air and ran a great risk of setting fire to something. The flame brushed his hair and Oliver was about to shout out, when at the very same moment an oily rag caught fire on the workbench. The man quickly tried to switch off his torch but in the process knocked various bottles over, some of which spilled their guts and the rag began to burn more intensely. He finally got the torch closed off, but the burning rag had fallen to the ground and set fire to a puddle of liquid on the floor. The man began swearing and stamping on the rag, but then the fire jumped from the rag to the trouser legs of his overalls. Oliver watched in horror as the man was being transformed into a live bonfire. The man began to yell and curse in a language he didn't know, but Oliver knew that if he didn't act quickly, the whole garage would burn and the man could die. He kicked the door open with all the force he could muster and created a gap wide enough for him to jump through. Without thinking, Oliver grabbed a blanket that was lying over an old car in the garage and flung it over the man who was still jumping up and down as the flames ran up his overalls.

'Lie down, you have to roll, put the flames out.' Oliver shouted. He spotted a bucket of sand hanging on a wall and he ran over to it. It was way too heavy to lift, but he could scoop the sand out with his hands and throw it. This he did, throwing it, first at the burning puddle of oil, then at the man, who had the sense to fall to the ground and begin rolling to extinguish the flames...He was still shouting, but at least he was covered up and the flames were smothered. Oliver put out the last of the flames with the sand and it was over.

The man angrily flung off the blanket. He was black from the smoke and fumes, coughing and spitting as he tried to grab some air. He looked at Oliver with pure anger and Oliver stepped back. 'I didn't do anything.' He protested. 'Are you alright?'

The man was still cursing, examining his hands and overalls for damage.

Oliver was worried. Perhaps it was a bit his fault. He had distracted the man, he had chosen not to go away when the man asked. 'You'd better go and see a doctor.'

'No doctor.' the man said with quite some force. 'You made the flame grow. You witch. I saw you make the flame grow.'

Oliver didn't take too kindly to that. He was most definitely not a witch and he most certainly hadn't made the flame grow. The man wasn't going to thank him for saving his life. He could see that. Something else he could see too was that the garage was full of owls. Huge models of owls, all facing towards Grandma's house. He was just about to say something before leaving when the man tried to get up, then, silently, passed out, falling back loudly against the garage floor, scattering some empty cans.

Oliver ran over to him and felt his pulse. The man had fainted, that was all. The fumes from oil and gas were still incredibly strong here and Oliver realised what the problem was. Some incredibly strong liquid had spilled in the fire and was dripping from the workbench down onto the floor beside the man. Already Oliver's own eyes were sore and he could feel his breathing getting difficult.

With some effort he pulled the man clear of the area, then went back to the work bench and put a cap back on the bottle of liquid. He thought it might be hydrochloric acid, but it wasn't labelled - definitely a strong acid of some kind. Then, remembering a Doctor was needed, he went into the man's house to look for a phone.

The kitchen adjoined the garage and was filled with packets of dried food and hundreds of cans of bean sprouts. Oliver moved on into the first room and was again surprised to discover it too was full of owls, all pointing towards Grandma's house. In the next downstairs room, he found one big owl in the process of being carved from driftwood, all the tools lying where they had been left on the floor. But no 'phone. He realised that he wasn't going to find a 'phone, and the man probably needed water more than anything else. Oliver rushed back to the kitchen, found a cloth, made it damp and filled a glass of water from the tap . He noticed that there was a newspaper cutting of the man in the garage, stuck on the fridge door, in it he was standing by a huge owl and smiling.

Back in the garage, the man was still lying there unconscious. Oliver knelt beside him, wiped his face and waited. At last he began to stir. Oliver bent his head, slid the goggles from his face and gave him a sip of water. The man drank it, then, quite without warning opened his eyes, fixing them on Oliver. Even though still dazed, the animosity was still there.

'You!'

But he didn't attempt to move.

'You spilled some acid. The fumes made you faint.' Oliver informed him, making him drink some more water. 'Do you feel better now?'

The man didn't say anything. Oliver could see he was going to recover, so he stood up and began to walk towards the back door. He'd wanted to ask about the owls, but he didn't think the man would tell him.

'Wait.' the man growled.

Oliver turned and watched him struggle up, watched him wince as he discovered raw, burned skin on his hands.

'What's your name?' he asked finally.

'Oliver.'

The man nodded and began to walk towards his kitchen door, seeming to ignore Oliver. Then, at the door, without turning his head, he said 'Thank you.'

Oliver needed to get out of the garage. The fumes were deadly. He shrugged and made for the door. As he entered the bushes again he began to think 'Was it my fault?' 'Had I really caused it?', but he had done his best to save the man. He'd done all the right things. Done all the things school had taught to him to do if there was an emergency.

Flop was there to greet him in the garden, nervously following his trail. So glad was the cat to see him, he allowed himself to be picked up and hugged (although he didn't at all like the smell that was on Oliver and soon forced him to put Flop down).

'There was a fire, Flop. And acid. There's a weird man in there, he makes owls.'

Flop had already decided that everything around here was weird, including houses that were the wrong way around and loud noises coming from the scrapyard every five minutes that were calculated to make cats have heart attacks. He let Oliver fight the way back through the wilderness to the other side for him. He didn't know what had happened to Oliver, but he wasn't about to let him escape for so long again.

'Got to wash, Flop, then join the library. You want to join the library?'

Flop wanted to lie down and think of supper. That's what cats were good at.

Still, Oliver was in a funny mood. He couldn't help thinking that the accident in the garage had been his fault and he felt very guilty.

Libraries held no mystery for Oliver. He'd been a regular at Louth library since he was a kid - and he hadn't just stuck to the kid's fiction either. He liked to explore, read different things - history, mystery, adventures. He'd once tried a sexy book but some of the stuff in that had made him want to throw up, all that tongue kissing and licking the rude bits, yuk! (Never mind, the emotional stuff.) When it came down to it this boy preferred the kind of book where some guy kicked a door down and stood there with a gun in his hand...if he absolutely had to be nice to a girl, he'd just give her a quick hug before going back to killing the bad guys.

That and discovering the world. At school he'd explored Encarta '98 on the PC (when it didn't crash) and he'd loved mining all the details from differing parts of the world on the Internet, but today he wanted to find out about a particular place. He was still feeling the effects of the afternoon's fire. Somehow, the man in the garage burning like that had reminded him of his father. He remembered the dreams he'd had of seeing his father burning in Bosnia. He'd seen a film on TV called 'Underground' about some people living underground during the second world war. They were still down there, hiding, fifty years later when the Serbs and the Croats went to war. He had fixated on a scene where the 'bad' guy and his wife had been shot whilst he was sat in his electric wheelchair, then, with his dead wife on his lap a soldier had poured petrol over their bodies and set fire to them. He'd dreamt for weeks on end that his father had suffered a similar fate. Today, in the garage, his dream had been rekindled, and he wanted to see the map of Bosnia again.

He was trying to ease a huge atlas from the top shelf – one of many fat books about worlds, space and oceans when the whole top row came crashing down upon him, knocking his hat flying and sending him sprawling.

Oliver sat there in the pile of books, dazed and not a little sore from the blow to his head. He was embarrassed and knew people were looking at him and mocking him. Confused, his eyes a tad out of focus, he looked up and saw a boy in a tatty 'Skunk Ananse' T-shirt studying him and an old man bitterly saying 'Fuckin' kids' as he turned away back to his local newspaper.

Suddenly, a young woman crouched down beside him asking, 'Are you alright? Hello? Can you hear me? Are you alright?'

Oliver abruptly realised that he'd lost his hat and quickly scrabbled amongst the fallen books for it, locating it and hastily clamping back on his head.

The young woman was still there and Oliver didn't want to make eye contact, he felt so embarrassed. She put a hand on his shoulder, she was trying to be nice to him. 'Perhaps you should ask for help before taking the books from the top shelf. They're a bit heavy. Are you sure you're alright? You got quite a knock on your head.'

Oliver frowned. He knew that voice. How could he? He was in London now. How could he know anyone's voice? He looked up and saw he was looking at a Celtic cross and Mr McTeal's daughter. She was still dressed completely in black, but her long black hair was tied back now and she was smiling at him, not at all cross with him. She too had a moment of recognition, but had difficulty in placing him. 'I've seen you before today, haven't I?

'You're...' Oliver realised that he didn't know her name.

'Aura McTeal.' She reached down and began to pick up the books.

'You work here?' Oliver asked getting up off the floor. He realised that his legs were shaky.

'I'm a library volunteer, well sort of volunteer. I'm helping with the literacy programme here.'

Oliver bent down to help her with the books but just dropped to his knees, clutching his head. He had a sudden shooting pain and stars in his eyes. Although he hadn't made a sound, Aura McTeal had noticed the pain in his face and she steadied him, held him close to her. 'It's OK, you've had a blow to your head. You're dizzy, that's all. Your head must be very sensitive.'

Oliver felt her arms around him, felt her warmth, sensed the genuine concern she had. He was like two people suddenly. This one, with a headache, being held tight, and the other, standing beside them saying 'Wimp! Get up, be strong. You think she really cares?' But it was so long since he had been held, it was hard to pull back.

'Your face is really white. You want me to walk you to the hospital? It's just around the corner?' Aura was whispering in his ear. 'What did they do to you? Was it a tumour?'

'I'll be fine.' Oliver told her, pulling back, but very reluctant to do so. It felt good to be held when he was feeling bad.

'You only just got out of hospital didn't you?' Aura asked him.

Oliver nodded. 'I'm feeling better now. I'm sorry. I didn't mean to be so...'

'Come on,' Aura said. 'Let's go and get a Coke. There's a place next door.'

'I'll be OK really,' Oliver declared. 'Thanks.'

Aura realised that Oliver was embarrassed to have caused so much fuss. She smiled at him and released him, picking up and replacing the books.

'What were you looking for anyway?'

'Map of Bosnia.'

'You should use the computer. It's got all the maps on it.'

'I get headaches when I look at the computer now.'

Aura nodded. She could understand that. The kid in the T-shirt was still watching and Oliver felt uncomfortable about that. Why didn't he just go away.

'Any particular country?' Aura was asking, as she opened the atlas for him.

'Bosnia...my father, he's in Bosnia. I mean...he went there...' Oliver told her, then in a smaller voice '...he never came back.'

Aura looked at this bald kid in his funny cap and pensive face and her heart skipped a beat. Not only had he had a tumour, he'd lost his father too. She wondered how it was that some people got all the bad luck. She took his hand and squeezed it, noticing a fresh burn mark. 'What happened to your father?'

'He's a photographer. He went to Bosnia to take pictures of the ruins after the war ended.' Oliver coughed, then continued. 'It's nearly been three years now.'

'Three years?' Aura exclaimed. 'He's been missing three years?'

'The war was supposed to be over. He didn't even write. He should have come back and...'

Aura squeezed his hand again. 'I think you should wear a shamrock or something. Your head and your Dad – you couldn't be much more unlucky.'

Oliver smiled at her and shrugged. 'My doctor, that's Dr. Campbell, he said. 'Oliver, you're very lucky, that's all that's keeping you alive.'

Aura nodded. She understood that. 'What scares you most?' She asked. 'Never hearing from your father again?'

Oliver considered the question quite seriously and shook his head. 'Never having hair again.'

Aura regarded him with surprise, then laughed, revealing her sharp, ultra white teeth, squeezing his hand again. 'Want to know a secret?'

Oliver nodded, not really understanding why she was being so friendly to him. He wanted her to be friendly, but he wasn't used to people taking him seriously.

Aura leaned in close to him and whispered, 'I was like you once. When I was thirteen. It's my secret.'

Oliver pulled back from her, confused. He looked at her. She was teasing him, he knew it. No way she had ever been like him.

Aura shook her head. 'Serious. I had chemo and everything. See this?'

She guided Oliver's hand under her hair and at touch, everything came clear. The long black hair was a wig. Under it was hair, but short and spiky. Aura smiled. This was to be a confidence between them. Oliver's heart beat a little faster. She had hair under there. It had grown back some. It had grown back!

'I wore a hat for three years. Slept with it on.' Aura confessed, her eyes a little glazed with emotion as she recalled those sad days.

Oliver felt like crying. Too many shocks in one day. Aura could sense he was disturbed. 'Come on, I'm taking you home. That bang on your head won't have done you any good. You live close?'

Oliver nodded. Somehow, embarrassment notwithstanding, he allowed her to lead him down from the mezzanine and out of the library into the late afternoon air. He wasn't going to say 'no'. He didn't know why exactly, but the moment he'd seen her at the McTeal house, he'd somehow sensed she would be a friend of his - how he didn't know, why he didn't know - but he knew, as she walked beside him, that she would be his friend.

'God, I need a smoke,' she declared wistfully.

'You smoke?' Oliver asked, horrified. She'd had cancer and she smoked?

'Don't look at me with such accusing eyes kid, I didn't say I was going to smoke, I just said I needed a smoke. A girls got to have some vices, y'know.'

Oliver understood that. The doctors had all told him no sugar, no chocolate, absolutely no sweet stuff for the first three months after the operation, and everyday he'd fought a burning desire to eat a giant-sized bar of Cadbury's chocolate. He'd weakened one day, eaten the whole bar and then lay in darkness waiting for something terrible to happen. Nothing. Not a single reaction. He awoke the next morning feeling pretty pleased with himself and then promptly threw up. Lesson learned.

They walked to Aura's car, a battered red Golf with a bent radio aerial. She unlocked it and opened the door for him. 'Get in. Was that your mother you came with today?'

Oliver sighed. Did he have to tell her about his mother too? 'No, my aunt. I live with my Grandma now. Do you like living with your Dad?'

Aura waited until the doors were shut and she'd started the engine before replying. 'He's not my real father, he lives in Newcastle. My mother left him for Denis, that's my stepfather's name. He was telling fortunes at Gosforth races and she fell for him. She'd have left my brother and me behind too - if my real Dad hadn't shipped us down to her. We had to change our names to McTeal too. I'm going to move out when I graduate. I don't get a grant, so I have to stay, and Denis won't let me borrow from a bank.'

'He's a bit strange.'

Aura laughed. 'He's a bloody nutcase, that is what he is, but when my mother ran off with someone else he was very good to us. I have a stepmother now who's only six years older than me, but she's fun. Don't know why she married Denis McTeal, but a lot of women seem to like him. God knows why. Now, where am I going?'

Oliver looked ahead and signalled left. 'It's near a pub by the river. By the power station.'

'The Cutty Sark. I know it. It's not far at all.'

Oliver was glad of that. He'd meant to remember the road and everything, but somehow what had happened to him this afternoon made him forget.

'You know what I found in the river today?'

'What?

Oliver looked at her as she turned towards the power station. 'A pair a man's shoes with the feet still in them.'

Aura looked at him suddenly, then looked away, disbelieving. 'Is that true?'

'Yep. My Aunt Harriet was with me, you met her. The Detective said someone had cut them off with an axe of something. It was deliberate.'

Aura shuddered. It made her own feet feel strange. 'It's scary. All kinds of things turn up in the river now. You be careful. You've come from up North somewhere, haven't you.'

'Lincolnshire.'

'Thought so. Things are different here. Don't trust people. Be careful and...', she darted a look at Oliver, '...hang on to your feet.'

Oliver laughed. It was so infectious that so did Aura and, together, they approached Grandma Otis's house in a better mood than when they'd left the library.

Aura dropped him off right outside the house and gave him a big smile. 'I have to do the library three days a week, or else Denis won't give me my allowance. Come in tomorrow, OK? Bring some identification so I can register you. We'll find that map and speak to Old Joe.'

'Who's Joe?'

'He's a refugee. From Croatia, I think. He knows how to find people. Or he knows people who know how to find people. Perhaps he'll talk to you? He's pretty old, but his brain is still going.'

Oliver smiled a goodbye, her words, 'he knows people who know how to find people...' ringing in his ears. He watched Aura drive off, then ran into Grandma Otis's house, a glimmer of hope in his soul for the first time since his father left.

He opened the back door. The smell of dinner cooking greeted his nostrils and Flop ran to him with a loud 'miaoaw'. All was well.

Lena looked at him without smiling. 'Mr Ng was looking for you.'

'Mr Ng,' Oliver didn't know anyone called Ng.

'Our neighbour. The Chinaman who's always writing letters to the council about your Grandma. He came by here and left you something. He looked pretty neglected. His wife left him, y'know. Went back to China. She came to see Grandma Otis and told her she had to go. She didn't like it here and he's been holding a grudge against us ever since. You watch out what he's put in that box. I don't trust him. How he knows you are here beats me. I mean, you've only been here a day. Bloody neighbours watch this place sharper than council tax officers.'

'Where's the box?' Oliver asked, looking around the kitchen.

'In your room. Don't disturb your Grandma. She's got a client in. Still got ten minutes. Dinner in half an hour. I hope you're hungry.'

Oliver gave Flop a hug then ran up to his room. There, on Oliver's bed, sat a shoebox. Oliver quickly opened it, forcing the lid off. A beautiful painted tawny owl lay there in a bed of green tissue. Oliver smiled and lifted it out of the box. A note lay underneath. On yellow paper, all it said was: 'For your protection.'

Oliver stared at the owl and wondered for a moment what the message meant. The door opened behind him and Flop dashed in, skidding to a stop when he sniffed the painted owl in Oliver's hand.

'It's for our protection,' Oliver told him. 'I think it's sort of like a rabbit's foot or something.' Flop didn't like the sound of that. He disappeared under the bed and Oliver heard him going a little crazy under there, clawing at the canvas lining. 'Rabbit's foot, not cat's foot,' Oliver reassured him. But Flop wasn't having it, he was staying put.

'You're honoured.' Grandma Otis declared, from behind Oliver.

Oliver turned and there she was, wearing a mauve shawl and black dress. She smiled at him. 'Mr Ng came to the house and delivered it personally. I don't know what you did, but he was very keen for you to have his box. He prizes his owls a great deal. He believes they protect him from evil spirits.'

Oliver nodded. 'They're all over his house and they're pointing at your room.'

Grandma smiled, a look in her face that seemed to say, 'I thought so.'

'Why?' Oliver asked. 'Why?'

'In his culture owls protect. He thinks I'm a witch. He's written to the council to complain about me, many times. Lena writes to the council to complain about his chanting and the lack of maintenance on his house. Fortunately, the council leader is one of my regular customers and just to save face, I made him buy one of Mr Ng's owls. Does that explain everything?'

Oliver shook his head. 'What about this owl?'

Grandma smiled. 'Put it in the window, aim it at his owls. Fight fire with fire, I say. Now, tell me more about these shoes you found. Quon tells me that there's more trouble to come and I want to know what it is before it gets out of hand.'

'Trouble?' Oliver asked, as he placed his new owl in the window, carefully aiming it at the room full of owls. The idea of his owl facing all of Mr Ng's amused him.

Grandma Otis had already left his room. 'Trouble with you. You're a magnet for it, Oliver, it's hovering, waiting, looking for an opportunity. It's one of the hazards of the trade.'

Oliver frowned. Certainly a lot had happened since he'd arrived, but how was it possible it was connected with him? Surely the shoes would have been at the beach, even if he hadn't gone there? Maybe Mr Ng would have burned himself anyway today? And what about Aura? He'd already met her twice and made her his friend. Was that a good thing or a bad thing? Things didn't happen this fast in Louth, that was for sure.

'Come on,' Grandma Otis called him from her room. 'I want to talk to you.'

For a moment, Oliver contemplated joining Flop under his bed, but one look at the six inches of space there and he knew that Flop was on his own. It was time to face the firing squad. He turned and left his room.

He crossed the landing to Grandma's room and she was sitting there, at her dressing table, with a crystal in her hand. She looked up at him as he cautiously approached. 'I'm going to take a look at your aura. I want to see just what it is I have invited into my house.'

'I met a girl called Aura today. She's beautiful and she's an actress and she had...'

'Hush,' Grandma Otis told him, 'hush....let me work. Come closer.'

Oliver did as he was bid and gingerly approached her. Ridiculous to be scared of a crystal, but he was. What was it going to say? What did it do exactly? Grandma Otis was scanning his whole body with it, watching the crystal, and the air between him and the crystal, very intently.

Oliver caught sight of himself in the mirror and was surprised to see a green glow with a tinge of crimson all around him...more intense where the crystal passed over him. He was going to remark on it, but thought better of it, just in case he was the only one who could see it. He'd made a fool of himself enough times for one day.

Grandma sighed and let the crystal fall to her lap. 'You've a long way to go before you're healed, but I can say one thing for a 'green boy', there's not a mean bone in your body. You're more your father than your mother, that's for sure. I don't like the crimson emanations, but they're there and we will have to deal with them. Now get you to a bath. Didn't anyone tell you that you smell of fire? Give those clothes to Lena to wash. Get going now. Get a bath in before dinner.'

Oliver walked to the door and looked back at her briefly. 'Did you see a colour?'

Grandma Otis looked at him with her pale, puffy, blue eyes. 'Saw the same as you in the mirror. Green and crimson. The colour of trouble to come. Don't worry. It's not you, but watch out for your trusting nature. Don't always believe everything your new friends say.'

Oliver left for the bathroom. Grandma had seen the colours too. How was it possible that one could see his aura? Why had he never seen them before? In the bathroom mirror he looked again, but he could see nothing except his dirty hands and face. He ran the bath and puzzled over all of this.

In her bedroom, Grandma Otis puzzled over it all too. Oliver's aura was powerful. He had the gift, alright, but what was happening? What had she invited into her house? Why was he green and crimson? She'd seen this before, on a man – an evil man, a condemned man – but what did it mean when it surrounded a child, an innocent child? How would she correct it? What could she do to make him safe? That he was in danger she was absolutely certain, but what could it be? How would it come? These were the real questions. When trouble came, how would he know it?

She looked up, beyond her bedroom door momentarily. She caught a glimpse of Flop, slinking out of Oliver's room and dashing into the bathroom. She smiled. As much as she didn't like cats, she knew that Flop was good for Oliver. The one certain thing in his life, the one thing from his past that he could be sure of. Grandma Otis was jealous of that. If only she'd had someone love her as much as that cat loved Oliver. 'But', she sighed, 'Best to forget all that. She'd had her turn'.

CHAPTER SIX

Oliver got a letter from the hospital at the breakfast table. He'd been referred to the Royal Marsden Hospital in Chelsea. His new specialist would be a Professor Imai, and he had an appointment with him in two months time. Lena seemed impressed by the hospital's name, well, as impressed as someone with a sherry hangover could be in the morning, but she was thinking practically, too. 'Now you've got a letter addressed to you, you can join the library. Take it along and get yourself enrolled. Just because you aren't at school yet, doesn't mean you can't read. I'm all for keeping you out of trouble.'

Oliver had fully intended to go back to the library. He wanted to see Aura again and find that Old Joe who, perhaps, could help him find his father. He couldn't wait to get to the library. Lena was a tad suspicious of a boy who actually wanted to read, but glad he'd be out of her hair all the same – especially the way she was feeling this morning.

'Your Grandma has a busy day today, so it's good you're out. Be back for tea, mind. Tomorrow we'll go shopping, get you some clothes.'

Oliver nodded. Some clothes would be good. So far, living at Grandma's wasn't so bad. He got fed and had his own room and school wasn't really a factor until September (and that was the whole summer away). Perhaps his hair will have grown a bit by then. Oliver was nothing if not an optimist.

'Flop come down yet? He was gone when I woke up.'

Lena made a face at him. 'He was waiting for his breakfast when I came down at seven. Made a bloody racket too. I hope he hasn't got worms.

He eats like a dog!'

Oliver grinned, proud of his cat. 'He can eat. Is he out?'

'He's out. Leave him be. He's safer there, I have to clean the house today.'

Oliver grabbed some toast and dipped the edge of it into the marmalade as he rose from the table. 'I have to go. Do I have to pay anything? Will I need money in the library?'

Lena frowned, remembering. 'That's something else we have to discuss – pocket money. Grandma Otis says you're to have ten pounds a week and you must keep to a strict budget. She wants to see a proper accounting. She wants you to learn the proper value of money.'

Oliver couldn't believe his luck. Ten pounds! His mother used to give him a pound; (if she remembered), usually he never had any money.

'I used to get five shillings.' Lena added, thinking back. 'Of course, five bob used to get me into the cinema and buy me all my sweets for the week. Couldn't ask a tenner to do that now. Now, don't forget your coat, and take care. Remember, this is London and you mustn't believe everything people tell you. And watch out for Mr. Ng, he's a weird one, that one. Nearly gave me a heart attack, yesterday, when he appeared from the bushes.'

Oliver had absolutely no intention of going anywhere near Mr Ng, ever again. Still, he had given him one of his owls and that was nice of him.

'Going now.' Oliver declared, grabbing his coat from the corridor.

'Don't forget your envelope, the library will ask for it.' Lena called after him.

Oliver quickly went back for it and then escaped. He was free for another day. Greenwich was for exploring.

It was raining. Naturally. Rain was there for a reason – to keep people depressed and miserable, to keep them at home or at work or, leastways, away from the library.

Oliver arrived, dripping wet and smug. Old-age pensioner faces stared at him as he turned aside and dodged behind a screen so he could wring the water out of his sopping hat. Oliver wasn't down however, he was back in the warmth of a civic library and if no one was smiling at him now, at least someone would, soon. He resolved to find Aura quickly, but a quick walk around the building soon revealed the truth: she was not there. Perhaps he'd come too early? Perhaps she was sick? Or the rain had put her off? Within five minutes of arriving, he was as depressed as all the other sad sacks in their grey mackintoshes and black cracked leather shoes. Oliver went up to the mezzanine where the atlases were, and sat at a table, resting his head in his hands. It was his own fault, he shouldn't have gotten his hopes up of seeing Aura. She didn't have to be there just because he wanted her to be there.

'She ain't here.', a voice told him.

Oliver looked up and discovered he was looking at the same boy in the scruffy 'Skunk Ananse' T-shirt as the day before. He didn't look healthy and was way too thin. His jeans had holes in the knees and his fingernails were black. He looked like he didn't give a damn about himself.

'Don't worry, she'll be here. She's a volunteer. Comes and goes when she likes. It was Aura you was waiting for?'

Oliver nodded. Why was this boy taking an interest in him? Oliver guessed he was about fifteen. His teeth were yellow and neglected. Didn't he know you had to look after your teeth?

'I'm Bullet.' The boy told him. 'Got shot in the neck.' He pulled out a bullet affixed to a shoelace he had tied around his neck. 'This is the bullet, another centimetre to the right and I'd be dead.' Bullet pulled a face. 'Sometimes I wish I was. Fuckin' rain, makes me depressed.'

Oliver was sort of impressed. 'Who shot you? Why?'

Bullet laughed, revealing more of his bad teeth and a pasty, white tongue.

'I was sleeping in a doorway, right, in Lewisham, 'cause I got thrown out by my old woman, right. These fuckin' punks go by, shooting anything that moves, and – wham – I got shot. This woman sees it and she calls an ambulance, right, they saved my fuckin' life. They could have left me, I bloody would have.'

Oliver was transfixed. He could see the scars for himself, there was no way Bullet was lying. 'You didn't want to live?'

Bullet made a face. 'You spend a fuckin' year sleeping in doorways, you don't give a shit what happens to you, do you? What would you know, anyway? Bet you got a nice warm bed and someone to tuck you in at nights. 'Night-night sweetie.'

Oliver ignored the taunting. 'You quit school?'

Bullet laughed, sitting on the table. 'Chucked me out after I burned the gym down. Served them right, wouldn't let me play volleyball in my DMs. Didn't even ask me if I could afford trainers. Just said no. So I burned it down. I was sniffing glue then, makes you a bit crazy.' Bullet made big eyes at Oliver and laughed again. 'I'm the original fuck-up. My Grandad's in jail, my father's a drunk, my mother's out of her face on tranqs most of the time. It's a sort of family tradition. I turned fifteen last month and forgot about it, 'till the cops stopped me and pinned me up against a fuckin' wall and beat me.'

Oliver looked at him in wonder. His own life wasn't great, but this boy's life was a complete mess. Bullet shifted position again. Oliver noticed that he had problems in sitting still, as if he was on edge all the time, expecting trouble to come from any direction.

'What you in here for anyway?' Bullet asked him.

'I wanted to look at the atlas. Bosnia...'

Bullet wasn't interested in that. 'I want to travel. I'm fuckin' sick of the rain. I want to go to Africa and see the lions in Kenya. I'll get there one day. Even if I have to stow away on a plane.'

'How come you're in here?' Oliver asked.

Bullet shrugged. 'It's warm, it's free, it isn't raining in here and I like to read. Just because I'm homeless, don't mean I don't read. Only, I like weird stuff. Just read a Japanese book - 'A Wild Sheep Chase' - but don't ask me who wrote it, 'cause he was Japanese and I don't speak Japanese.'

Oliver was impressed. This was the first person he'd met who'd ever read a Japanese book.

'He giving you trouble?'

Oliver turned around and there was Aura, standing right beside him, still wearing her wet red raincoat, her nose dripping with rainwater. 'Can't believe this bloody weather. Heard on the radio that's there's still a drought order on, can you believe it?' She smiled at Oliver and removed her coat.

'Bullet has read a Japanese book.'

Aura was not so easily impressed. 'Bullet has read every book in this library - correction - stolen just about every book in this library.' She gave Bullet a sharp look. 'Leave this boy alone, Bullet. He's a kid and he's been sick, OK? Come on with me, Oliver. Got someone you might want to talk to. Got to get you a library card. Did you remember to bring something to identify yourself with?'

Aura walked away and Oliver stood up to follow. Bullet held him back a moment as he watched her go. 'She thinks she runs this place. You watch out for her, she's always giving orders. She'll have you as a slave before you know it. People like her are all alike.' He gave Aura the finger behind her back.

Oliver shook Bullet off and followed after Aura. Bullet was wrong. She was

OK, it was Bullet who scared him. He wondered if he really did sleep in doorways. He looked as though he did, but everyday? What about winter? How many other kids slept rough? London was scary.

Aura steered him towards Joe, an old man who looked so tired and frayed he resembled a ghost, a living ghost reading a newspaper in a library. His skin was so creased and his suit so crumpled, with shiny elbows in his faded pin-stripe jacket, he was almost like a scarecrow. Aura sensed Oliver's reluctance to meet with the man. 'It's OK, he's a Croatian refugee, he speaks good English. He was a schoolteacher until he had to flee the fighting. He's exactly the person you need to speak to, he knows Bosnia.'

Oliver looked up at Aura and was about to protest further, when he saw a red weal on her face. It was so fresh he could see the imprint of a hand. He was so shocked that someone had hit her, he said nothing at all. She noticed he had seen her mark and quickly spun him around towards Joe. 'Go fix your own problems, I've got enough already.' With that, she was gone and Oliver was left on his own, just feet away from Joe, the mad, old Croatian.

Joe saw him staring and he nodded at Oliver, smiling to reveal a brand new set of totally white teeth. Opening his mouth was like cracking open an egg, it completely transformed him. 'You're the boy with the missing father?'

Oliver was astonished to discover that Old Joe spoke perfect English, with just a slight accent. He wasn't scary at all. Oliver moved towards him and Joe indicated for him to sit opposite him at the table. Oliver moved cautiously forward and pulled out a chair to sit on. 'How old are you?' he asked.

Joe shrugged and turned his palms up on the table revealing huge lumpy scars. 'Not as old as you think, then again, sometimes I feel older than the stars.'

Oliver was looking at the man's hands, his eyes growing wide, Joe noticed his stares and quickly turned them over again.

'Sometimes people can be very cruel. Sometimes people you think are your friends, can be evil. I survived. I am here. The British Government has found me a place to live, they have given me clothes, some money and yet...', he sighed, 'I am alone. My wife and daughter and my son are dead. My niece Greta, it is possible she survived and I would like to go back to find her. But...' he shrugged again.

'All your family were killed?' Oliver asked.

Joe brought his fist down on the table with a loud bang, his eyes suddenly aflame. 'Burned in their home. I was teaching when they came and set fire to the school. I was trying to put out the flames there when the Serbs came to my home and killed everyone. Everyone. Cut their throats, left them to bleed to death. All my family.'

Oliver stared at him in astonishment, a vision of horror in his head. All of them dead. He's never met anyone who'd been through so much Hell. He tried to think of how he would have felt if he had come home to find everyone murdered, but the thought was so alien to him he just couldn't. Old Joe was watching him, letting his words sink in. But what Oliver was thinking was, if there were people like that, killing children and everything, perhaps his father had been dead all this time. All Oliver's hopes that his father would return were for nothing.

Grandma Otis was in her garden, dressed for Antarctica, even though the weather was quite mild. She'd seen from the window that her roses needed attention. Black spot had got in amongst them and it would be hard to eradicate. Spraying each rose bush quite methodically, a sudden twinge of pain stabbed her left shoulder. She let escape a cry of distress and stood up as straight as possible, but the biting pain seized her shoulder again. Gritting her teeth she let the spray canister drop to the ground. (Grandma Otis knew what this was; bad news. Bad news was coming and it was close.) She'd experienced this kind of pain before and she concentrated very hard on trying to blot it out. She turned towards the house and with a heavy sigh began to walk towards it, her gaze distracted by the sight of an old station wagon being crushed in the scrapyard. The squeal and crunch of metal seemed to echo her own grinding bones.

Lena was coming out of the door with a mug of hot tea. She saw her and stopped short. 'What is it? What's wrong?'

'Pain. Trouble's coming. Find me the tiger balm, it's my shoulder again.'

Lena hurried back indoors all wide eyed and panicked, as Grandma Otis reached the back porch, where she picked up the hot tea mug and pressed it against her shoulder to ease the pain. Something bad was going to happen and she knew, although she couldn't be certain, it would concern Oliver. Worse, there was nothing she could do about it.

Oliver sat before a computer screen and stared at the web pages of the

International Red Cross. Old Joe was pointing to names on the screen as Oliver was scrolling down the pages and noting e-mail addresses.

'Now you try Amnesty International. You will have to e-mail them all, if you want to find your father. Everyone, not just once, but many times. Ya, you have to annoy them, work at it, so that in the end they will help you, just to make you go away.'

Oliver turned to Joe asking, 'How come you know how to do this Joe?'

Joe shrugged. 'I didn't know. First I wrote letters that got ignored, then I discovered e-mail. They read it. I know my niece is alive and I want her to join me here. I wrote to everyone. The Prime Minister, presidents. You can't just ask them to help you because your father is missing or you're unhappy.'

Oliver frowned. 'I can't?' It seemed pretty reasonable to him.

Old Joe shook his head quite emphatically and rubbed his face a moment, to help his concentration. 'No, I can tell you, they aren't interested. You have to let them know how much profit there is in it for them.'

Oliver was really confused now. 'Profit?'

'Ya, it's true. These are important people, politicians and bureaucrats, and where I come from, politicians will only listen to you if they think by helping you they will get on television when your father steps off the airplane. That is how you get their attention Oliver. Is like playing the piano; no. Play right tune, people will listen.'

Oliver was beginning to see the light.

'Make it sad? I could tell them my mother is sick and they just took a lump out of my head the size of a tennis ball.'

Joe nodded wisely. 'Yes, Oh...la-la-la, I can hear the tune already. I think we begin to write the letter.'

Oliver smiled and opened up a text box for them to write in. He'd never met anyone so old before who could use a computer as well as Old Joe. He was smart, even if he couldn't see the screen so well.

It was gone five o'clock before Oliver was finished with Joe, and the library was emptying. Aura was finishing up a literacy class with some immigrant children and Bullet was asleep at a reading table. Old Joe was pretty tired himself, but they'd gotten a letter written and e-mailed it to all kinds of places all over the world. Aura had paid the library charges, she felt it was the least she could do for Oliver. She came over to them both and rested her hands on Oliver's shoulders.

'We're closing early today. Short-staffed. Has Joe been helpful, Oliver?'

Oliver gave her and Joe a brilliant smile. 'Joe's been fantastic. He really knows how to surf the web. He knows how to get into almost anyone's home pages and we've sent letters to everyone, even the President of Serbia.'

'Good, let's see what comes back. I'll check our e-mail on Friday.'

Old Joe smiled, wiping his eyes. 'If I had had this technology when I was Oliver's age, I think I could have been President by now.'

'At least you guys are using the Internet for a purpose. Mostly we just get kids in here looking for X-Files and cyber-babes. Go home now Oliver. You've done well today.'

She turned to Old Joe and gave him a quick peck on his cheek. 'Joe, that was really sweet of you to help him.'

Old Joe shrugged. 'He wants his father back. We shall find him. Now, I must go home. My eyes, they give me so much trouble when I look at the screen.'

Aura looked over to where Bullet was still sleeping. 'Hey Bullet, wake up. We're closing. Doss somewhere else.'

Bullet opened one eye. 'Who cares?' But Aura had already moved on and out of the building.

Oliver was busy making sure he had noted down the names and addresses of all of the people he'd written to and, when he looked up, was surprised to discover that Old Joe had already gone. Indeed, he was passing by the library windows as Oliver looked up, giving him a little wave. Oliver waved back, suddenly aware that Bullet had come up beside him and was yawning.

'You're in pretty tight with the Princess.'

Oliver looked up from his computer screen and frowned at him. Bullet mimicked some Hollywood trailer.

'The Princess In Black: The Bitch Who Does No Wrong.' He laughed. 'She's rich too. Seen her car? Bet she's loaded.'

'She's nice.' Oliver declared, defensively.

'You think? She's rich. She goes home to her big house and her big bed. She's just down here to make herself look good. That's all these people ever do; come here, smile at us, then go home and wash themselves with fuckin' TCP.'

Oliver shook his head, but didn't say anything. He didn't want to get into a fight over this.

'I gotta go to work.' Bullet abruptly announced.

'Work?' Oliver asked, unable to hide the doubt in his voice.

Bullet smiled. 'Wanna see? It's uptown. You can come.'

'Got no money,' Oliver told him, hoping that would end things. Bullet still scared him.

'Nothing to pay. I nicked some rail passes. Never pay. Come on, you ain't seen nothin' in this city, mate, and I know you wanna.'

Oliver had to admit that he did want to see more of the city. 'OK, but I have to get back to my Grandma's soon, she'll worry.'

Bullet grinned. 'You'll get back. Grandma's do too much fuckin' worrying. You'll get back. I promise, I'll protect you.'

Oliver didn't really know how to say no, so he nodded.

Bullet grabbed his arm and pulled him away from the computer desk. 'Come on then. I'll show you London and how to make money. You'll be perfect.'

Somehow, Oliver didn't especially know why he'd be perfect. Perfect for what? He sensed he'd just made a terrible mistake by going with Bullet, but that was the way with fate. You had to go all the way with it, then see where it has taken you.

Oliver did have more doubts as he was hustled towards Greenwich station, but he was very impressed at how cool Bullet seemed to be and confident. He had them both on a train and travelling towards Kings Cross within ten minutes of getting Oliver to agree to go and once the train had gotten going, there was no turning back anyway. Bullet explained to him exactly how the ticket worked and how it was still valid for the rest of the month – free travel. He could go uptown anytime he wanted, that had to be a good deal. Oliver didn't think too much about the person Bullet must have stolen it from. He watched Bullet bum a cigarette off one of the passengers and although Oliver had to stand, Bullet just squeezed himself next to someone by the window and lit up, right under the 'No Smoking' sign. Bullet winked at Oliver, and although Oliver knew everyone around him wanted to shout at Bullet to make him put his cigarette out, no one did. Bullet just seemed to enjoy them glaring at him, and he didn't get unnerved, not even when the man next to him got up and moved to get away from the smoke. Travel was free on the train for him and Oliver, but it wasn't exactly comfortable. Everyone was packed in like pilchards and although the woman opposite him was standing, she was attempting to read a book entitled 'The

Innocence of Roast Chicken' which seemed like a weird title to him. She was reading with one hand holding onto the parcel rack and one foot braced up against the door. This was a determined reader.

The train began to slow at Waterloo East and Bullet signalled to Oliver to move his arse. Oliver began to sense everyone was ready to move and once the train had stopped, he found himself swept along with the flow and carried out of the carriage. Bullet was the last to emerge, still smoking. He handed a smoke to Oliver. Oliver shook his head. Bullet shrugged. 'Won't kill you. You don't believe all that shit they put on the package, do you? Hey I'm really scared of harming my pregnant child. I've already been shot and that didn't kill me. Anyway, who the fuck wants to live forever? Anything that helps you die when you're young can't be all bad.' Bullet laughed. 'Come on, got places to go, people to see.'

Oliver crossed his eyes and made Bullet laugh again. 'Can we get something to drink soon?'

Bullet nodded, pleased that Oliver seemed happy and curious enough to see his 'manor'. He walked off towards the exit with Oliver trotted alongside him, his head practically spinning as he tried to take everything in. Oliver was thinking that Bullet wasn't so bad a friend to have, and he was probably going to have some fun. 'Where are we going?'

'Need to see someone. You just keep your eyes open for cops and keep your mouth shut, OK? This is my deal, you just look and learn. OK?'

Oliver gave Bullet a quick look, but knew right away from one glance that Bullet meant what he said.

'We get off at Waterloo East, 'cause the cops don't watch as much as they do in Charing Cross.'

Oliver nodded, but didn't know why the cops should bother them, they weren't doing anything wrong. He noted that Bullet certainly had a strong effect wherever they went. People seemed to veer off as he came towards them. He didn't know where they were going, but Bullet seemed to be sure and quite purposeful. As they emerged into the main Waterloo station Bullet signalled to Oliver to walk on. Oliver did so, but out of the corner of his eye he suddenly saw Bullet dart forward towards a crowd of female tourists, laden with bags, looking up at the train schedules. None of them noticed Bullet running towards them and when he dashed into their midst, they were too confused, too startled to realise what was happening. Bullet was already on his way running towards the far end of the station carrying two snatched bags, before one of the women cried out the alarm. Oliver witnessed all this with complete astonishment. Bullet was a thief, a bag snatcher. What had he gotten himself into? Oliver watched the women stand around in complete confusion, another burst into tears. With a sigh he walked towards the far end of the station where Bullet had disappeared, and where a sign read 'Festival Hall & National Theatre'. It was only as Oliver was half way to the end that he realised that he was in the Eurostar station and that there was a train waiting to go to Paris. He felt a surge of excitement. He could travel to France from this very spot. He desperately wanted to go to look at the train, but the police were on the station now and he didn't want to fall under suspicion. Now he was beginning to regret accepting Bullet's invitation to go with him, this wild kid was going to get him into trouble, he could sense it.

Oliver reached the end of the station and entered a short tunnel which headed towards the riverfront and crossed the busy road that ran alongside Waterloo station. Even here there was trouble. A couple were stood arguing, the young girl's possessions lying on the tunnel floor. The young man was out of breath and Oliver guessed that here too Bullet had snatched something and the man had given chase. But where was Bullet? As Oliver emerged into the sterile backyard of the Shell building there was a new surge of people coming towards him and the station. Bullet was no where to be seen. Oliver stared at the river and the buildings. On one side, the railway bridge ran beside the Festival Hall and then diagonally, across the river to his left, lay the House of Commons and Big Ben. He'd seen all this on TV and in pictures, but here it was for real. It wasn't as big as he expected, but then, he'd never actually expected to see it. He walked on, taking the natural inclination of the elevated pathway towards the Festival Hall. Oliver was just thinking that he'd like to live in a home with this kind of view when he heard, 'Hey, fuckhead, where were you?'

Oliver looked around and there was Bullet grinning madly, appearing from behind a brick pillar. He approached Oliver and together they began to walk towards the Festival Hall. Oliver could see Bullet's was counting a wad of notes and credit cards.

'Fuckin' traveller's cheques. Got a whole bunch of them. I think I can sell them and the cards for something, but all we've got is 500 french francs and a hundred dollar note. Bloody tourists don't carry much cash anymore, pisses me off.'

'You stole their money.'

Bullet looked really shocked. 'I found it on the ground. It's shocking what tourists will throw away, isn't it.' Then he laughed, digging Oliver in the ribs. 'Of course I bloody stole it. How the fuck do you think I live? I'm fifteen, they don't give kids any jobseekers allowance and if you want somewhere to live they stick you in a foster home with a lot of junkies and some fat creep who cruises your arse every night. I live on the streets, got to make a living best you can. Come on, I got to speak someone inside here.'

Oliver was definitely worried now. What if Bullet was on a video? What if the cops saw him with him? Would he be put into a home too?

Bullet began to run towards the Festival Hall, Oliver keeping pace beside him. A cool blast of wind grabbed them and Oliver noticed the weather was changing, clouds were building over the city. 'Besides,' Bullet suddenly told him, 'didn't I tell you I'd give you a good time? Can't do that without money, now, can you?'

There was logic to this, but Oliver knew now that he was running with trouble. Something bad would definitely happen. Sooner or later.

Bullet led him into the side entrance of the Festival Hall and made him sit and wait in the chairs provided for a café that was closed for the evening. Oliver didn't mind waiting. He was just as happy to see all the people gathered in their black ties and elegant evening clothes. He surmised that something special must be going on and he watched as people drank at the bar and examined strange objects on display in the exhibition area. Bullet had disappeared in the direction of the bookshop and Oliver sort of expected the worst. He wondered if he should go home right then and there, get away before something stupid happened. But he didn't. He sat there, like a dummy, waiting for Bullet. He knew he was being stupid, but then again, he didn't want to seem like a total wimp.

Two overdressed women walked past him carrying violin cases. Oliver suddenly remembered exactly what the Royal Festival Hall was used for – music concerts. All the more strange for Bullet to have dragged him into there. What could he possibly be doing?

Bullet was back and in a hurry once more. 'Let's go. Bastard cheated me, only gave me ten percent of what they're worth.'

'You sold that stuff?'

'Know a bloke who can use them, as long as you get them to him before they report them. You have to move fast. Takes the cards too, but he doesn't pay much for them. I know I can get more for that stuff, but I haven't found anyone else who'll take em yet. They have to work close to the station so you don't lose time.

They were outside again and moving towards the Hungerford footbridge, which lead to the Embankment and Charing Cross station. A train was drawing out of the station, slowly trundling past them on the bridge to stop again at Waterloo, a little way behind them now.

'Where are we going?'

'Across the river, got to get to Covent Garden. Lot's of people to see, you know, the usual shit.'

Oliver just nodded. Whatever; he was just tagging along. Bullet was travelling pretty fast however and he was struggling to keep up. 'You have to walk so fast?'

Bullet smirked, but didn't cut his pace. 'Got to move. Didn't anyone teach you anything? You move like you're going somewhere, got something on your mind. Move slowly, people and cops gets suspicious, they stop and bother you. You could learn a lot from me. I've been living on the streets a long time now. Got to survive, know where the warm places are, who to trust, who's going to sell you out, who's got the best deals, who can get you stuff. Lots to learn.'

Oliver was listening and thinking. Bullet was the kind of kid who always got into a lot of trouble at school, but knew how to get out of it, knew how to get around the teachers.

They took the steps up to the bridge. Oliver noted it was high tide and the river was churning in the wind. There was a kid begging at the top of the steps, sat squatting under a tartan blanket, silently sat there, his hat beside him contained with a few coins. He fixed his eyes on Bullet who stopped before him.

'Where's Fraser?' Bullet asked.

The kid shrugged. 'Said he'd be here at five. His loss.'

Bullet seemed to understand and moved on, Oliver having to virtually jog beside him to keep up. Oliver was fascinated with the river and the buildings on either side of it, all of which were beginning to shine as the lights switched on at twilight.

'What did he mean?' Oliver asked.

Bullet didn't reply, so Oliver tried again.

'That kid back there. What did he mean?'

Bullet frowned, then finally realised what Oliver was asking. 'Well, Fraser bought that spot, paid a lot for it too. Anyway, he sublets it to some other kid for part of the day.'

Oliver had a problem getting this one through his head. 'Someone pays to beg on a bridge?'

Bullet put an arm around his shoulders. 'You think you can just sit down in a nice prize corner like that and not get the shit kicked out of you? If you're going to beg in this town, you have to pay. Spot like that takes nearly £300 a day, more in summer. Fraser has to pay someone, so someone has to pay Fraser, it's the system.'

Oliver still had problems with the whole concept. It didn't make sense. No one owned these places in the street. Yet, you had to pay someone to beg there and then there was the other thing. 'You said £300? A day?'

Bullet shrugged and turned to Oliver. 'Figure it out , hundreds of people cross this bridge everyday, thousands probably. The more pathetic you look, they more they'll give you. If every twentieth person gives you 50p you're going to make a lot of money. The colder it is, the more sorry they feel for you. Fraser once took £500 and got frost bite. He's the best beggar in the city.'

'How do you know that?' Oliver asked.

''Cause I got my own spot.'

Oliver frowned. 'You have your own spot?'

'Well not officially. I can't afford a spot yet, but I'm working on it. I sort of freelance.'

They reached the other side of the river and were now walking into the entrails of the Charing Cross building. Oliver was astonished to discover they were walking alongside a gym and where people were sweating it out on exercise machines behind the glass windows. Some woman with huge muscles in her legs was crushing the life out of some equipment and Bullet pulled a face at her. She instantly lost her concentration and nearly crippled herself as she involuntarily let go. Bullet laughed and ran off, Oliver quickly in tow, not wanting to be hunted down by a woman who looked tougher than any 'Gladiator' on TV.

Bullet paused when they reached the down escalator to the street level. 'People got so much money they have to waste it on getting sweaty. You know what I want to waste my money on one day?'

Oliver shook his head. He didn't have to reply, he knew he'd tell him anyway.

'I want my own place, right up above this station. They've got Penthouses up there with views of the river, you can see for miles and I want a rifle.'

'A rifle?'

'Yeah, a fuckin' rifle. I'm going to shoot all the rich, just one at a time. No one will ever know where the bullets have come from. Just one poxy bloke in a suit a day, get 'em in the arse.' He looked at Oliver with a serious expression on his face then suddenly broke into laughter. Oliver's face was a mixture of horror and confusion and Bullet was enjoying ripping this country boy.

Oliver kept his silence, for his part, just noting that here was one more clue that Bullet was a tad crazy. They merged onto busy, sloping Villiers Street, running alongside Charing Cross station. The smell of urine and cooking seemed to ooze from every pore and people hurried by towards the Embankment Tube station or meandered up towards Charing Cross road with soggy kebabs dribbling down their jackets. It reminded Oliver that he was very hungry.

'You hungry?' Bullet asked.

Oliver nodded and he was about to tell Bullet that he hadn't got any money when Bullet clapped a hand on his shoulders and gave him and quick friendly squeeze.

'We'll need some more money. Got to work, come one, we're going to Covent Garden.'

Oliver frowned as Bullet steered him towards the dense traffic on the Strand. 'What exactly do you do there?'

'Same as everyone else, annoy the fuckers. Come on, you'll like it. You don't have to do anything, just watch.'

Oliver knew that wasn't true, but he was curious. What could Bullet do that was any more annoying than he was already?

'You know how to drive?' Bullet asked abruptly as they weaved their way through the stationary traffic.

'I've driven a tractor,' Oliver replied.

'Good enough,' Bullet replied.

'Why?'

'Just in case,' came Bullet's enigmatic reply.

Oliver pondered this 'in case'. In case generally meant 'maybe' or 'soon'. What was Bullet planning now? And why did they need a car?

He ran alongside Bullet who was striding out with a sense of purpose now, navigating the streets with confidence. Oliver noticed all kinds of places he'd either read about or seen on TV. Publishers of books he'd read, massive restaurants such as TGIF filled with young people enjoying themselves. He was quite excited to be in London, in Covent Garden, especially at night. He didn't know what he expected, but it was more fun than being in Greenwich with Grandma Otis and he had Bullet to thank for this.

'I've got some business to do, then we can go to Old Compton Street. I know a lot of people there. You'll be surprised, famous people too, seen them on TV. Everyone goes there at night now.'

Bullet had stopped momentarily in a shop doorway to look at his face. From his back pocket he took out a little plastic bag and extracted something that looked like human hair. He pulled this over his head and attached it by a slim hook over his ear. He smoothed it over his right cheek, then turned to Oliver. Oliver immediately jumped back with revulsion. Bullet looked hideous. He had a fierce scar running down beside his eye and his upper lip was drawn back to reveal some teeth. He looked as though he had been slashed with a knife and he had never had it treated properly. It utterly transformed his face and Bullet seemed really pleased with himself as he placed a finger under the hair and made some final adjustments. He narrowed his eyes and hunched his shoulders forward. 'Look great, don't I?'

Oliver couldn't hardly bear to look at him without wanting to throw up.

'Now I'm ready for work,' Bullet declared, moving off again, expecting Oliver to catch him up.

They came to a halt outside a restaurant that looked very expensive to Oliver's eyes. Inside, rich tourists were eating off candle-lit tables covered with white tablecloths. One thing was for sure, they wouldn't want Bullet in there. Bullet winked at Oliver and produced a tin cup from inside his expansive sweater. 'Wait across the road and watch,' Bullet hissed at him. Oliver backed away and left Bullet to position himself right outside the window where the diners were eating. He didn't face the street, like a normal beggar, but the window so that the diners just couldn't miss him. Every time they would look out or look up from their meals, Bullet would be standing there looking at them, his hideous face and hunched shoulders, dribble spraying from his upturned lip. He was a truly ghastly apparition. Even from his position across the road Oliver could sense that the diners were repulsed by Bullet. A gust of wind took his spittle and sprayed it against the window. Oliver watched the diners' reactions, a woman nearly gagged and stood up angrily, calling for a waiter or the manager's attention. Some potential customers came to the restaurant entrance and took one look at Bullet then immediately turned away. Inside, Oliver could see that the receptionist had seen the incident and called someone to deal with it. Any minute now someone was going to come out of the place and beat Bullet up, he was sure of it. They wouldn't stand for it. Oliver couldn't but help feel a little bit sorry for the diners. All he knew was, that he wouldn't be able to sit there and eat if someone as hideous as Bullet was dribbling outside the window. Bullet didn't budge however. He wasn't even looking at anyone. Just standing there drooling, making himself look as hideous as possible.

A group of four businesswomen arrived in their stylish suits, all of them animated, laughing, ready to dine. They caught sight of Bullet and one woman nearly retched right there on the spot. 'Oh my God.' Oliver heard her cry out. She turned away, but another of the women put her hand into her shoulder bag and produced a five pound note, crushing it into Bullet's tin. Then, she too ran off to join her friend as they began to search for another place to eat.

Oliver was beginning to understand just how smart Bullet was. Six customers turned away in less than ten minutes. This restaurant was losing money because of him.

Oliver could now see some reaction within the restaurant. The manager had finally been summoned by the diners nearest the windows and they were being quite vocal in their distress. Any moment now Bullet was going to be in big trouble. The manager began to walk towards the front entrance, stopping a moment to talk to the receptionist. He then headed on outside, aiming towards Bullet.

Oliver would have liked to have heard what the manager was going to say, but a motorcycle started up nearby which distracted him and when he looked back, Bullet was gone, the manager was walking back inside and the situation was over. But where was Bullet?

Oliver was about to walk back across the road when he felt a hand on his arm. He looked around and Bullet was standing there, his fake scarring gone, only the red marks of the tight hairline still remaining. There was a wet stain on his sweater from all the spittle, yet he looked pretty pleased with himself, couldn't stop grinning.

'Fifty quid, plus a fiver. Not bad for twenty minutes work, eh? It's fuckin' ace.

Did you see their faces? Practically puked on their lobsters, works every time.'

Proud of himself, Bullet led Oliver away from the area, pointing out the Rock Garden Café as their destination. 'Of course, you can't do this outside the same place again, but there's hundreds of restaurants in this city and it's really quick money. I mean, some people beg down in the tube for hours an' only make sixty quid....you got to use ingenuity to make money in this game. I got paid £40 to move away from the queue outside Mezzo a week ago. Only been there five minutes. Some guy actually puked when he saw me.'

Oliver was proud of Bullet in a funny kind of way. At least he was doing something different. 'How did you get the idea to make yourself so ugly?'

'Read this book about beggars in India, and how they deliberately cripple themselves and their kids, 'cause they reckon begging is their career, y'know? I mean, is that totally fucked up or what? People cutting their limbs off, breaking their hands, slicing their ears off...So I got this idea of making myself look like shit the easy way.' He rubbed his face. 'Leaves a scar though, takes time to go...wouldn't want to do it too often. Shit, I'm hungry, let's get a hamburger.' Oliver was starving, but he didn't have any money and kind of felt guilty because Bullet had gone out and 'earned' his. 'I haven't got any money.'

'I told you I'm paying. It's your first time in the city. My treat.'

Oliver stopped to watch a fire-eater impressing a crowd of tourists. One thing was still bugging him and he turned to Bullet to ask, 'Why don't the police arrest you when you do that stuff outside the restaurant windows.'

'You think they want to be seen arresting someone as pathetic as me? They'd rather die than be seen beating up a spacker.'

Oliver digested that, it seemed reasonable, the cops probably wouldn't, but what if they found out Bullet was faking it? They'd beat the life out of him then.

Bullet was grinning again as they approached the Rock Garden terrace. 'Did you see the face on that woman who came to eat at the restaurant? She nearly had a heart attack when she saw my face. Bet she has nightmares for months. People just hate people to look like crap. They think all the people who look weird should be locked up.'

Oliver thought about the people who looked strangely at him when he'd had his head shaved and knew that Bullet was probably speaking the truth. People didn't like other people looking different to them, it unnerved them.

'You do this everyday?'

'Most days. Unless I get lucky in the station first. I have to make at least two hundred quid a day or I'm not really operating.'

Oliver didn't think he'd heard that right. Bullet, the kid who sleeps rough earned two hundred a day? 'I thought you just sat around the library.'

'Yeah, well that just where I sleep. It's warm. I'm telling you kid, you can make a career out of this. You'd be good. You've got a cute girly face and you're bald, you wouldn't have to do anything, just sit in this square and people would cram money into your fist, really.'

Bullet led Oliver to the terrace and signalled a waiter that they were going to sit down. The waiter shrugged. Oliver's head was still full of this concept of him sitting in the square begging for a living. He resented the remark about his 'cute girly face' too. There was no way on Earth he was going to beg. Maybe Bullet didn't know it was wrong. In fact, Oliver had begun to comprehend that Bullet didn't have any idea of what was right and wrong at all. He just did whatever he wanted. There were things he said that didn't quite match up, however. Did he really make two hundred a day? What did he do with it? Why didn't he live somewhere? Why did he go back to Greenwich every night? Yes, there was a lot that didn't add up. Oliver watched Bullet reading the menu and snatching quick looks at the other diners situated both in the open terrace and inside.

'Do you save any of the money you make?' Oliver asked him.

Bullet looked at Oliver with surprise. 'You think I spend it all? You think I'm that stupid?' He shrugged. ' Lots of kids just blow it all on gear and get wasted on other shit, but I've got a bank account and when I've got enough I'm going to drive to Africa. The whole way.'

'Africa?'

'Fuckin' right. I'm going to drive all the way. Ferry to Spain, then Morocco, the Sahara, Kenya, Zimbabwe, Mozambique, South Africa...I'm going to see every place I can, all the way to Cape Town.'

Oliver was impressed. It was a good ambition. Africa, driving across the Sahara, that was great. 'How much have you got saved?'

'About £2000, saving takes time. I reckon I'll have enough in two years and besides, I've got to learn to drive.'

Oliver smiled. Yep, that would probably be helpful. If you're driving to Africa, learning to drive would be a damn good idea.

'Got to learn how to fix cars too, things always break down. I read everything

I can about people who've done it and they're always breaking crankshafts and cylinder heads and if they don't break down they get attacked by Africans with guns, so I guess I'll have to learn to shoot too. Now what are you going to eat?'

Oliver looked at the menu and the bewildering choices. 'Hamburger and fries, have they got onions rings?'

Bullet grinned. 'Got whatever you want. We got the money. I'm going to have the chicken.'

Thirty minutes on, their food served, their stomachs filled with Coca-Cola, Oliver knew something for sure – he was enjoying this. He liked the music, the people eating and talking around him, the huge twelve-ounce burger and the fries, more than he could ever eat. He liked the building, the fact that it was in London, right in Covent Garden where thousands of people milled around watching each other, watching jugglers, fire-swallowers and listening to street musicians. He felt like they were sat at the very centre of London and he wasn't missing a thing. Everything was new to him and he liked it. Alright, he did feel a bit guilty that Bullet had stolen the money that paid for it. He also wondered why it was that Bullet had invited him along. Perhaps Bullet needed a friend? Perhaps...well anyway, Oliver was happy and that made him feel good all over.

But happiness is a transitory thing. It was when he had to go to the bathroom that things changed. Alright, he'd had to pee more than once (Coke always did that to him) but he did have to go again and it took ages. Bullet had laughed at him that he'd had to go again and run for it, as it was so sudden, but Oliver wasn't embarrassed, worse things had happened to him in hospital. He'd gotten used to sudden things happening to his body.

He'd washed his hands and gone back upstairs when he was brought to an abrupt halt at the top of the stairs. Bullet was no longer outside but inside, sat at a table with two overweight men, one with a spiky moustache, the other had a hand on Bullet's shoulders. Oliver didn't quite understand what was going on, but instinctively knew something had changed. Bullet was laughing and smiling with the men, as if he knew them and when Oliver walked across the restaurant to go back outside, Bullet pretended not to notice him. Oliver sat at the outside table and noticed the bill had arrived. Since it was for twenty-five pounds, he grew a little bit worried. Was Bullet coming back? How could Oliver pay? He sat there and looked a bit lost and when he looked back at Bullet's new table he was embarrassed to discover the men were looking right at him, as if they were discussing him. Oliver grew distinctly uncomfortable. Worse, Bullet got up and came right over, he was wearing a different kind of smile and Oliver knew that he wanted something. He didn't know what, but he just knew he wasn't going to like whatever it was he was going to say.

'Got some business, you could make some money, help pay me back for the food you just ate, if you want.'

'What?' Oliver was on full alert now.

'They're Americans. Want to have a good time, get drunk a bit, y'know?'

Oliver didn't know. Bullet could see that. ' Listen, they'll pay you fifty quid to hang out with them, cash, you could use the money. You could probably get more if you let them do what they want...'

Oliver might have been a naive kid from Louth, where not a lot went on in life, especially for a young kid, but he instinctively knew what the words 'let them do what they want' meant. They wanted sex. It was the grossest thing he had ever heard, worse, they wanted sex with HIM. He must have turned deathly-white because Bullet didn't press it.

'OK, you're new, you don't know stuff yet, I'll find someone else. You're blowing off a lot of money Oliver. They'll pay a lot for a virgin. A lot.'

With that Bullet was gone, back into the restaurant and towards the telephone. Oliver's heart was beating fast, he felt nauseous. Bullet was going to have sex with those two fat men, for money. He'd actually expected Oliver to do the same and what did that mean? Did that mean Bullet was gay? Did it mean Bullet wanted sex with him, too? Oliver was beginning to sweat. He felt dizzy. He was angry and confused. He gripped the table, aware that he was swaying a little and...

A waiter came over to him and Oliver could see that he had a worried expression on his face... 'Oh shit, are you OK? You've gone white. What did you eat? Was it the fish?'

Oliver was beginning to sense that he was going to be sick, if not right there, any minute now. He knew the waiter could see this...

'Oh fuck, get up, come on, don't be sick here, don't be sick here. What did you eat?'

He had Oliver up out of his chair and virtually frog-marched to the ladies, which was nearest, and shoved him in there. 'Don't come out until you've got rid of it.'

Oliver just got there in time and promptly unloaded everything. He must have sounded pretty bad to the people on the other side of the door. He was sweaty and it never seemed to finish, wave after wave of puke came up, his head buried in the loo, his legs shaky and sweat pouring off his face, dripping off the end of his nose as he heaved one more time.

Outside the waiter had to divert some women to the men's toilets and just hope no customers could hear the kid inside puking his heart out.

Oliver felt it was over and washed his face in the sink. He was still stunned. Not so much at what Bullet had asked him to do, but how stupid he'd been to let himself be led all over town by a kid who was obviously trouble. He should have known from the moment Bullet gave him a stolen train ticket that no good would come from it. He still couldn't believe that Bullet thought he was going to say 'yes' to going with the men.

'You OK?' The waiter asked outside the door.

'Better now.' Oliver replied. 'I'm coming out.'

He was about to leave when he remembered to dash back into the loo to flush it. It stank in there, and it was a waste of a good hamburger too.

Oliver emerged from the ladies to find a queue of women waiting to get in. He was acutely embarrassed, but one look at his pasty white face told them the story.

'What did you eat?' A woman asked. 'Was it the fish?'

'I need some air...' Oliver muttered. The waiter just grabbed his arm and shoved him out of the door. 'Don't worry about the bill, go home.'

And that, was that. He was out on the street. He didn't have to pay the bill, he'd been deserted by Bullet, he'd thrown up...OK, he did feel better, but he was still in shock.

The crowds swallowed him up. There seemed to be more people on the street than before and it was dark now, cooler. As he walked away from the restaurant he looked back and glimpsed the two fat Americans walking away with Bullet and another kid, a thin kid with a Nike sweatshirt. Oliver pressed into the shadows so he wouldn't be noticed. His heart began to beat faster again. Suddenly Covent Garden seemed less exciting, a little menacing now. He was suddenly aware that he was on his own in a place he didn't know and not sure of which way to go to get back home.

As he walked he tried to make sense of what had happened, how quickly everything had changed. 'Out of my way,' someone shouted at him. Oliver moved aside as some kids barged their way through the crowds. Oliver noticed a hand dipping into a tourist's pocket, another snatching a camera off someone's shoulders. He heard a shout as someone raised the alarm, but the kids had moved off, instantly becoming invisible in the crowds. Tourists were easy meat. Oliver could see how simple it was for people like Bullet to survive on the streets, how he could see it as a way of life. It was like living on a huge garbage pile. You just had to reach down and pick up whatever you wanted.

'You alright, dear?' A woman asked him, bending down to stare in his face. 'You look a bit peaky.'

Oliver backed away, taken by surprise. For a second he had thought it was his mother staring at him, her eyes alive, questioning, concerned. 'You sure you're alright dear?'

Oliver blinked. It wasn't his mother, someone much like her, but taller - yet she had looked so real....This woman was dressed in such a short dress he could see her underwear.

'I ate something,' Oliver informed her, ' I feel dizzy..'

The woman seemed to understand and dug into her shoulder bag. 'You've got a touch of food poisoning. It can be serious, love. You'd best be off home. Here...' She offered Oliver something from her bag. 'It's something for your digestion. It's alright, it might help. Suck it, dear. Alright?'

Oliver found she'd shoved the tablet into his mouth and he recognised the taste as a Rennies. He'd had enough of those when they'd fed him in hospital.

'Best go home, love. Your mother will be worried.'

Oliver began to suck on the tablet and the woman left him. He looked back and saw her wave a motorist down. The car slowed and she seemed to crawl half-way into the car talking loudly to the motorist, her scantily clad backside hanging outside the car. She must have said something right because she backed out and walked around the car to get in the other side. As she was getting in the car she gave Oliver a little wave and Oliver waved back.

The Rennies began to work its effect on his stomach and it did seem to help some. The woman had been nice. He wished he'd asked her where he was, which way to go to the station and felt stupid he hadn't.

He walked on and saw a parked police car with two cops watching the crowds. Oliver was going to approach them, then remembered he had a stolen railway card on him and he wasn't even supposed to be in Covent Garden. Suppose they asked questions and called his Grandma? Uh-uh. He couldn't let Grandma Otis know he'd snuck off to the city, or befriended Bullet. She'd be horrified.

'Station's just down to the Strand, then turn right,' Oliver overheard someone tell a group of tourists, who seemed to be as lost as he was.

Oliver began to follow them. His legs felt decidedly wobbly. He remembered they always felt like this when he felt sick. A street singer suddenly struck up 'Hi-Ho Silver Lining' off-key and Oliver was happy to get away from Covent Garden, even though he was going home and there would be hell to pay there. It was nearly ten o'clock, Grandma Otis was going to have a fit, he knew it.

There was a man walking his dog near him now. A small man with a strange hat and a white dog that limped. Oliver watched the dog as he walked behind the tourists and sensed how unhappy the dog must be to live in such a noisy city. There was no grass or trees, just people, traffic and... Suddenly, Oliver realised that he was feeling a bit better, the tablet had worked. He was missing Louth. He was walking in the centre of London at night and missing Louth. That had to be the weirdest thing. Maybe London was great, maybe it was big, but it was also so very scary.

The man with the dog turned left when the tourists turned right onto the Strand. The traffic was dense now, but Oliver could see that they weren't far from Charing Cross at all. He was going home. All he had to do was catch the right train.

In the station concourse the crowds were looking at the notice boards. Everyone was trying to figure out which train to catch, what went where and at what time. Oliver was studying the form as hard as everyone else, trying to make sense of it.

'You dropped your ticket.' A voice told him, very close to his ear.

Oliver turned around and a tramp handed him his ticket. The man looked unsteady, terrible, dirty and haunted, but his clawed hand proffered him his ticket that had somehow fallen.

'You ought to be more careful, no fun getting stranded here.'

Oliver took back his ticket and muttered his 'thanks'...but the tramp had spotted a burning half-consumed cigarette on the floor and moved off to seize it. How did a man get to be like that? Oliver looked after him. London was becoming like a hologram. With one look the city of the postcards stared you in the face, then, it shifted and the Bullets, the prostitutes and tramps revealed themselves and they were everywhere. No one had actually harmed him, no one had even scared him, in fact most people had been friendly, but Oliver was beginning to grow wary of the city. He wasn't ready for it yet. He didn't know enough.

A surge of people headed for the barrier and Oliver felt tempted to follow, but he still couldn't make out which platform he was supposed to be on for Maze Hill. He found it. Platform One, 22.12hrs. Oliver looked at the clock. It was 22.11. He panicked. He ran for the platform, but half-way up to it he became conscious of a sign that read 'To reach Platform One, passengers must use Platform Three'. Oliver changed course and dashed for gate three, running alongside several others who had made the same mistake. Someone was looking at tickets, but Oliver ducked through and ran, reaching Platform One just as a whistle sounded. Even here it was confusing as he couldn't understand which was Platform One and which was Two, especially as both trains seemed to be leaving at once and there was another sign which read 'Only the front six coaches...' something or other. Oliver ran on, even though the train was now actually leaving, and he jumped up on the last carriage, struggling with the door as someone from the platform was shouting 'Oi' at him.

Oliver got into the carriage and flopped down on a seat. He had no idea if he was on the right train and right at this moment he didn't care. As long as it was going closer to Grandma's he was happy.

The train stopped at Waterloo and Oliver thought he heard the announcement which included Maze Hill, but he wasn't entirely sure. The train left the station again. This time someone was aboard shouting 'Tickets'!

Once again Oliver worked up a sweat. He had a stolen ticket. What would happen?

Would he be arrested? Would he...?

'Where are you going?' the Inspector asked.

'Maze Hill.'

'This ticket's for Gravesend.'

'My Grandma lives in Maze Hill.'

That seemed to satisfy him. But Oliver was still nervous. 'This is the train for Maze Hill?'

'If it isn't you're going to be in trouble, lad.' As a reply it was less than useful.

As the Inspector left him, Oliver became aware of a drunk asleep three rows on. How would he know which station to wake up on? Or did he ride the train to the end?

London at night looked beautiful. St Paul's was lit up just before London Bridge and just after that he glimpsed Tower Bridge again. He knew that his next visit to London would be a very different one. He wasn't going to be with Bullet, for sure. And he wasn't coming up without money. He wanted Maze Hill station to come up quickly. He willed Grandma Otis to be asleep and the back door open so he could sneak in unnoticed, but he instinctively knew that Grandma Otis was probably up and fretting, and he'd be lucky if he wasn't locked into his room and fed bread and water for a month for giving her such a scare. Kids disappeared everyday now, he knew she'd be worried. As the train sped through the suburbs, he speculated on what kind of punishment they'd visit on him, what Grandma would say to him, what he'd tell her. Should he tell the truth? Everything? Or lie. Grandma might be shocked if he told her everything...

Greenwich Station stop. One more stop, then home. No matter what, no matter how angry Grandma Otis would be, he was glad to be going home and to be seeing Flop. Flop would certainly be angry with him. He hadn't told Flop not to worry and Flop always worried if he didn't tell him where he was going, but at least he would always forgive him and curl up and purr. Yes, Flop would be there for him, he was always there.

CHAPTER SEVEN

Ten minutes later, but still nearer eleven o'clock than ten, Oliver disembarked from the Maze Hill train. The station was dark and misty, only one other passenger got off, from a carriage near the front and she seemed to vanish off the face of the earth the moment the train departed the station. He was alone, cold, and he didn't have a clue which way to go.

This was the worst he had ever felt since leaving Louth. Cold and late, knowing that when he did finally get home he would be punished, that he completely deserved it. It was not the certainty of disgrace, but the sheer stupidity of not actually remembering the way. Hardly surprising as he'd never actually been to this bleak little station before. It was more of an afterthought than a station and, as far as Oliver could tell, looking back across the rooftops, not even near Greenwich, not least the Greenwich he knew.

Instinct told him which way to go: find the road which headed down towards the river. As he emerged from the railway property onto Maze Hill road, Oliver grew uneasy. He couldn't say why exactly, but he had the premonition of danger. It was late, the few people that were still about were mostly returning from the pub and had had a bellyful. Uptown, Oliver had been surrounded by strange people, but he never was afraid, never felt like he did now. As he approached Trafalgar Road, the main route that took all the through traffic to Woolwich or back to town, he could hear the thunder of trucks sailing on through, the hiss of their airbrakes, and saw, in the shadows, kids, bored kids, kicking bottles and cans, looking for trouble, looking for one bald kid who'd be good for a laugh.

Oliver willed himself invisible but he knew eyes were on him as he approached from the opposite side of the street. He knew he had to get across the busy road, he knew he mustn't make eye contact. Louth might have been a backwater, but it had its fair share of bored kids who liked to kick the windows in at night and terrorise each other. Oliver had seen them, seen the fights between Monks' Dyke school and King Edwards Grammar school...

A huge articulated truck was wading through the street, so large it seemed like an ocean liner. Oliver could see three boys and a girl detach themselves from the group, begin to walk towards him as he waited to cross the road. Oliver just knew he had to ignore them, couldn't let them begin talking to him. They'd kick the shit out of him for sure, they'd know he was a country boy. The truck was getting closer, its engine roaring as it accelerated and changed gear. The other side looked clear of traffic...Oliver ran for it. Right in front of the truck. There was a hiss of brakes, tyres skidding and screaming, a blast of a horn as the whole truck jinked, then shot forward again as the driver gunned the engine. The driver swore in German out of his window. But Oliver had made it to the other side, and as the truck rolled on by, he didn't break his stride, just kept on running, turning only once he'd reached the shadows to make sure he wasn't being pursued.

The kids were still there, watching his side of the street, but jeering motorists now, giving them the finger, having 'fun'. Oliver had had enough of fun lately. Way enough.

He made one false move, mistakenly turning off Hoskins Street and finding himself in a dead-end street. Miserable and cold now, he retraced his steps, looking up into the orange light of the street lamps for the familiar power station chimneys that overshadowed his new home. 'Oh that way.' he told himself. 'The river is over there.' He wasn't used to streets that went off at all kinds of angles.

It was getting later and later. He began to worry that Grandma Otis would have called the police; that they'd be looking for him. He began to grow very uneasy and noticed it was getting damp and misty again. He knew now that this was a good sign, it should be cooler by the river. Truth was, it couldn't get cool enough. Grandma Otis would make sure of that. He speculated on how she'd punish him, if she'd try to beat him...no, she'd get Lena to do it, Lena would like to beat him, he was sure. A dog barked as he passed by an enclosed front yard and a light came on. Oliver hurried on, concentrating only on getting home and curling up with Flop.

He finally found the right road, with its uneven cobbles and was approaching Grandma Otis's house when he noticed a number of cars were parked in the road and inside her yard. New cars. One was a Jaguar, another a black Mercedes. Oliver knew that these cars didn't belong to anyone around here, so why were they there? What was going on?

As he drew closer he noticed that all the rooms at the bottom of the house were illuminated, and a curious glow seemed to light up Grandma's window. Was Grandma Otis having a party? If so, it was very quiet. Either way, it was spooky and the fuzz hair on Oliver's neck seemed to bristle.

He took the cautious approach and aimed for the back door. Someone was waiting for him. From out of the shadows two arms grabbed his foot, then dashed away. Flop!

'Flop, Flop', Oliver whispered. 'Come here, tell me what's going on?'

Flop came back to him, let out a hesitant cry and allowed himself to be picked up and cuddled. Flop had known Oliver would come back. For more than an hour he'd been waiting, knowing Oliver was trying to find his way home...

'Can we go in? What's happening? Is Grandma mad at me?'

Flop purred. He was happy. He felt safe now.

Oliver opened the back door and peered in. The light was on, the kitchen looked a mess and, as he inched it open some more, he could see Lena, asleep and sprawled out across the table top, snoring. Oliver's heart soared. He could get in. With luck he and Flop could get all the way to his room without anyone noticing. He could even pretend he'd been there for hours.

'Let's get in, come on,' he told Flop.

Oliver entered and set Flop down who made a dash for his bowl, diving into a plate of prawn flavoured biscuits. Oliver shut the door and locked it behind him. As quiet as he could, he removed his shoes and took off his jacket, hanging it up behind the door. It was warm in the kitchen, and (aside from Lena's snoring) a friendly place to be. He stood up again and knocked into a bottle on the floor. It seemed to him to make a terrible crash, but it didn't disturb Lena. When he picked the bottle up, he knew why. Sherry. Smelled bad too.

Flop took a sip of his water then came back to Oliver, wanting to be carried again. Oliver picked him up and snuggled him. 'Come on, let's go to bed.'

Flop miaowed as if to say 'At last...'

Oliver could hear footsteps upstairs and he wondered what was going on. The quietest party on earth, that was what. He wondered if he should go up at all, but decided it would be OK. Grandma Otis was busy, she wouldn't want to be bothered. He'd sneak up and slide into his room. He walked over to the stairs speaking softly to Flop. 'I've been to London, Flop. You would have been really scared. Went by train too.'

Grandma's own room was tight with people, the only light (a soft green glow) that seemed to emanate from Grandma Otis herself. She sat up in bed with a shawl wrapped around tight around her as she concentrated hard on the job in hand. The people in the room sat around her with intent gazes, barely breathing. Two tall men in Hugo Boss suits hung back against the outer walls with bored expressions on their faces, only mildly interested in the proceedings, probably only there to accompany their wives or girlfriends. At the end of the bed sat a woman with stooped shoulders, dressed in a orange cotton dress, with a skimpy woolen cardigan barely disguising her anorexic figure. As she sat, silently sobbing, two of her female companions tried to comfort her. There was the overwhelming element of sorrow in the room and altogether too many people for comfort. The atmosphere was close, humid and electric.

Grandma Otis let out a sigh, then released a disembodied voice that came from her mouth, but was most definitely not her own or Quon's. It was the voice of a child, a male child, a boy aged ten or younger.

'Susan? It's me, Steve. Susan? Can you hear me? It's me, Steve.'

The woman in orange sat bolt upright. It was she who was named Susan and it was clear from her total astonishment that she clearly recognised the voice calling her. The transformation in her face was instantaneous. She immediately became animated. 'It's Steven, it's Steve,' she cried out to everyone. 'It's his voice, it's him. Steven? It's me, Susan.'

'It's dark Susan, why is it so dark? Where are you? When are coming to get me?'

The young child's voice was piteous and realistic. Even the two men who had been acting so bored earlier were now listening with interest and keenly watching Susan and Grandma Otis.

Susan was shaking her head violently now. 'Why didn't you wait for me? I told you to wait. I told you not to swim alone, there's undercurrents. Oh, Steve, if you'd only waited.'

There was a sudden creak on the stairs and everyone jumped as they strained to see out onto the landing. The green glow surrounding Grandma Otis flickered and began to fade, yet simultaneously, an apparition appeared at the top of the stairs: a vision in yellow, a young boy, glowing in the reflected light from Grandma's room, revealing his startled face.

Susan leapt up from the end of the bed and cried out: 'It's Steven, it's Steve, he's come back to me, he's come back.' She ran forward and wrapped her arms around the apparition she thought to be Steve. Immediately there was a hissing and a loud cry of pain as a cat landed clumsily onto the floor. A struggle had begun between Susan and the apparition. The more she squeezed, the more violent the struggle became.

'Steve?' wailed Susan.

The others in the room began to rise, spooked and not a little concerned for Susan's safety. The atmosphere was one of nervous expectancy tinged with growing scepticism.

'Steven!' Susan cried out once again and this time there was an immediate response as the child in question managed to get his head out from under her crushing figure.

'Leave me alone, leave me alone, I'm not bloody Steve!'

Everyone froze to the spot. The last fragment of light surrounding Grandma Otis died and Oliver broke free of Susan's grip. Susan, however, still did not realise what had happened.

'Steve, you came back to me, you...'

'I AM NOT STEVE!' Oliver shouted angrily, evading Susan's hysterical clutches.

Oliver found himself facing a room full of adults who were all experiencing a rising tide of anger. Behind them Grandma Otis lay slumped in her bed only slowly coming back to herself.

One of the men came to Susan's side and took her by the arm. 'Come on Susan, obviously you've been victim to some terrible, malicious fraud. It's not Steven, darling, it's not Steven.'

Grandma Otis finally found her own voice, though it croaked and sounded frail when she finally uttered: 'Oliver? Are you there? What's happened? Are you there?'

Susan broke free of her escort and turned on Grandma Otis, her nostrils flaring, her eyes mad with grief and anger. 'You wicked witch, you cruel woman. I came to you and you did this, you...' She spat as she spoke, she was so angry. 'What kind of trick is this? You stole my Steve. He was coming back. He was ready. You stole him.'

Oliver rocked back on his feet, standing right on the edge of the top stair, not at all sure what had been going on, or what was happening now. He recognised that the atmosphere had turned very ugly and, somehow he was involved.

Grandma Otis sat up in her bed, tight-lipped and flushed, unaccustomed to being called a cheat. She lifted her stick into the air and pointed it at Susan. 'Mrs Ford,' she snapped, 'you can think what you like, but no one ever comes back, not in the flesh, never.' She turned to Oliver and tried to rein in her anger a little. 'Oliver get to your room, you've no part in this.'

She turned back to Mrs Ford and her anger returned. 'That's my grandson and he's got enough troubles without you adding to them.'

'Steven was here.' Susan hissed at her. 'You let him go.'

Susan's escort put an arm around her and pulled her towards the stairs, but she wasn't finished yet. 'I'll sue you. He was here, he was here!'

Grandma Otis slammed her stick down on her bed, startling the other two women who had remained still and tightlipped until this moment, completely confused by the evening's events. The women stood up and grabbed their coats. 'He was here.' they confirmed in unison.

'They can't come back,' Grandma Otis insisted, her own anger rising once more. 'Anyone who says so is a fool, anyone who believes it is a bigger fool. You can sue me all you like, but it was you who came to me to hear your son one more time. If you heard him, you heard him, but I'm no magician. If you want to raise the dead, get yourself a bloody witch doctor!'

Oliver took this opportunity to duck into his room, quickly closing the door behind him. To his relief, a cross looking Flop was sat on the bed, frantically licking his paws, looking up momentarily, as if to say, 'About bloody time, lock the doors, pack the bags, they're all mad!'

Oliver joined him on the bed and discovered that he was shaking. His back hurt where the woman's hands had gripped him. Just what had been going on? Was Grandma Otis really trying to bring people back from the dead? Like

Frankenstein? He didn't know whether to be frightened or impressed. 'Granny Frankenstein' would be pretty amazing really, but he knew he'd probably gotten the wrong end of the stick.

He heard them talking outside and going downstairs. The front door slammed and soon after he heard car engines being started. Flop and Oliver listened as the last car drove away leaving just the silence of an old house and the sounds of a distant foghorn on the river. Flop leaned into Oliver and Oliver tickled the top of his head. Both of them were confused and anxious. Oliver whispered into Flop's pink ears. 'It's pretty scary Flop. I think everyone in this city is seriously weird.'

Half an hour later the pipes were rumbling somewhere in the house after Grandma Otis's bath and although she was calmer now, inside she still seethed. Her reputation would survive this, there had been moments like this before. Her regulars would come, they knew she was the real thing. She'd never wanted to see these people in the first place. She'd instinctively known that these people would be trouble. They'd been referred. Well, she'd not do a favour for that quarter again, that was for sure. People missed the dead all the time, but it was unhealthy to obsess about it. That woman Susan was driven by guilt. She knew that she'd let her attention wander and her child had drowned. That was all this was, a saga, a charade to deflect her guilt, to avoid the blame for her carelessness. Downstairs she heard Lena coughing and dragging her body off to bed. There had to be a way to wean her off the sherry, it was going to do the woman in one day. Grandma Otis sighed as she shuffled from the bathroom to her bedroom, plonking her aching bones down in front of her dressing table mirror.

She let down her long, grey hair and began to brush it out. A nightly ritual in front of her mirror. For her, no matter how late the day ended, it wasn't finished off properly unless she gave her tresses fifty hard brushes. That's the way it had always been, since she'd been a child. Always fifty brushes with her mother-of-pearl brush. She looked up into the mirror and started...it was not herself looking back but a young boy, a leering, sullen, wild young boy. He looked directly at her and mouthed 'Oliver'...then winked at her.

Grandma Otis was so shocked, she was so completely taken aback she dropped her hand brush onto the carpet, her hands instinctively shooting to her neck, clasping the small gold cross she had there holding it tight. The vision disappeared, it had only lasted a second – or less – if it had ever existed at all – but it left Grandma Otis thoroughly spooked, there was no other word for it. Oliver was in danger, whoever the boy was, he had nothing but evil intentions upon her grandson.

She was up on her shaky legs as fast as she could rise and walking towards Oliver's room. She pushed open his door and the light fell upon his bed. He was lying still fully clothed across his bed with the cat curled up in his arms. Flop looked up at Grandma Otis and let out a tiny warning cry to Oliver. He awoke instantly and blinked as his eyes adjusted to the light from the landing. He knew immediately that he was about to be punished for his adventures that night, and for causing trouble when he got home.

'I didn't mean to cause trouble,' he began. 'I was just coming up the stairs and...'

Grandma Otis waved the remark. 'Who's the boy, Oliver? Who is he? A thin boy with a mean look, a permanent sneer on his face, looks bitter and he's got a scar...'

Oliver blinked at Grandma Otis with utter confusion. How was it possible she could describe Bullet so accurately? It was impossible she could know Bullet, impossible.

'You know Bullet?'

Grandma Otis steadied herself by holding onto the door. She knew she'd hit a mark. He had met this boy. 'He is evil, Oliver. He isn't your friend, even if he pretends to be. He means to harm you. I don't know why, but I have had a warning. Do you understand me? A warning. He wants to harm you.'

Oliver nodded his head. A warning. Well he'd had one too! Bullet was no friend, he'd knew that well enough. He couldn't tell Grandma about Bullet without telling her where he been or what he'd done and he wasn't going to makes things worse than they already were. He tried to change the subject.

'I'm sorry I upset everything here tonight. Will you get into trouble? Will she really sue you?'

Grandma Otis pulled a face. 'She could try, but she won't. They aren't my regulars, friends of a friend.'

'What did they want?'

'The impossible. Some people can't live with their guilt and they want to talk to the dead...some people just want to make sure their loved ones are safely over and others...well, they just want advice. I couldn't help them tonight, they wanted more than I can give them. If they think I'm a fraud, then I've survived worse. No one likes you if you won't give them what they want.'

Oliver digested this. 'Bullet isn't really my friend, he's...'

'He's mean, that's what he is and he wants to get you into trouble.'

Oliver frowned. 'Well he can't. I don't ever want to see him again.'

But Grandma Otis knew otherwise, it wasn't something Oliver could choose. 'You know, your mother made a friend once. She was called Allison. She was the nicest girl you could ever want your daughter to be friends with. Then Allison discovered boys and pills and she'd steal money to pay for everything. She stole from everyone but she was very clever because she made everyone believe that it was your mother, my Sophia, who was the thief. She even had me convinced, I am ashamed to say. I thought it was my own daughter taking money from my bag and others pockets. When Allison pointed out that your grandfather's gold watch had gone we all accused Sophia of taking it, and she had a new record player that I hadn't paid for...well, we all liked Allison and no matter what Sophia said, we just didn't believe she was innocent.'

'Is that when my Mother ran away from you?' Oliver asked, familiar with this story, but interested to hear it from Grandma's side.

Grandma Otis looked away for a moment, a tear welling up in one eye as she recalled the terrible incident so long ago. 'Yes, but of course, that is when we discovered Sophia was innocent because Allison went on stealing from us and although she tried to blame it on all sorts of people, we knew better.'

'When Sophia came back, we tried to make friends again, but,' Grandma Otis rubbed her eyes and sighed, 'she never forgave me, never.'

She looked at Oliver's face and saw how tired and pensive he looked. She knew right then that something bad had already happened to him. Perhaps he'd tell her in time. She hoped so. She hoped he'd learn to trust her. 'This new friend you have made. He's a lot worse than Allison. He seems friendly, but...' she searched her mind for the right thing to say, 'but he wants you to be as unhappy as he is, he's jealous of you.'

Oliver looked up at her with genuine surprise. 'Jealous?'

Grandma Otis smiled at him, a moment's genuine affection showing. 'You have something he hasn't got Oliver. People like you. Did I tell you Harriet has fallen for you?'

Grandma Otis registered his embarrassment and turned away, adding as an afterthought as she pulled the door to: 'Did I tell you how happy I am you came to live here? I always wanted to see you, y'know, but Sophia refused to bring you to me. I once came to Louth, but she wouldn't let me see you. I waited, but she wouldn't even let you out of the house that day. 'Grandma Otis sighed. 'This is your home now Oliver, you will be safe here.'

With that said, she was gone and Oliver was left sitting up in bed in darkness. Flop lay across his lap, solidly asleep, only the fading luminosity of the new owl on his window ledge was there to keep him company. He'd expected a telling-off, at worst a beating, he wasn't sure how to deal with what Grandma Otis had actually said. He was happy to know she wanted him to stay, but he was still unnerved by her description of Bullet. She was right, no matter how she'd known about him. He was definitely going to avoid him, big time. He lay back down on his bed and snuggled up to Flop who put out a paw to his face again and left it there. Sleep wanted him and he was ready.

CHAPTER EIGHT

Lena was making breakfast, nursing a severe hangover as she made the scrambled eggs. A glass of bubbling Andrew's Liver Salts sat fizzing on the table with a small stack of paracetamols beside it. She turned from the pan and picked up the glass, knocking it back and swallowing four of the pills, as Oliver wandered in, lobster-red from the hot shower towelling his wet head dry.He could see Lena looked as though she was really suffering.

'Did you see Flop yet? Did he eat?'

Lena stirred the scrambled eggs some more as the toaster flipped up, exposing the over-done toast. 'Get the toast won't you. Your breakfast is nearly ready. Your cat already ate. I dropped a raw egg and he was all for scoffing it down.'

Oliver pulled a face. 'Yuk, he never ate an egg before, but once he eat my mother's corn on the cob. He stole it off the table and wouldn't give it up. He ate all the corn off it too.'

Lena screwed up her face with pain as she shovelled out the scrambled eggs from the pan onto a warm plate. 'That's a strange cat alright.'

Oliver could see that she was having a hard time looking at and smelling the food. He busied himself with buttering the toast. Lena was clutching her head as she lowered the pan into the washing up basin.

'I don't know what they put in the sherry these days, but it sure isn't what it used to be. Never used to get a head like this. Never.'

As Oliver put his toast on the table and sat down to eat as Lena sat down and buried her head on her arms, groaning loudly.

Oliver began to eat, he pondered what it must be like to make yourself drink so much you would wake up with a headache, and why people did it. 'Lena? When you were young, did you ever think about the future?'

Lena didn't reply immediately, or stir from her position on the table. Oliver thought she was probably too ill to answer, so he started eating, enjoying his hot food.

'We didn't think much about the future when we were young.' Lena remarked eventually, her fingers going out in the space directly before them as they searched for her pack of cigarettes. They found the pack and Oliver pushed the pink lighter into her hand with his toast. As if in slow motion she sat up and one sweeping action lit a cigarette and sat perfectly still, blowing smoke towards the ceiling with her eyes tightly closed.

'We all thought the bloody world was going to end any day soon; so we didn't make any plans. All of us were the same. We didn't need to get a mortgage, we didn't need to do anything boring. We could be actors, or artists, or singers and it didn't matter if you didn't make any money, because the Russians or the Americans were going to blow up the planet, sooner or later. I knew the world was going to end when I was five years old and even when I was thirty, I was still waiting.' She opened her eyes and looked at Oliver, studied him, making Oliver feel uncomfortable. 'You don't know what it's like to grow up in a world that could end at any time. I used to laugh at people who made plans for the future. I told them, 'Why bother? You'll be dead. Spend your money, don't save. When the bomb drops, you'll regret not having a good time."

She laughed, but it was bitter and painful for her, for she soon stopped and clamped a hand to her temple again. 'I was wrong, of course. Stupid. The world's still here and I'm broke, got no future, no life. I suppose my world did end after all. I suppose all the bloody optimists were right. Everything did come right in the end.'

Oliver swallowed the last of his scrambled eggs and went to the counter to switch the kettle on, checking to see if it had water in it first. It had. He flipped the switch. 'I dreamt about the world ending once. Big explosions and people vapourised onto the pavements. I saw this film about the war in Japan. My doctor told me that the reason I'm still alive is because I have a destiny and God wants me to stay alive long enough to meet it.'

Lena looked at Oliver and frowned. 'I used to think I had a destiny. I used to think I would be discovered one day, that I'd be wanted, loved but I always knew that the day it happened, that's the day all hell would break loose and the world would end.'

Oliver smiled. 'Maybe that's why you didn't become famous.'

Lena scowled at him. 'What do you mean?' Then; 'If you're making tea, I'll have a cup too. The tea bags are in the jar marked salt.'

Oliver busied himself with the cups and teabags as he considered his reply. 'I mean, maybe God couldn't let you become famous because if you had been, then the world would have ended.'

Lena blew a smoke ring at him and fell back on the table, burying her head into her arms again. 'Well, I still think the world's going to end...'

'Do you like milk and sugar?'

'...and I hope I die first. Milk, no sugar.'

'I went to the library yesterday and I met Aura there. She introduced me to Old Joe and we sent messages all over the world to see if anyone will help me find my father. That's the future. Joe says the Internet is going to take over everything.'

Lena just groaned. 'Make the tea. Make sure you wear a coat today, it's windy, might rain.'

Oliver looked out of the window and saw she was right, it was blowing the trees really hard. He wondered if there would be any waves on the river. He wanted to take a look.

Lena took a final drag of her cigarette and tossed the butt end into the sink. 'I suppose we'll have to think about a school for you soon.'

Oliver spun around and made an unpleasant noise. 'Next term, not now. When my hair grows back.'

Lena opened her eyes and was about to say something sarcastic but stopped herself. She hadn't really thought about what it would be like to go to a new school and have kids taunt you for being bald. Kids were cruel, she knew that and they'd sooner pick on you for being different, than not.

'Well, it had better start growing soon if it is going to be ready for next term. Besides, you'll be cold in winter without it.' Then she remembered something else and pushed the newspaper towards where Oliver stood as he made the tea. 'Take a look at page four.'

Oliver opened the local paper up and immediately found the relevant headline. Instantly his face broke into a grin as he read it out aloud. ' "Shoes In Mystery Death Riddle" Hey, it's the feet I found. There's a picture.'

Lena slumped back onto her arms and groaned again. 'Pass the tea, I need the tea.'

Oliver pushed the cup over towards her as he read out bits of the story. 'Police say they are looking for a man's body with a pair of missing size ten feet.' He looked disappointed as he continued to read. 'It doesn't mention me or Harriet.'

Lena grasped the tea. 'Good. Grandma Otis wouldn't like it if they made a connection to this house. She doesn't like publicity. It always brings the nutters out of the woodwork.'

'But why doesn't anyone know who he is? Someone must know he is missing. How did his feet get cut off?'

Lena was tired of his questions now. 'Why don't you ask Grandma Otis to see if Quon knows. He knows a lot of things.'

Oliver nodded. Yes, it was a good idea. Somehow Grandma had known about Bullet, so it was very likely she'd know about this mysterious man. 'I'll ask her to ask him. I still don't know how he knows things, but I'll certainly ask.'

'Now if you'd be so good as to finish your cup of tea in perfect silence I would appreciate it. And where were you last night? You're not going to get in the habit of roaming at night are you?'

Oliver was about to launch into an excuse when Grandma Otis rang her bell and Lena groaned very loudly. 'Oh God, she's awake already. You can tell me later, I have to make her breakfast. Are you going out?'

'I like the wind.'

'Wrap up, alright? And make sure you're back for tea. Five o'clock sharp. Not a minute past.'

Oliver nodded and sipped his tea, glancing out of the window a moment to examine the weather more closely. Yes, the river, he wanted to explore the river today, see where it went, what was sailing. Lena got up from the table and put more bread in the toaster. She looked very pale, very sick and suddenly very old. Oliver knew that he'd never, ever, want to drink sherry, not if it made a person look like that.

The tide was out, far out, and there was a huge mud bank below the river walkway. Virtually nothing was sailing on the river, which left Oliver feeling a little bit disappointed. He was walking with his coat on with the hood up to keep out the biting cold wind. He'd taken the upriver walk, discovering that on the other side of the defunct power station lay an old hospital that had been in use in the eighteenth century, long before the power station that had been plonked next door to it. He knew from history that back in Queen Elizabeth the First's time this had been the most important place in England, where Nelson's Navy was based and he tried to think what it must have been like to live in Greenwich back then. He couldn't see much of the white plastered hospital building, but he had glimpsed a little courtyard through an open door and it looked very inviting. He knew there was a lot to discover and he wondered if there were pictures of the port back in those times. Had Grandma's house been standing then? Were there secret passages, smugglers' tunnels? If there were, he intended to find them.

He'd walked towards the buildings and pubs that overlooked the river, where squeezed in the middle was Crane Street, a narrow passage between the river buildings and a row of small terrace houses on one side. He was fascinated by the place. He'd had in mind a visit to look at the Cutty Sark and perhaps walk along the foot tunnel that runs under the river, but that was before he'd noticed the wooden floodgate was open to the river and someone had left a racing rowing boat on the pebbles. Oliver walked out onto the pebble beach and contemplated walking alongside the river for a while. As he approached the river though, he noticed just how squishy the mud was and he was not really prepared to ruin his only good pumps for this. He looked across the river at the other side. A four-man crew was rowing upstream, struggling in the wind as the spray engulfed them. In the distance a tug, seemingly drifting on the water, its crew lolling about out on deck. He turned, nothing very interesting today, he'd go to the Cutty Sark after all. Oliver moved back towards the slipway, and was about to break into a run, when he stumbled and fell headlong onto the hard pebble surface. He swore, slipping again as he tried to rise, and slid back a couple of feet. He was covered in mud now and he'd only been out of the house fifteen minutes. He was thinking irritatedly that he just couldn't go anywhere without getting into a mess of some kind. He turned his head and instantly received a jolt. He had discovered what it was that had tripped him. He was looking at a decomposing human head. A man's head.

'Shiiit!' Oliver yelled. He looked around to see if anyone could see him in any of the houses or pubs overlooking the beach area, but he couldn't see any faces.

He looked at the pulpy, pasty, bloodless head again and nearly threw up on the spot when a black eel slithered out of an eye socket and slipped back into the half-open mouth . 'Eeyuk!' Oliver cried out, scrabbling up on his two feet at last. He looked down at the head again with disgust and fascination. Now he could see it more clearly, there were all kinds of slug-like things attached to it as well. He nearly tasted his breakfast again, but managed to keep it down. He would have to report it to the police, he had to get away from it. A severed head, just lying on the beach...he knew, as he ran towards the floodgates facing Crane Street, that he was more than likely looking at the head that had belonged to the pair of feet he'd found in the shoes. Greenwich was the scariest place on earth. Someone was chopping people up around here and leaving the body parts for just anyone to find.

It took an hour, but the police finally arrived and were none too pleased to discover the tide was coming in. But it was they who'd wasted time not believing anything. Oliver had waited at the beach for ages before they'd sent one bored cop. He'd shown more interest when Oliver had finally persuaded him to venture out onto the beach and then turned very pale before leaving Oliver in charge as he went to call others. Now, Oliver sat in a police Range Rover, out of the wind at the end of Park Row overlooking the river, watching policemen in muddy shoes and boots going over the pebbles and surrounding area to see if there were any other body parts. They'd missed the head before; it was possible the hands and torso might be lurking somewhere. Oliver was interested to watch how methodical the police were, but he tended to think they were wasting their time. He knew (but couldn't say how) that all they'd ever find was the head and shoes, the fish had got the rest.

A woman opened the car door and came inside to sit next to Oliver. He immediately recognised her as being Detective Kray, the woman who'd spoken to him after he'd found the shoes. 'Other kids go around smashing up windows or stealing cars around here. You just turn up body parts. What next, Oliver? A whole family with their legs missing?' Oliver smiled and shrugged. 'I was only going for a walk on the beach.'

Detective Kray nodded and put her head to one side. 'And you're thinking this head belongs to the feet, am I right? You wouldn't be playing detective would you? Not that I'm criticising you, but there's dangers in finding stuff. Lots of people don't like anyone poking their noses into things and they'd just as soon chop you up and throw you into the river as anyone else.'

Oliver frowned, he was confused. 'I was just taking a walk. Shouldn't I have called the police?'

Detective Kray shook her head. 'No, you did right. It's me. I'm not used to kids doing the right thing. I'm taking you home. I don't want you telling anyone about this. I don't want anyone knowing it's you who found both bits of this bloke's body, OK? Just in case this gets ugly. No need for anyone to know. You understand?'

Oliver understood. She was giving him a message: stay out of it. He was disappointed. Obviously something was going on here he didn't have any business knowing about. It made him want to know more, of course, but he wasn't going to tell her that.

'You'd be surprised at just how many bodies do end up in the water every year. Most people think that it's an easy way to get rid of someone.' She started up the Range Rover and made a three-point turn. 'But the tide is a funny thing. Things go down the river and they come back. They go one side, they come back. And sometimes we find them. Found a torso ten miles down river last year, no head, or legs or hands, but forensics discovered he'd eaten a curry just before he died and they tracked that curry right down to Lambeth and the restaurant that sold it. Got the switch number of the man who ate it and within ten days we knew who had been murdered and probably why.'

'Did you catch the murderer?'

Detective Kray drove off up the street towards Trafalgar Road. 'Well, that's usually the hard part. Take this head you found – that's great. A head's got teeth, at least this one has. The man will have a dentist somewhere and that will definitely identify him, but, even if we didn't have teeth to go on, he might have a scar or a mark. Or we could reconstruct his face using computers, and show some pictures of what he really looks like to people and we'd get a name that way.'

'But it doesn't tell you who killed him, or why.'

'No, it doesn't. But when we know who he was, we might find out the why.'

'Could be he was cut up by the mafia. I saw a film on TV.'

Detective Kray shook her head. 'Not their style here. If they wanted someone to disappear, they'd disappear. You think you'd make a good detective?'

Oliver thought about this for moment as Detective Kray negotiated her way into the traffic. 'My teacher said that being a policeman, or a teacher, was a bad idea, you never make any money and no one ever says thanks'.

Detective Kray snatched a look at Oliver's serious face and knew immediately that he wasn't being sarcastic. 'Well, I suppose your teacher is right. It's down here, right? I've heard about your Grandma. She's the one who tells peoples' fortunes isn't she?'

'She gives people advice,' Oliver corrected her, remembering what Lena had told him to say if asked.

'Take my advice Oliver, you stick to the library on a cold day like this and stay out of trouble. There's a lot of mean people out there these days.'

Oliver nodded. Yes. A lot of mean people, with very sharp knives.

'Nice neighbourhood your Grandma lives in. I bet half the hot cars in London end up here at night. Your Grandma doesn't sell car spares by any chance does she?'

Oliver didn't get the joke but detected the mocking tone in her voice. Detective Kray was amused by her remark, however and continued to smile to herself as she brought her car to a halt outside Grandma's house. 'Come on, I'd better meet your Grandma.'

Grandma Otis wasn't very pleased when he was brought back by a policewoman, a detective no less. She was even less charmed to discover that Oliver had found yet another body part on the beach, less than 200 yards from her house. They were talking in her hallway. Grandma Otis had felt obliged to come down the stairs for this.

'Detective Kray, this boy has only been here three days and he's already done more than I have in ten years.'

Oliver thought this was a criticism, but wasn't sure.

'Well Oliver's done all the right things, but I think he should keep it to himself for the moment. Don't want people to think that he knows more than he does, do we?'

Grandma Otis understood, even if Oliver didn't.

'I was thinking Quon could help,' Oliver remarked to Grandma Otis. Grandma Otis gave Oliver a very black look and he didn't pursue it..

Detective Kray looked interested, 'Quon?'

Grandma Otis just smiled. 'A friend. He likes to play amateur sleuth.'

Detective Kray shook her head and smiled. 'I knew as soon as I saw this old place that Miss Marple might live here. But leave the investigating to us. We'll know who it is soon enough. And Oliver? You call me if you ever get into any trouble alright? Here's my card again. Don't go looking for trouble, but if it finds you, call me.'

Oliver felt quite important taking her card, but he had to go to the bathroom. Perhaps it was the cold wind or something, but he had a pain. It was embarrassing, but he had to run.

When he'd gone, Detective Kray walked to the front door, pausing a moment, looking back down the passage where Oliver had just quickly disappeared. 'He's been sick, I can see that. Will he get better? He's very thin.'

Grandma Otis smiled. 'Thank you for taking an interest, but Oliver's stronger than he looks. His father was tough and quite a survivor, I believe. He's a good boy. He's curious though, and it's going to get him into trouble.'

Detective Kray shrugged. 'Better than apathetic like most of the kids 'round here. He's bright. Keep him away from some of the kids who hang around the streets, if you can. There's some kids out there that just live for trouble.'

Grandma Otis nodded. She knew that well enough, (didn't she see mother after mother looking for guidance on how to deal with that very problem?) 'But you can't make them a prisoner in the home.'

Detective Kray nodded. 'More's the pity. Good day, Mrs Otis.'

Grandma Otis stayed in the hallway for several minutes after the policewoman had gone. Three days and Oliver had turned her life upside down. God wanted her to wake up or go to an early grave. She didn't know which. Heads and feet washing up on her riverfront. It was getting to be like the violent London of old. A hundred years of civilising forgotten in one generation.

'Lena?' She called out. 'Let's have some tea.'

Oliver found himself trapped by his own success now. Grandma Otis had insisted that he had to get cleaned up after his river escapade and then discovered that she'd decided he couldn't leave the house for the rest of the day. Her heart couldn't take it apparently. She asked him at lunch to contemplate what he'd seen and learn from it. Well, as far as he could see, he'd found a head and that was that. Grandma Otis didn't see it that way of course. The fact that he'd found the man's feet was bad enough, but to find his head, it was fate alright, but bad fate. She was keen for him to break this bond between him and the dead man. She didn't know how it had happened, but it had and some might argue that since he had just arrived from the North, there was something to this fate; that he'd been sent to London for a reason. Grandma Otis didn't think so. She didn't like it one bit. She knew things didn't happen by accident, but she didn't want Oliver overwhelmed, didn't want him put in the way of forces he didn't understand.

However, Grandma Otis might be used to contemplating in her room in an afternoon, but Oliver was not. Oh, he could daydream with the best of them, but actually 'contemplate'; well, he wasn't sure he knew how to do that. What is more, he couldn't stay indoors. He just couldn't. He had to beg Lena to let him out into the garden and even then had to swear on Flop's life that he wouldn't leave it.

So that is how he found himself in the back yard with Flop doing his best to contemplate life and death and...

'Hey, you, you help me?' A voice announced.

Oliver looked up and Flop made a break for it to the bushes. Mr Ng was on the roof of his garage fixing a hole. He didn't look so frightening anymore. He was wearing overalls and a funny hat with purple stripes.

'You unhappy?' He asked Oliver.

'I liked your owl,' Oliver remembered to say. 'It's keeping my room safe.'

'Need more than one,' Mr Ng declared, but didn't specify how many would do.

'You help me?' Mr Ng asked. 'I need tools.'

Oliver leapt up. Grandma Otis couldn't complain if he helped a neighbour. Anything had to be better than trying to contemplate anything.

'What do you want?'

Mr Ng nodded. 'Tools on workbench. Pass them up.'

Oliver dove in through the bushes and entered Mr Ng's garage. It was quite changed from his last visit. Gone was the fire damage and all the things that he'd been making there. In its place was a huge fibreglass horse astride a trailer. Mr Ng was working on horses now.

'The sealer. Pass up the seal-gun. That's what I need,' Mr Ng called down.

Oliver found what looked to be a seal gun and took it up the ladder with the sealant. The wind was howling around the ladder, but Oliver enjoyed being up there and getting a look at the breaker's yard beyond. They were crushing another car and it was making a terrible din.

Mr Ng took the sealant from him and Oliver stayed up in the hole through the roof watching him fixing the gaps in his old roof.

'Why did you come to live here?' Oliver asked.

Mr Ng didn't reply straight away as he was trying to get the liquid to come out of the seal gun in a smooth action. He placed a tile on the roof and ran the sealant around it, smoothing the seal with his thumb. 'Why you come here?' he asked Oliver.

'I had to come and live with my Grandmother.'

'I came to study.' Mr Ng declared earnestly.

'Study?'

'Yes. I was to be Doctor, but I make mistake. I get sick. I fall in love. I did not study. I marry. I have to make animals for people to sell. My wife, she dress windows. My animals go into windows. My wife, she gets sad, she wants to leave. She goes. I still make animals.'

Oliver realised that he'd just heard Mr Ng's whole life story. It was quite sad. It explained the horse downstairs too.

'I like your animals. Don't you?'

Mr Ng took another tile and filled another gap, sealing it with the same smooth expertise. He looked at Oliver. 'I wanted to be Doctor. A man should do what he should do. What do you want?'

Oliver was sort of hoping he wasn't going to ask this question but he had an answer ready. 'I want to live in the mountains with the trees and animals. I don't want to have to get a job. I just want to live in the forest and listen to the trees, swim in the rivers ; explore things.'

Mr Ng smiled as he took the last tile and slotted it into place. 'You must go live in China. You will find many forests, many animals.' He laughed revealing his stained teeth.

'Yes, live in China. You replace me. That's good, very good. I like that.'

Oliver smiled. He hadn't planned to live in China, but he was glad he had made Mr Ng smile. Now he really had something to contemplate. Poor Mr Ng. Wanted to be a Doctor all his life and ended up making models of animals for window displays. He wondered if he would ever get to visit a mountain, or live in a forest. Or would he end up working in a shop or worse, Burger King? (Which was the worst job he might end up doing he could actually think of at this precise moment) But at least he was thinking now, he actually had something worth contemplating.

'I have to go now,' Oliver told Mr Ng.

'Thank you. You help good.'

Oliver smiled and descended the ladder. In the distance a police siren reminded him that the rest of the world was still out there. Somehow, Grandma was right...it did feel safer at her house. Almost like he was already living in the past. He could blink and instead of breakers yards, there might be fields, trees, sailing ships, sailors and many horses. What would it sound like then. No cars, no electricity, how did people know what was going on?

'That's what I want to be,' he told himself as he emerged from the bush between Mr Ng's house and Grandma's garden. 'I want to be a time-traveller.' It seemed a perfectly reasonable idea. Someone was bound to invent a way of going back or forward in time in the 21st Century. He wondered if they already had and how old you had to be to apply. Time travelling was probably going to be a good career choice one day. He made a note to make sure that he continued to study history in school in case they asked awkward questions when he applied for the job. In fact, the more he thought about it, you'd have to know so much about history, you'd have to know everything, all the politics, all about money and religion and...Oliver suddenly realised that he needed to know a million things and that was just from one second of contemplation. What had Grandma Otis started? Still, history seemed a very good thing to study.

With that settled he went back inside to make himself some tea. Time-travellers needed food, lots of it.

The sky was darkening and the wind was getting stronger. Somewhere outside, a church clock struck ten o'clock and a car horn sounded for an unnecessarily long time over in the next street. Suddenly, a face appeared at Oliver's window. The face was calling to him and when Oliver looked more carefully, he saw that the face had no body and the person calling was in pain. He looked again by the light of a car's headlights and immediately took an involuntary sharp intake of breath. Bullet was looking at him through his window.

'Ha! Open up stupid. Open up.'

But Oliver was transfixed. Bullet was nothing more than a severed head with worms crawling over it. Blood seemed to drip from his neck and his eyes bulged.

'No, no.' Oliver shouted loudly. 'Go away.'

There was a crack of lightning, his window swung open. Bullet was laughing crazily, his head suspended in mid-air outside his window. 'Let me in arsehole. Let me in.'

Oliver scrabbled forward to close the window, aware that it was raining hard now and he was getting wet. Behind him he could hear Flop miaowing and spitting. Oliver reached for the window to close it, but Bullet was in his face again, mocking him. 'Think you're so fuckin' smart, don't you? Think you're better than me. Well you are nothin', worm. You're less than nothin'.'

'Fuck off!' Oliver yelled at Bullet. 'You're not my friend. You're never going to be my friend.'

Bullet laughed at him and Oliver lashed out at his head. Only when he touched it, it was his own head he was staring at. Dead, mute, bleeding; a huge swelling on one side.

Oliver drew in his breath again and felt hot tears on his cheeks. He was crying. Not out of fear, but because he knew he was dead. The tumour had come back, it had come back.

He reached for the window again and managed to grasp it, but he wasn't strong enough to shut it against the wind. He looked out again, his head was gone, but now he could see Mr Ng was still on the roof of his garage, waving and pointing at something behind Oliver. Oliver glanced behind him- his owl was glowing. That's what Mr Ng meant: the owl, grab the owl. Oliver lunged for the owl and held on tight...

All was calm. The window had shut all by itself, the rain stopped outside and there was no longer any scary head looking at him through the glass. Flop jumped up beside him and put out a paw to the owl. The owl glowed and Oliver could feel his breathing returning to normal...

'There you are. Why are sitting out here? It's cold. Come on in. Grandma Otis wants to see you before you go to bed.'

Oliver looked about him. He was on the stoop, sat on the old swing chair. Flop was nowhere to be seen and there was no owl, no head. Not even a window. He had been dreaming. But what a dream. He could still see both Bullet's and his own head in his mind's eye.

'Are you alright? You didn't eat much of your supper. Oliver? You look very sweaty. You haven't gone and got a fever have you?'

Oliver looked up into Lena's eyes and saw her genuine concern. He smiled. 'Had a nightmare, I think. It was scary.'

Lena put out a hand to his shoulder and gave him a squeeze. 'I have them all the time. God, you're sweaty. You really did have a nightmare. Let me guess. Was there a severed head in it?'

Oliver nodded. Lena smiled knowingly. 'Go up and see Grandma Otis. She's in a better mood now. Might as well make the best of it.'

As Lena left him Oliver decided to go to the bathroom. He wasn't ready for Grandma yet. He needed to wash and change. The dream had left him feeling strange and apprehensive.

In the bathroom the hot steam in the basin sort of helped a little and he sponged himself down thoroughly. He hardly dared look in the mirror in case he saw anything strange, but when he cleaned his teeth, nothing frightening occurred, so he began to gain his equilibrium. He could explain Bullet's head appearing in his dream; that was because Bullet had betrayed him and he was thinking about him a lot. And he could easily explain about the severed head, it was just the head he'd found on the beach, but seeing his own head suspended outside the window, that was what had unnerved him. Why was he dead? Why the swelling and the blood? Was something bad going to happen to him? Was he going to get sick again?

A few minutes later, he appeared in his pyjamas outside his Grandma's bedroom and she beckoned him in with a friendly smile.

'Sit on the end of my bed. Mind my toes.'

Oliver did as he was told and moved into the room. Almost immediately Grandma Otis noticed he was troubled by something. 'Lena told me that you looked feverish. You're not sick are you?'

Oliver shook his head. 'I had a weird dream, that's all.'

Grandma Otis pursed her lips. 'I'm not surprised. You have been a very busy boy since you got here and everything must be so different to Louth. Not many bodies washing up in your little river there I suspect. Do you miss it?'

'Louth?'

'Yes. It was your home, after all. Where did you go, what did you like to do?'

Oliver thought about that for a moment. Everything he did was always before he got sick. He hadn't really done anything for so long. 'I used to go to the canal a lot. There's a place you can ride your bike to. A big ditch alongside the canal where someone has tied a rope to a huge branch of a tree and you can swing out across the ditch and back to the canal bank. James Swain has got some horses and he was going to teach me to ride last year, but now I won't be allowed to ride. When my Dad was there, he'd sometimes take me to Cadwell Park to watch the motor racing. He's got a friend who races his old MG and a Lotus. He never wins, but I like going to the pits and,' he grinned, 'there's always lots of crashes.'

Grandma Otis smiled. She could see Oliver visibly relaxing before her, calming down as he remembered Louth. She knew from her first glance at him that he'd had more than just a dream. Now, for the first time she was beginning to sense that Oliver may have inherited some of her own talents. She recalled the terrible nightmares she'd had as others thoughts first invaded her dreams. Was that what was haunting him now? Was it beginning for him? If so, how could she tell him not to be afraid? Would the knowledge of what will happen to him and others scare him? Would he close his mind to it? He was naturally curious, but when it had happened to her she was so young, it had become part of her life so quickly...would it be good for him to get involved at all?

Oliver was still talking about Louth.

'When it snowed two years ago, I went tobogganing on Hubbard's Hills. That's just on the edge of town and it's a kind of valley that was formed by ice during the last ice age. Anyway, we were having a great time and getting really wet, when Michael Lester got out of control and crashed into the river and broke his arm. I had to walk him all the way to the hospital on the other side of town in the snow and he kept saying the same thing over and over. "They're going to cut my arm off, they're going to cut my arm off." Oliver laughed. 'They didn't, but Michael was called Bandit from then on. Y'know-One-armed-Bandit.'

Grandma Otis smiled. It was good to hear him tell a story, see his face and eyes come alive. He was so different to his mother in so many ways.

Oliver sighed and looked at his Grandma with a curious expression. 'Do you ever see anything about yourself? Does Quon ever tell you things about yourself? Warn you, or something?'

Grandma Otis nodded. 'Just little things. He would never tell me if I was going to have a heart attack or anything. I'd probably worry myself into my grave just thinking about it. No, he just tells me little things. Perhaps warn me about people, or once, when I was younger, he told me not to go to a dinner they were having at Lady Fenster's. There was a terrible fire and three people died of smoke inhalation. Quon wouldn't have known how they were to die, or why, but he'd knew there'd be trouble and I listen to him. One should always listen to warnings, no matter how they come to you.'

She could see Oliver digesting this. She knew he had another question too.

'You think Quon could help me find out who the man was who died on the beach?'

Grandma Otis shrugged. 'Perhaps, but why?'

'Shouldn't we help the police?'

Grandma Otis pulled a face and reached for her inhaler, always kept ready by her bed to help with her breathing. 'I tried offering my help once. They didn't respect Quon, or his help. They'd rather not solve a crime than admit they had to use a clairvoyant.'

'Yes, but was Quon right?' Oliver asked, very interested now.

Grandma Otis sat up in her bed a little higher and pulled some pictures from a pile beside her bed. She began to sort through them as she spoke.

'Quon is rarely wrong. He told them where to look for a missing child once, but they didn't listen, or didn't believe him. Quon insisted the child was in an abandoned car, standing no more than fifty yards from her home, and she was still alive.'

Oliver looked at Grandma Otis with rapt attention. 'And was the girl in the car?'

'The police said there was no abandoned car, the newspapers laughed at me and one even printed an article saying that I was exploiting the misery of the young mother who had lost her child and I should be prosecuted. This made me very angry, but Quon was both angry and insistent. He made me send Lena to look for the girl herself.'

'She found her? She found her, didn't she?'

'Indeed she did. She was right where Quon said she'd be. Trapped inside a car in someone's yard. The police had been looking for an abandoned car on the street, not an old car dumped in someone's yard.'

Oliver's brow furrowed. 'They found her alive didn't they? She was still alive?'

'Well, it wasn't as easy as that. Lena found the car, but it was locked and the owner was away. Lena called me in tears and I called the Police Commissioners wife. She comes to see me from time to time, you see. She made the Commissioner himself go and rescue the child. There were some red faces I can tell you, but yes, the child lived. In fact...' Grandma Otis handed Oliver a photocopy of some 'A' level certificates with a photo attached. 'The child sent me these only last year. She knows Quon saved her life and every year she sends me a card to say thank you. It's been eight years now. She knows how precious life is, like you.'

Oliver was glad the child lived. Happy for Grandma that someone still knew how to say thanks. He took a deep breath. He wanted to ask about his dream, about how he saw himself dead, but couldn't bring himself to ask. Instead he thought again about the head on the beach by the river. 'Well, maybe Quon does know who the dead man is and I could tell Detective Kray without telling her who told me? Maybe his family don't know he's dead? Maybe they're thinking he's gone away and...'

Grandma Otis raised her hand and made as if to tell him off, then smiled.

'Curiosity killed the cat, don't you remember? Didn't the policewoman specifically say that you shouldn't get involved?'

'Yes, but if Quon knows, then we could tell his family, at least. We don't need to know why he died.'

Grandma Otis frowned. 'Quon isn't a detective, y'know. He shouldn't be used for such things either. But, if you want I will ask him, but I can't guarantee he'll help you, or the dead man. He might not know. Sometimes if someone hasn't passed over or...well anyway, I'll try. You go fetch Lena, she wanted to have a word with Quon herself, then come back and sit still, alright? No talking, you listen and be still.'

Oliver grinned and jumped up off the bed, excited now. He dashed out of the room and practically flew down the stairs to find Lena. Behind him Grandma Otis took off her glasses and prepared herself for the session by taking deep breaths and muttering her usual prayer for God's protection.

Lena sat with her knitting as Grandma Otis gathered her 'energies'. Oliver sat at the end of the bed once again, trying desperately hard to be quiet and still, the two things he'd never been particularly good at. In the silence of the house he could hear many sounds. Lena's clacking knitting needles in the corner and the clock striking the half hour downstairs, the rumble of the wind in the fireplace where Grandma Otis kept her dried flowers and the sound of his own heart, thumping hard in his chest, the blood banging in his ears.

Imperceptibly at first, the light began to change in the room and he recognised that the familiar green glow was beginning to shine around Grandma Otis. She was getting to that place where Quon was waiting for her. Oliver began to gently rock himself from side to side, just like he'd always done when a small child. It was soothing, even if it did make the bed creak a little. As the green light was spreading around Grandma Otis, Oliver fell to thinking about the man's head on the riverside. He could see it now with immense clarity, almost as if he could pick it up and make it talk. It wasn't at all scary now, just a severed head, a specimen. He could see things now that he hadn't noticed when he fell. The shape of the man's nose, the tiny diamond stud situated in one nostril.

Grandma Otis opened her eyes. Quon was with her and ready to speak, but neither one could, for they were both watching Oliver at the end of her bed, his mesmeric rocking from side to side, him thinking, totally oblivious to his surroundings now and there, spreading softly all around him, a diffused indigo light. Oliver was the one making the connection, not her, not Quon. Here was the confirmation she needed that Oliver had the gift. He was the genuine article and glowed indigo, no less, one of the strongest. Of course, he wouldn't be conscious of it yet, but it was there, whether he wanted it or not, to be nurtured, to guide him through his life or...she didn't want to think about the downside. No need to inject any negative thoughts.

Oliver started abruptly and, in doing so, fell backwards, sliding off the bed and landing hard on the carpet below. 'Waah,' he shouted, as if waking from a nightmare. 'Waah.'

He lay there, on the carpet, completely motionless, unable to speak coherently, or move. Lena didn't move a muscle. She could see with her own eyes what was going on and she knew better than to intervene.

Grandma Otis hauled herself to the end of the bed to look down over the end of it at Oliver. She had expected something like this. Quon was still with her, he watched and waited. Grandma Otis took a deep breath and leaned on the edge of her bed, closing her eyes to let Quon through.

'Stay calm, Oliver.' Quon told him. 'We're here. You're safe. Tell me, you saw the head, didn't you? You saw the man's head.'

Oliver could feel salt on his tongue, it was such a strange sensation. He could see Lena watching him, knitting, studying him, he in turn studying the room from his horizontal position. He remained mute a few moments more. Something was happening to him, everything felt so strange, almost as if he were floating on a cloud, yet, a part of him knew he was lying on the floor in Grandma's room.

'I saw his head move.' he whispered, at last. 'He opened his eyes.'

'What colour eyes?' Quon asked carefully.

'Brown, black...dark. He looked at me.'

Grandma Otis had been completely taken over by Quon now and Lena sat with her knitting, transfixed. Two of them, there were two of them like this, in the same room. She felt the hairs on her neck rise and she could see sparks of colour between them, green, indigo, a flash of yellow...

'He said a name, he said a name didn't he?' Quon was asking Oliver.

Oliver tried to remember. He suddenly felt a gripping pain in his heart and lungs. He felt agony, fear, surprise and suddenly, he realised that it wasn't his own pain he was feeling, but the man's, the heads, the dead man's pain.

'He doesn't know he is dead. He doesn't know.'

'This is normal, he hasn't had time to pass over yet.' Quon told him. 'He's caught. He was surprised. Is he still there, Oliver? Is he still there?'

Oliver closed his eyes again. Yes, the head was still there. The man was looking at him with curiosity and confusion in his face. 'What is your name?' Oliver asked.

The face looked back at him with genuine surprise and somehow, he didn't know how, Oliver instantly knew that the man's reaction was something to do with television. Oliver was supposed to know the man, he was famous, he was on TV.'

'He's on TV,' Oliver whispered. 'He's famous.'

Lena abruptly dropped her knitting. The wool fell to the floor crackling in the electric atmosphere down there, sending sparks of multi-coloured light everywhere.

Quon pushed harder, enjoying the intensity of the moment, Oliver's strength, the diamond bright curiosity. It was so different to Grandma Otis's, strong, but well-defined and controlled powers. Grandma Otis had capacity, but Oliver had raw and uncontrolled energy peaking at such an incandescence Quon could see with immense clarity, almost like his first time with the young Grandma Otis.

'Make him talk.' Quon urged Oliver. 'Make him talk.'

'I can't.'

'You can.'

'I can't. I...' Oliver closed his eyes once more and found himself not back at the riverside, but in a room, a huge white room. He was inside the man's head and the man was alive! It was a studio, a TV studio. There were chairs, cameras, people walking to and fro. A girl in tight jeans came up to him and smiled as she fixed her blonde hair up into a pony-tail. 'Good-morning Mr Michaels. Great show last night. Shall I do your face now?'

The room changed. Oliver was looking at a long table. Many men were playing cards, someone glanced up at him then nodded in recognition. 'Twenty-five grand. Think you can play with the big boys now?'

A beautiful red-headed woman with brilliant white teeth leant over and kissed him on the cheek, the smell of her body scent was almost overwhelming. 'Go home, Mitch. I'll join you later. Go home. I'll tell Robin I've got a headache.'

Oliver experienced a weird kind of feeling, one of intense expectation and pleasure. Then, quite abruptly the room changed again and he found himself in an apartment, high up, overlooking London, it was night, the city glowed below him, in the distance lay St Paul's dome. He was entering a room, taking off his jacket, he felt tired and grumpy.

'Mitch.' a woman's voice called out with a tinge of anger in it. 'Where the hell have you been?' A hand came out of nowhere and slapped him on his face, hard.

Oliver opened his eyes. He blinked, rubbing the side of his face where he had just been slapped. Slowly it became clear. He had been the man . He had been inside the dead man as he went about his life.

Lena was holding him in her arms, softly calling his name. She looked very worried.

'Oliver? Can you hear me? Oliver?'

Grandma Otis appeared at the end of the bed once again and looked down at him, handing a glass of something to Lena to give him. Oliver could see all this, but he felt that if Lena wasn't holding him he would float up to the ceiling, he felt so lightheaded. Lena lowered the glass to Oliver's lips and he sipped. He swallowed and a red hot glow slipped down his throat, setting fire to his stomach.

'God, Lenaaa...yuk, what was that?' Oliver cried out, trying to push away the glass.

He sat up and heard the downstairs clock striking midnight. He looked at Grandma and she smiled at him, putting out a hand to stroke his head.

'Welcome back. You've been gone over an hour.'

'Are you feeling OK?' Lena asked him, giving him a quick squeeze.

Oliver struggled free. He didn't need a squeeze now, he was fine. His mouth was still on fire from the alcohol.

'Mitch Michaels.' Oliver told her. 'His name is Mitch Michaels.'

Lena knew the name immediately. 'He's got that TV show on Channel 4. 'Michaels' World'. He exposes all kinds of people on TV. If it's him that's dead, you would think it would be on the news.'

Grandma Otis sighed. She didn't care who it was, just that Oliver had got through his first time in one piece. 'You did very well, Oliver. Do you feel alright? Do you feel light-headed? Do you feel as though you could fly?'

Oliver smiled. That was exactly how he felt. 'You know? What happened? I was looking at him, and then I was inside him, walking with him. No...I was him.'

Oliver looked at Grandma Otis and Lena. He could see they had been worried, but he could also see Grandma was excited, there was something very different about her now.

'How could I be someone else Grandma? How could I be him?'

She smiled and sat down in Lena's chair. 'It used to happen to me all the time. Remember the story I told you about the little girl trapped in the car? I was inside there with her. I was as breathless as she was. I felt her desperation. I knew her panic. I knew she felt she was going to die. I felt as if I would never get out of that car alive and it was every bit as real as the real thing. I can tell you, it took more than a sip of brandy to get me right after that. Welcome to the family, Oliver. You're one of "The Clan" alright, and I think you're going to be someone very special.'

Lena was still worried about the dead man.

'He doesn't know they cut off his feet and head then?'

Grandma Otis pursed her lips. She was thinking the very same thing. 'I doubt he'll know anything about it. It was probably so fast he'll never realise what has happened to him, or else be traumatised. His whole psychic karma will be in shock. It will take some time to make a connection. I have been in contact with murder victims before and it's a terrible thing. The whole experience haunts them in the afterlife. Your man, Oliver, will be looking for the door back to consciousness and he's not going to find it.'

Oliver frowned. 'Isn't there anyway we can help him?'

Grandma Otis shook her head and began to settle back into her bed. 'No, and don't try. You hear me? There's enough warning signs around you without you trying anything foolish. You might have a gift, but it is going to take years to learn how to use it responsibly. You get off to bed now.'

Lena rubbed her neck, remembering as she did so to tell Oliver something. 'I put some milk and biscuits out for you downstairs. Go down and have them, but don't let your cat have them. Flop eats everything. I'm going to have to check that cat for worms.'

'He just likes to eat. I'm sure he'd tell me if he got sick.'

Lena looked at Oliver and for a moment she actually considered that he probably could talk to his cat, then she shook out the notion. 'Just go and have your milk.'

Oliver finally got the message that they wanted him gone. He got up and headed for the landing, announcing, 'I'm going to the library again tomorrow. I'm going to study all this stuff . What section do you think it's under?'

'S,' Grandma Otis replied with a smile. 'But you won't find what you've seen today in a book. It's not something you can talk about either. You understand me Oliver? People will think you're strange enough because of your head, don't give them a chance to mock you.'

Oliver turned around, his feet sliding on the polished landing floor. He was about to say something, but one glance at his Grandma and he knew she was right. There were some things you just didn't tell people. Nevertheless, he was puzzled by one thing. 'What happened when you first started to glow green like that Grandma? Didn't people say anything?'

Lena smiled knowingly and stopped down to retrieve her knitting from where it had dropped. 'There's only so few who can see the light, Oliver. Me, your Grandma, now you. That's how you know, that's how you know it's real.'

Oliver was confused. 'You mean, no one else can see it?'

'Not even your mother,' Grandma Otis confirmed. 'Now go and have your milk and biscuits and mind you brush your teeth afterwards. You have to look after your teeth.' She looked up at Lena. 'Lena, Quon tells me that there's someone waiting to talk to you.'

Reluctantly Oliver left the room, his head still spinning with all the things that had happened to him. He certainly had a lot to tell Flop, but whether Flop would believe him or not was another matter.

CHAPTER NINE

Flop woke him the next morning after returning from his breakfast downstairs. He'd already been outside. He jumped up on Oliver's bed and began to lick himself clean. Oliver could hear Flop's tongue combing his fur, when he opened one eye he could see Flop who'd positioned himself just below his chest.

'Flop?'

Oliver looked up at his beside clock. It was only eight. Usually Flop would wait for him to get up and they'd have breakfast together. 'What's going on?'

Oliver was about to stroke Flop when he noticed a piece of paper tucked under his new collar. 'What's this?'

Flop let him take it, licked Oliver's hand, then dashed off the bed again. As Oliver unravelled the paper he could hear Flop thundering down the stairs again and seconds later Lena's voice calling up. 'Breakfast.'

'Coming.' he answered, a bit puzzled that everything was so early today. He stretched and climbed out of bed. Then remembered the note again and stopped to read it. It was a computer printout.

At first he was completely baffled, then he realised what it was. Old Joe from the library had sent the note. Must have seen Flop and stuffed it under his collar. Oliver was impressed. There were few people that he'd let touch him, let alone put something under his collar. He studied the paper and realised that he was looking at some replies to his e-mail messages.

'Sorry we cannot help, no record of this man's name on our lists. Try Red Cross.'

'We regret there is no record of this name on our records.'

'No record. Can't help.'

'Suggest you try UN relief agency for area.'

All four of the replies were negative. No one had heard of his father. Oliver's heart sank. How was it possible he could have disappeared so completely? He noticed a scrawl on the back of the paper from Old Joe...

'Come Friday to the library. We will try other people. I have ideas. Joe.'

Oliver stood up and pinned the note to the wall. He resolved to meet with Old Joe. There had to be some way of finding his father. Even if he was dead, surely someone must have found his body? Someone must know what happened to him. Then he shook his head, stating aloud, quite firmly. 'No, he's still alive. I know it. He's still alive. They'll find him and he'll come home.'

Oliver went to the bathroom, still feeling down, but resolute. If you wanted something to be, you had to keep your hope alive. He knew that. He'd stayed alive to prove to his father that he could beat the tumour. Well, now he knew he had to keep his hope alive that one day they'd find out what happened to him.

'He's still alive.' Oliver repeated as he looked into the bathroom mirror. As if just saying it kept his father safe.

At breakfast Oliver remained quiet and thoughtful as Lena read her Daily Mail with meagre attention.

'You alright?' Lena asked eventually.

Oliver nodded as he sipped his tea.

'Who was the old man I saw talking to your cat. He put a note under Flop's collar. The cat just sat there and let him do it.'

Oliver shrugged, he'd already considered that, but realised that Flop must have known that Old Joe meant no harm. 'That was Old Joe. He's helping me look for my father.'

Lena didn't even look up from her paper. She just pulled a face and shook her head. 'He's gone, dear. Probably got himself another woman and living the life of Reilly in Dubrovnik.'

Oliver looked at Lena in horror. It was almost as if time had stopped. The whole kitchen was frozen around him, the air solid. How could she have said that?

How could she say his father would just start up with some other woman and not ever write to him. There was no way his father wouldn't write to him if he was able.

Lena seemed quite oblivious to the effect her remark had made on Oliver. She yawned and stretched in her chair.

'You're going to the library today?' she asked.

Oliver could hardly bring himself to reply. He merely nodded and Lena seemed to be happy with that.

'Well, don't do anything crazy today. Your Grandma is only just getting over the head incident. I have never known anyone who could let so many things happen to him in such a short time. That poor man not knowing he's dead still makes me feel queer.'

Oliver finished his toast and looked out of the window to see what sort of day it was. It was cloudy, but there was at least a patch of blue. Right then and there he decided to find out where Mitch Michaels lived and go to his home. He'd find out for sure that he was dead. It was one thing to dream you saw a dead man live, but quite another to prove it.

He didn't know what he would do exactly, but he'd find out where he lived, go there and try to prove he hadn't imagined the whole thing.

'Looks like a nice day for once.' Lena was saying to no one in particular.

Oliver got up from the table and went to put on his jacket. 'I'll be going then. I'll be back for tea.'

Lena looked up at him and smiled. 'You have some money?'

Oliver shook his head. Lena pointed to the window ledge by the door.

'Take the coins on ledge. Can't have you out there without anything.'

Oliver took the few pound coins he found there and pocketed them. Lena stood up and adjusted her hair in the kitchen mirror. 'Grandma Otis has got an important visitor this morning, so no shocks, alright?'

Oliver nodded, tying up his shoelaces.

Lena thought of something else. 'If you really want to find your father, you should send a photograph to the newspaper in Dubrovnik. Of course, he might not thank you for it. Who knows, you might have a little brother by now.'

Moments later, stood outside the house, Oliver was angry and upset. Lena had no call to mock his father like that. Now she was even suggesting he'd started a new family. 'A little brother.?' Oliver was really upset now. Did Lena know something about his father that she wasn't telling him? Could it really be that his father had abandoned him? No matter what, he resolved, there was no way his father would do that without writing to him, to let him know what was happening. Still there was that doubt now. Surely he wouldn't start a new family knowing he had an old one, would he?'

Flop ran out from under a bush and brushed against his legs. Oliver crouched down to hug him. 'You wouldn't run off and live with someone else without telling me, would you, Flop?'

Flop just fell over onto his side and invited Oliver to tickle his tummy. 'I'm going to find the dead man's house today Flop. I'm going to just see the place where he lives and ask if anyone has seen him. I want to know if my dream was right or not. Do you think I could have seen him in my dreams?'

Flop placed his teeth over one of Oliver's fingers, but didn't bite. Just held his fingers with his teeth, not biting hard. He didn't let go either.

'Ow, let go.'

Flop let go, but he knew that Oliver was troubled and shouldn't go off in a mood.

'It's a weird day Flop. No one has seen Dad, I don't know what's going on, I'm having visions- everything is so spooky.

Flop sat up and began to lick Oliver's hand. Oliver rubbed his head in return. 'I'll be back later. Take care.'

Oliver stood up and looked back at the house. He had an odd feeling, those fuzzy hairs on the back of his neck stood up again, but he couldn't exactly say why. He turned and walked towards the road.

It was at that precise moment that Grandma Otis abruptly opened her eyes.

'Lena? Lena?' She called out as she struggled to sit up. 'Oliver?' She called. 'Lena? Don't let him go. Don't let him climb. Don't let him go near any tall buildings...'

She fell back against her pillow again, exhausted and confused. Lena had rushed up the stairs and appeared at her doorway, slightly out of breath. 'What? What is it?'

Grandma Otis opened her eyes again focussing upon Lena.

'Where's Oliver? I had another dream. He mustn't climb today. He is in danger. Great danger.'

'He's gone.' Lena informed her. 'He said something about the library.'

Grandma Otis frowned and shook her head. 'The library?'

'He got some sort of message about his father. No trace of him yet, not that I'm surprised.'

Grandma Otis succeeded in sitting up this time. 'He's not going to the library.' she declared emphatically. 'He's not. Oh, I just know something is going to happen to him today. I just know...'

Lena sat on the bed and took Grandma Otis's hand. 'He's gone to the library. I'll go up there after breakfast to make sure, alright?'

Grandma Otis nodded. Yes, best to be sure, but there was that emptiness in her heart. She knew trouble was coming, she just knew it.

Three heavy construction trucks drove out of the University of Greenwich grounds, loaded with rubble. Oliver had taken the Maritime Museum route along Romney Road for his walk, which lay opposite the site of the new University, busy being hollowed out of the old Naval College buildings. He briefly speculated whether he would be able to attend there when he was older. He considered studying in such a beautiful place; such an old place, would be good. He was certain he would go to University one day and he wondered when it was you were supposed to decide what it was you should study. Perhaps studying the curious things that his Grandma did would be the thing to do. He wondered if that was the kind of thing you did at University; study people, fantastic things.

At the corner, he saw a newspaper hoarding was headlining something about the 'Millennium Dome disaster.' Oliver stood waiting for the traffic to slow so he could cross. He could see someone was reading about the Millennium Dome as they waited. He picked out the sub-headlines about leaks, fire and delays. "Won't be ready 'till next millennium," says local MP!

'Waste of bloody money,' a woman was saying as she looked at the hoarding. Oliver gathered she was talking to him. 'Eight hundred million pounds to build a plastic Pantheon and it won't even last ten years. Why couldn't they build new hospitals and schools with the money?'

The traffic came to a brief halt and Oliver took the opportunity to hurry across the road. The woman followed him, but she'd said her piece. Oliver had another thought. Never mind the schools, what about the traffic choking Greenwich? Why didn't they get rid of that? Eight hundred million pounds would build a new road, wouldn't it? It seemed like a lot of money to him. How could they have all these historic buildings and all these cars and trucks constantly going by? But that was the extent of his thoughts, because now he found the passage to the covered market and he was thinking ahead. He wanted advice, and possibly a hug. Lena's unkind remarks about his father were still stinging. He knew there would be one person he could talk to.

'Excuse me.' Oliver asked a young woman dressed in a mediaeval costume advertising a local store. 'Do you know which is Frock Lobster?'

He need not have asked. Before the woman could answer there was a shriek from inside a shop two doors down and Harriet herself came rushing out towards him. She grabbed him, scooped him up and hugged him as if he were her long lost son. 'Oliver, my little prince, my baby.'

Oliver was acutely embarrassed by this, but happy to be welcomed, nevertheless. Harriet dragged him towards her shop and he saw the pink logo of Frock Lobster on the striped awning. Her shop looked warm and inviting and he quickly found himself plonked on a stool by the cash counter being introduced to the two girls dressed in black inside. They were smiling at him and laughing at Harriet as she prattled on and made a big fuss.

'This is Kit and Kelly, they help me here. They're students. Kit's at Greenwich University studying media and Kelly is studying to be a fashion designer so that she can steal all my clients when she opens her own place. Girls, this is Oliver, my new boyfriend and we are going to teach him to respect women and treat them right, aren't we girls?'

Kit and Kelly laughed and Oliver could immediately see that Harriet had been talking about him. But although he was embarrassed, he didn't mind. At least he was welcome here and Harriet looked happy.

'I was going to call Grandma Otis to invite you out next Sunday. I've got some tickets for Alton Towers. Kit and Kelly are coming. We thought it would be fun.'

Oliver nodded, finding himself grinning like mad. Walking into Harriet's life was like wading into a pool of sunshine on a cold day. She just smothered you with sunlight.

'Will I be allowed?' Oliver asked. 'I don't think I'm supposed to go on some rides.'

Harriet suddenly remembered. 'Oh shit, that's right. Well I'm sure there are things you can go on. You could wear my old scooter helmet. That would keep you safe.'

Oliver laughed, agreeing that that would work. 'OK.'

'Good that's settled. Now come into the back room and see what I've done. I've had it with fortune-tellers. I'm going to take charge of my life and change things. You're going to think I've gone completely mad. Did you want a Coke? Kelly, get him a Coke, or did you want coffee? We have great Kenyan coffee.'

'I'm not allowed coffee, my mother said it was bad for you.'

Harriet looked at him in amazement. 'She did? What did she want you to do? Go straight onto hard drugs?'

Oliver thought about it for a moment, giving the question more serious consideration that was intended. 'Well, I like tea – but not with sugar – and I like Coke, but it's got sugar in it and I don't like Diet Coke, because I read somewhere that it's bad for you, too.'

Kelly laughed now. 'You didn't say he was so serious. I'll get him a Coke. Your teeth can survive one Coke.'

Harriet wagged her finger. 'Your mother must have been so strict, but she wasn't wrong, believe me dentists are no fun, I've screwed enough to know.'

Oliver found himself in the back room of the shop where clothes – racks of clothes – were stored and all around the plain white walls Harriet had pinned up photocopies of palm prints. Each print had names and short biographies attached to them and Oliver understood immediately what they were. Harriet stood beside him and waved her hands in the air saying 'Ta-da!'

Kit came in and shook her head at Harriet and Oliver. 'She's mad, y'know.'

Oliver grinned. He knew that. That's why he liked her.

'These are Elizabeth Taylor's hands, see they're all puffy. These are Julia Robert's hands, but I don't think she quite ended up with the right man, do you? One look at her hands and you can see trouble.' She walked to another pair and peered at the name. 'Oh yes, these are Winona Ryder's, she's got no problem in getting men to fall in love with her, but I'm never going to have such cute hands anyway, so I don't know why she's on the wall at all. These, here are Kate Moss's hands, but I'm not sure I'd like men with tattoos. Oh, and these are Claudia Schiffer's, but I don't think I'd like to end up with a man who likes to put people in boxes and make them disappear.' Oliver laughed. He understood that remark. He was enjoying watching Harriet being so serious about these hands. Harriet sighed as she moved over to the far wall. 'I didn't like Cindy Crawford's hands at all, all that dieting I suppose, but I really like Claudia Mason's hands. I'm told men are intimidated by her, but then, so they should be. She was on the cover of Vogue last month and looked absolutely gorgeous. Kit got me a copy of Liz Hurley's hands, but who needs to attract unfaithful men? I am a specialist in unfaithful men. I wouldn't need to change an inch of my hands to attract them. All these women have really emotional lives...I mean, all I want is one perfect love-life.'

Oliver heard one of the girls snigger at the front of the shop.

'I heard that!' Harriet said loudly.

Oliver went closer to a pair of hands and compared his own palms to the picture. 'What about these?'

'Those are Minnie Mouse's hands - Meg Ryan. Do you know how hard it is to get hold of these palm prints? I had to pay a fortune to get them. Look, she's happy, but maybe too happy. I don't think I could cope with that.'

Oliver sighed. Perhaps Harriet was being a bit too picky. 'Well, I like her hands. You should choose beautiful hands, maybe someone will fall in love with you anyway?'

Harriet looked at Oliver more carefully, then held up her own hands for him to see. She had big hands, her fingers covered with many gaudy rings. 'You see my problem? She's got small hands. Winona has small hands, everyone famous seems to have small hands, or long thin elegant hands. I am wearing tennis racquets at the end of my arms. I could guide airplanes in with these hands. I could catch them with these hands.'

Oliver smiled and turned to see Kelly coming back with a Coke for him. 'Is she on about her hands again? I've told her, it's not the size of the hands, it's the fingers. Men love long slender fingers.'

Harriet made a rude noise. 'It's all very well for Kelly. She's got hands a man would die for. I've got bloody pancake hands.'

'But, it's not the hands.' Oliver questioned. 'Is it? It's the lines on the hands.'

Kelly grinned. 'He's as bad as you. I've told her Oliver, it won't work. You can't change your life by changing your love lines. If you could, everyone would do it.'

'They just haven't thought of it.' Harriet asserted, somewhat defensively.

'Well, what will you do to your hands, exactly?' Oliver asked, as he opened the Coke can, which fizzed loudly and began spurting its contents everywhere. Oliver took a quick gulp from the can and burped loudly , causing Kelly to laugh as she left the room. 'This boy's alright.' she told Kit, who was serving someone in the front.

Harriet leaned back against the wall and sighed, looking at the palm of one of her hands. 'Well, first, they erase the lines on my hands, the ones I'm born with, then they cut new lines into my palms.'

Oliver pulled a face, it sounded so harsh. 'Well, what if you chose this hand, right.' He pointed to a pair of hands on the wall. 'What if these hands are from someone who is really happy and everyone loves them, then they get AIDS, or run over and squashed? Would that mean you'd get AIDS or run over too?'

Harriet scowled, looking at the pair of hands Oliver had chosen. She shook her head.

'Those are Madonna's hands. I could develop problems they haven't invented yet with those hands. I could wake up a single mother with those hands. Oh God, you're right! I've got to make sure there aren't any fault lines in these hands. They could be happy then – Wham! – two years from now there's a huge truck just waiting for them to cross the road.'

Oliver sipped some more of his Coke. 'But how will you know that? How can you stop that?'

Harriet smiled. 'I'll get these palms read, just like I got mine done. It's a kind of insurance, y'see? I'll get them read, but I won't let them know whose hands they are reading, that way I'll know it's true.'

Oliver looked at more hands. 'I like these.'

Harriet examined them and nodded her approval. 'Katherine Hepburn. She used to be a famous actress. People used to talk about her romance with her husband. Tracy and Hepburn, big romance, only he dies early. Of course she's heartbroken, but she got to write his memoirs for big money. Hmm, you're on the right track, kid. Lot of happiness, some nice memories, he dies early so you don't have to worry about Alzheimer's...yeah, everyone loves a tragic ending.'

Oliver thought about it some more. 'And these?'

'Brigitte Bardot. No thanks. Too tragic. Lost her looks real early, then became a cat – hag living alone with her memories. Besides, it's too late for me to be a sex kitten. I'd be better off with Hepburn.'

Oliver sighed. 'It's scary. Nobody's perfect.'

Harriet's face lit up. 'Of course, there's always Marilyn Monroe. Men stuck to her like flies, but,' she suddenly remembered, 'she killed herself. Of course, she's practically a saint now, but...nah, I'd be miserable all the time. Perhaps I'll settle for Meg Ryan. She's happy at least.'

A customer looked in and waved to Harriet. 'Hello, you still trying to choose?'

'It's tough; Oliver here thinks I should go for Katherine Hepburn.'

'Sweet, but didn't she play a nun once? Listen Harriet, you can have my man, but leave me his credit card, OK?'

Harriet laughed as the customer twirled in the dress she was considering buying. Harriet cocked her head to one side and narrowed her eyes.

'Too flashy, Jane. Try the same dress in the blue. Kit, get the blue in size 12.'

The woman shook her head. 'I'm a fourteen now. I think my bottom is going to end up somewhere behind my knees if I don't exercise soon.'

Harriet put an arm around her and steered her back into the shop. 'Kit, put the size twelve on her. It's an incentive to diet, Jane. Don't give in, fight it, defy gravity.'

Jane sighed, looking over at Oliver. 'My husband says why can't I dress like I used to? I put on my mini-skirt and he says 'Yuk! Cover it up, you're not seventeen anymore. You can't win.'

Harriet sympathised. 'Maybe you should try changing your hands, too?'

'Listen Harriet, if you want a man in your life, get a man's love-line. The way things are in London now, all they're interested in is each other.'

Harriet smiled. 'I could get Pierre's hands. Then I'd get screwed fifty times a week. Of course, it might seem a little shallow.'

Jane whistled. 'Fifty times a week! If that doesn't make you happy, Harriet, nothing will.'

Harriet and Jane laughed together, but Oliver just stared at his Coke, embarrassed. Harriet noticed this and went over to him, hugging him hard.

'You didn't hear that, Oliver. Don't worry, kid. If I can't keep you on the straight and narrow, no one can. I've pledged to Kit and Kelly that I'll make at least one boy grow up straight in this city. Do you like Kit by the way? She got such cute blue eyes don't you think?'

Oliver immediately went scarlet and for once he was glad his face was buried into her shoulder.

'Now.' Harriet said, pushing him away from her and looking at his face. 'What is happening with you? I've been talking and I don't even know why you're here.'

'Can I take a look at your phone book?' Oliver asked her.

Harriet seemed surprised, but accepted it easily enough. 'Of course, finish your Coke, read the phone book, do what you want. I'd better go see my customer. She usually spends a lot with me. You like the idea of Alton Towers?'

Oliver nodded. 'Very much. Harriet? Have you ever heard of Mitch Michaels?'

Oliver immediately noticed a change of expression and mood in Harriet's face. She looked very annoyed he'd asked about him.

'Who's been talking?'

'No one. Is he on TV? Lena says he's on TV. Does he wear a diamond in his nose?'

Harriet must have got the wrong end of the stick. 'Don't tell me he's into little boys now. Did you meet him? What did he say to you? You stay away from him Oliver. He's a total bastard. You hear me?'

'Harriet?' Kit was calling her. Harriet went into the front of her shop to deal with her customer. Oliver was slightly shaken. She'd really reacted when he'd mentioned the man's name. He'd seen and felt a surge of anger in her voice.

Oliver found the phone book, but didn't find his name in it. In his mind he could still see him, still see his apartment, high up, overlooking the city. He was about to give up when he saw Harriet's pink, quilted address book. He knew he was being bad and nosy, but he took a peek at the 'M's. Mitch Michaels's address was the first one there.

Oliver heard Kelly's voice and he quickly closed the book and finished off his Coke.

'You coming to Alton Towers with us?'

'Yeah. I've always wanted to go.'

'What do you think to the hands? Crazy, huh?'

Oliver looked at the wall and smiled. 'I'd be scared.'

Kelly smiled at him and stroked his nose with her finger. 'Who's to say they've got a better future than you? That's what I keep telling her.'

Oliver nodded. The truck was probably waiting for him someday, somewhere. 'I have to go.'

'You take care Oliver. We'll see you on Sunday, OK?'

Oliver nodded and went out to where Harriet was closing the deal. He knew he'd have to face at least one more hug, before getting out of there.

Harriet grabbed him by the door and squeezed his hands. She leaned her face into his left ear. 'Whatever that snake wants, don't go near him, alright? He's trouble Oliver. Mitch Michaels is poison. I'm surprised no one has killed him yet. I'm surprised I haven't killed him myself.'

She let him go then, calling out a last 'Take care!'

But Oliver left Frock Lobster highly disturbed by Harriet's last words. 'I'm surprised I haven't killed him myself.' What had she meant? How did she know him? Had she known that it was his feet that had washed up on the beach when they'd been there together?

What was he heading towards? Should he go home now? Did Harriet kill him? No, that wasn't right, she didn't know he was dead. No one does, not even Mitch Michaels knows he is dead. That was the weirdest thing of all. To say Oliver was confused would be to understate things. He knew that going to find Mitch Michaels' home he was doing wrong, but something was compelling him. He told himself that he'd only look, perhaps ask someone if they had seen him and that's all. Nothing more. Then come home, even if nothing happened. That's what he told himself. He ran across the road heading towards the river and the Cutty Sark. The traffic was as dense as ever, the diesel fumes thick in the air.

Oliver was just disappearing from view when Aura drove past in her yellow Fiat Punto. She couldn't stop, had no reason to stop – but something in the way he was walking disturbed her. She'd really taken to the kid when he'd come into the library. He seemed quite different to other children who came in. She looked at her watch, contemplated going around the block and catching up with him, but she knew with the traffic this bad it would be a waste of time. Besides she had to get to the library, then rush to classes in Sidcup. Oliver would be back. He'd be OK.

CHAPTER TEN

The lift was free. That was the good part. Walking along the Greenwich Foot Tunnel under the river all by himself was kind of scary, but he liked the echo his footsteps made and terrorising himself with the idea of the roof suddenly caving in and the river flooding it all. Somehow Oliver had expected to find more people using the tunnel between the Isle of Dogs and Greenwich. Maybe everyone was at work. The white glazed bricks were strange. Almost as if you'd expect to run into an old hospital down here. He wished he'd brought some rollerblades. It would have been cool to zap along the smooth underground pathway.

Finally Oliver reached the other end and a lift was waiting. The liftman was listening to some play on the radio about ghosts, but it didn't seem to be very realistic. Even though Oliver did consider it to be a great coincidence.

'On your own then?' The liftman asked him.

Oliver nodded.

'Quiet part of the day this. Builds up later. OK then. Let's go.'

He closed the gates and the old lift began to ascend. Oliver mused on whether he was doing the right thing now. He should go back. Grandma Otis would be mightily upset if he got into trouble. He resolved just to look at the apartment block, at the very most just ask if he was there. That was all. No more to it. If he was at home, then he would accept that what he'd seen was just a dream, nothing more, that he wasn't psychic. Not like Grandma Otis at all.

'We're here.' the liftman declared. 'My, you're in a dreamworld, aren't you? Bin stood with the doors open for a full minute.'

Embarrassed, Oliver hastily walked out of the lift and into the cool, mid-morning air. God, where was he? He had emerged into some sort of little park called Island Gardens. He could see when he turned around, that the whole of Greenwich was on view from here. Straight across the river there was the Cutty Sark, the new University and the Royal Observatory up behind it on the hill. He saw movement, the big red ball dropped down the pole on the Observatory roof. It was midday. He knew about that. He'd read about it. An ancient signal to the navel vessels on the river. They always dropped the red ball when it was midday. The tide was quite high now. He would have liked to have stayed and looked at everything, but he had things to do.

Step one, he had to find the signpost to the Docklands Light Railway. That was easy. So was finding the station. You just had to follow the signs and there it was just across the road. It sort of stood to reason that Mitch Michaels would live in Docklands. He was rich, he was on TV, he would be living where rich people lived. Besides, he'd always wanted to visit Canary Wharf. It was the tallest building in London, or at least, he thought it was. Perhaps the other tower was... hmm, he would have to check that. He hated not remembering important facts like that.

Oliver was crossing the road going towards the station when he heard his name being called. He turned, sure that someone had made a mistake, for who could possibly know who he was? Bullet! He was there, just below the station, walking towards him. Oliver's heart sank. He'd deliberately not gone to the library so as to avoid him, and yet here, of all places, here he was.

'It's my man Oliver.' Bullet came over and put an arm around his shoulders. Oliver wrinkled his nose. Bullet stank of aftershave and upon closer inspection appeared to have a huge red love bite on his neck.

'Shit, what a bloody crap night I've had. This bloke, he said he was a sound designer, whatever that is, anyway, he says he wants to take me back to take some pictures. Well, I said he could do what he likes, but it'll cost him and right then and there he plonked £200 for me to pose. So we go back to his place, just over there, right by the river, and first thing he tries to rip my clothes off. Anyway, he's got his teeth in my neck and the biggest hard-on I ever saw, when he begins to choke, I mean, he turned blue, and I thought I'd better call an ambulance. They came really quick, which just shows if you live at a decent address they're just waiting around the fuckin' corner for someone to get sick. Five bloody minutes, that's all, five. When my cousin Lig got sick three years ago, they took forty-five minutes and he died waiting. Anyway, they cart him off on a stretcher and he's still got this hard-on; so it looked pretty funny with him lying on the stretcher choking to death with his dick standing up. The blokes carrying him out don't turn a hair though, didn't say a word. Anyway, I pretend I'm his son, so they leave me there and when I go to the bathroom I discover he's taken these weird blue pills, Stiffies they call 'em.' He showed Oliver a few that he had in his pocket. 'The bottle says it guarantees a hard-on for twelve hours, so I know I could sell these for a good price. I mean, twelve hours! Don't know what he thought I was going to do, because if he thought I was going to lie there and take it for twelve fuckin' hours he was going to get a big surprise. You should see his place, full of awards. He said he worked on the new Star Wars films. He's got a wife and kids, too. Bloody rich people all think they can do what they like. Nothing worth stealing though. So? What are you doing over here?'

Oliver looked at Bullet with a mixture of fascination and disgust. Oliver felt very uncomfortable when Bullet talked about sex, especially the stuff he was doing. He hadn't known anyone in Louth like this, except maybe his French teacher, who had love bites all over her, but she was a girl. At least Bullet had called an ambulance, he wasn't entirely heartless. Oliver was making a moral judgment here, but he was thinking that begging was more...well, he didn't know what it was, but it was something he could talk about. Sex wasn't.

'Look,' Bullet declared, realising that Oliver was less than pleased to see him, 'if you're still upset about the other night, I'm sorry. I heard how you puked up your dinner. Those guys were OK, they fell asleep right after they started drinking again. We took everything we could find. Paul got a digital camera and I got his Powerbook. Know anyone who wants a computer with Internet connection and everything? Paul says it's worth about £2000. You know how to use a computer. You can have it if I don't shift it.'

'You can't use the Internet connection, 'cause then they'd know where you are. You'd need a phone to use it.'

Bullet pulled a face. 'You can't just switch it on?'

Oliver shook his head. 'My Dad had an Apple and when it was stolen he paid someone £300 to get it back for him. Said that he would have paid a grand to get back the stuff he had stored on it. You could sell it back to the man you stole it from, probably. They're hard to insure. Dad said he couldn't get insurance at all'

Bullet looked at Oliver with surprise. 'Fuck, you're a budding master criminal after all. I'm going to have to start listening to you now. You're right. I should call his hotel. I bet he'd pay a lot.'

Bullet had followed Oliver to the ticket machine below the station now and Oliver felt kind of awkward. How was he going to get rid of Bullet. Oliver bought a return ticket. Bullet didn't bother.

'Who are you going to see?'

'I'm going to look for someone. That's all.'

'Who? Did you hear something about your father? They were talking about you at the library yesterday. That bitch Aura and the old foreigner.'

'No.'

Bullet caught his arm. 'Then where.'

'I'm...' Oliver tried to think of something that would discourage Bullet. 'I'm doing something for Detective Kray. It's important, OK?'

Bullet laughed. 'Important police work, huh.' He laughed again as he followed Oliver up the steps to the station above them where a train was waiting. Bullet was mocking him as they climbed. 'Oliver, the great detective. Where's your fingerprint kit? Did you remember to pack a gun? Lots of nasty people out there.'

Oliver stopped half way up and turned to face Bullet. 'I'm going to find out about the man who died. I found his head on the shingles and...'

Bullet looked at Oliver strangely, now more curious than ever. 'You found the head? Oh, right. You've been watching too much TV. Who cut it off? Ninjas? Where did you find it? In the rubbish bin outside the Chinese?'

Oliver turned and began to walk up to where the train waited. How was he going to ditch Bullet? Why didn't he just go away?'

Oliver reached the ticket barrier and just as he put his ticket in the slot, Bullet raced up to the platform and squeezed up close behind him. They went through together. Two other passengers were waiting on board the train and eyed them both with contempt and suspicion.

Bullet was about to mock Oliver further about the 'head' he'd allegedly found, when he noticed the first edition of the Evening Standard that one of the passengers was carrying. The headline ran bold across all the columns: MAN'S HEAD FOUND IN RIVER. Bullet snatched the paper from the female passenger who looked as though she was about to protest, but when she looked at Bullet she immediately thought better of it.

Oliver wanted to apologise to her, but knew that that would only make Bullet worse.

Bullet was reading the front page, oblivious to any mayhem he might have caused. 'This head? This was you? A member of the public? You found the head?'

Oliver looked at the headline, but noticed that there was no picture of the head itself.

'Wonder why they didn't print a picture? They took lots of pictures.'

Bullet read some more then folded up the paper again and handed it back to the astonished passenger. 'Thanks, sorry, but my friend here had some urgent business to discuss.'

The train doors closed then and the train gradually pulled away from the station.

'So what was it like?' Bullet asked Oliver.

'What?'

'The head, stupid.'

'Detective Kray said it was cut off by a real expert.'

Bullet smiled. 'Maybe it was a Ninja? Huh? They've got really sharp knives. They can cut through your bones with no trouble at all. So...', Bullet stuck his face right up close to Oliver's, 'tell me exactly why you're on this train and where you're going.'

Oliver detected the menace in Bullet's voice. He sighed. He knew he'd have to tell the truth to him. No one on this train would help him. It was his own fault for disobeying Grandma Otis. He should have gone to the library; none of this would have happened.

The train pulled into Mudchute the first station and Oliver contemplated running for it once the doors opened. He dismissed the idea immediately. Bullet was older, faster. There would be no way of shaking him off.

'I'm going to see if the man is there or not, in case I dreamt him wrong. I tried calling him, but he's got an answerphone. Besides, that doesn't prove anything. Then I called the TV station and they said he was at home, sick, so if he really is home, then I'm wrong and the head is wrong.'

Bullet hadn't exactly followed this. He looked confused. 'I don't know what the fuck you're talking about, mate. The newspaper said you didn't know who it was. You telling me you do?'

Oliver wished the train would crash, or something, or at least move. 'Kind of' was his weak reply.

Bullet was enjoying this now, watching Oliver squirm. 'And the head talked to you?'

Oliver gave Bullet a look to show that he understood that Bullet was mocking him. 'Might have.'

The train started off again and Bullet nearly lost his footing. 'Might have? You're even weirder than I thought. This is beginning to sound like a two-man mission. It's way too dangerous for one bald-headed geek.'

Oliver had known he was going to say that, but he had to at least try to shake him off. 'It's OK, I can go alone. It's going to be stupid anyway.'

Bullet nodded. 'Oh it sounds stupid alright, but I'm coming. We're talking about the living dead here. Do we get to put a stake through his heart?' Bullet laughed, pleased with his own joke.

Oliver sought desperately to put Bullet off.

'It's at Heritage Tower. It's a long way.'

'Heritage Tower? That's a cool place. That's where the rich people live. You won't get in there, they've got security and cameras, armed guards. I've been there. Got picked up by this bloke and his girlfriend. I got beaten up by them. They paid me a hundred to do it. Sick people, Oliver. I couldn't move for days after. I heard they do it all the time. Take homeless kids home, feed them, then beat them.'

Oliver didn't want to hear anymore about the terrible things that happened to Bullet. The train stopped at Crossharbour Station, then moved off again. No one got on or off. 'I'm just making sure he's there, that's all. I just want to see if he's really dead, or not.'

'Well, what's his name? You're the detective. Do you know his name? You said you called his number.'

Two more stops later, the train was finally pulling into Canary Wharf station and Oliver had a strong urge to step out and check out the station. He loved big buildings and the idea of a station running under such a huge building was impressive. He couldn't move, of course. Not with Bullet watching his every move. Maybe on the way back.

Some more people got on. Businessmen with overstuffed briefcases and gossiping secretaries, talking loudly about something that had happened at work. Bullet still wanted to needle him. He leaned in and whispered. 'I've seen these types. These blokes go looking for rough trade at night in their shiny suits. I should come here, save em the trouble. Tell me about the head again Oliver. What did it say? "'Ello, Ollie"?'

Oliver refused to be riled. He just wished Bullet would go away. The train doors closed again and the train moved off towards the city.

Lena was looking pensive. She'd been all over the library and seen no sign of Oliver, or the old man who brought him the note. Aura was leaving, lugging her heavy bag. 'Can I help you? I saw you wandering around.'

Lena looked into the face of a beautiful young woman and had an immediate flash of recognition. If Grandma Otis had been there, she would have known what it meant, but all it was was a flash, yet Lena immediately knew that she was looking at someone quite special. 'You know you look like Sara Simmons when she was young. I saw her on the stage, wonderful actress. I often wonder what happened to her.'

Aura smiled. 'That was my Aunt. I've seen her in a couple of films. She was beautiful. She's got arthritis now, sadly. Can't move.'

Lena felt a pang of remorse. 'No, really? But she's my age. I was her understudy in "The Rivals" at the National.'

'You should look her up. She's quite lonely y'know. She lives in Blackheath.'

'Still by the railway station?'

Aura smiled. 'She always says that she never had to walk when she came back from the theatre. She loves that cottage, she won't leave.'

'I'll definitely go.'

Aura smiled. 'But who are you looking for?'

Lena remembered. 'A young boy. Wears a hat all the time. Oliver, he's...'

Aura smiled. 'I know who you are – Lena, the housekeeper. He told me all about you all. Is his Grandma OK? She's not ill is she?'

Lena was so surprised to discover she was speaking to someone who knew who she was that she didn't know what to say next.

'He hasn't been here today. In fact, I saw him heading towards the Cutty Sark. Maybe he's still hanging out by the river?'

'He said he was coming to the library.'

'I know he's due to meet Old Joe here tomorrow. He's been helping him try to locate his father. Do you think he's alright? Oliver, I mean. Are you worried about him?'

Lena sighed. 'His Grandmother is worried about him. He's a bit wild and he's gone through a lot lately.'

Aura smiled. 'He'll be OK. He's so cute.'

'He's too trusting. He's not used to London. He could get into trouble.'

Aura conceded that. 'Still, he's got to learn. If he comes in I'll leave a message for him to say that you're worried. I have to go to classes now.'

Lena felt she hadn't said it right. She tried again, lowering her voice a little 'What I mean is, there is a specific warning for him to not go climbing. Definitely no heights.'

Aura looked at Lena and saw that she was very concerned. She suddenly had a worry and she went over to an older woman sat by 'book returns'. 'Have you seen Bullet today?'

The woman shook her head. 'Not today. He was in yesterday looking for that little boy, the one who wears the hat.'

Aura felt a momentary giddy sensation. Bullet. She hadn't liked the way he'd looked at Oliver. But what to do? Who knew where Bullet actually lived- if anywhere. She decided against saying anything to Lena, why worry her unduly? 'If the little boy comes in, tell him he has to go home. It's important. OK? Tell him his Grandma called.'

The woman nodded and Lena got the impression that she would remember.

Aura walked Lena out.

'We all like Oliver. Funny, isn't it? We get hundreds of kids in here and he walks in and you immediately notice. Something quite unusual about him.'

Lena sighed. 'He's shaken our lives up, I can tell you, never mind his cat.'

'Oh, his cat. I heard about his cat too.'

Lena and Aura laughed together.

Nevertheless, five minutes later when Aura was in her car and speeding across Blackheath she had a returning sense of guilt. She should be out looking for Oliver. Maybe he was in trouble, and if he was, she somehow knew it would be Bullet behind it.

Bullet was laughing as he climbed over a fence. 'See! It's not electrified. They just put the sign up to put people off. It's like the speeding cameras, they never put any film in them.'

Oliver clambered up the fence and slung his legs over, dropping to the ground beside Bullet. They were standing beside the river now. The Heritage Tower lay before them and they now stood in its grounds. The lawns and trees in huge ceramic pots were all new and you could tell from the metal grills in the gravel path that the greenery was built over a car park.

At least it was better than nothing and it gave good cover to would-be spies and burglars.

'It's bigger than I thought. Must be a lot of people living here.'

Bullet was scouting the surroundings. There were warehouses across the river from them, newly converted to flats. It was possible keen-eyed people could see something, but he doubted it. There were a few boats on the river, but they wouldn't be taking much notice of him and the kid. Bullet lit up a Marlboro Light and sat on a bench overlooking the river and Rotherhithe on the other side.

'Be nice here when the trees grow a bit taller. Hide all that shit over there'

Oliver didn't really think trees had any business growing in pots, though he actually liked the view and everything. 'Why did we have to come this way? We could have gone straight to the front door.'

Bullet sighed. ''Cause the front door won't help you. That'll be full of doormen and security people who'll take one look at us and call the cops. They'll never tell you if that man is there or not. Believe me, this is the best way.'

Oliver knew he was breaking the law now. It was OK if they were only trespassing. But he knew Bullet would want to do more.

Bullet was looking at him, pointing his cigarette at him for emphasis. 'So you found the head, right? Oh yeah, and the feet, and right away you know it's this guy on the TV. The head told you he's got this show on TV.'

Oliver sighed. There was no end to Bullet's questions. ' I just had a dream, that's all. I just heard someone call out his name...then huge worms crawled out his eyes and...'

Bullet abruptly stood up, flicking his cigarette away. 'Shut up about worms, alright? I hate bloody worms, right? Why do worms have to be in heads. People always bloody go on about worms crawling about inside of people's heads. I don't want to know about bloody worms.'

Oliver looked at Bullet with some surprise. This was the first time he'd detected any vulnerability. Just the word 'worms' seemed to affect him. Worms were a funny thing to get worked up about, but he guessed it was like himself and spiders.

Bullet suddenly began to cough and he spat, a huge wodge of blood splashed onto the gravel and Oliver looked at it with horror.

Bullet looked at it, then laughed. 'Bits of my lung, nice, eh? I should see a Doctor. Been coughing up blood for days now. I should go to a hospital, least it's warm.'

'Just don't eat the food. It can really make you sick, believe me.'

Bullet coughed again, then tossed away the cigarette pack. 'Bloody things kill you.' He spat again, but it wasn't as bloody as the first and he seemed encouraged by that.

'What's his name then?'

'Who?'

'The dead bloke.'

'Mitch Michaels.'

'I've heard of him. Never seen his show. Is he a singer or something?'

'Does a kind of news show. Exposes people doing bad things.'

Bullet looked at Oliver, then laughed. 'You said that just like a toff. I bet you turn out to be one of them. Go to University, get to make the bloody poxy rules.'

Oliver ignored him.

'So you think the head that washed up was this Mitch? Sure it wasn't a woman? How could you tell? What's a head look like when it's been in the water for hours?'

Oliver didn't answer. He was wondering how they'd get into the building if they didn't go through the front door. Bullet got up off the bench and began to walk towards it.

'Come on then. You know, if I was rich I wouldn't live here. I'd live in Hawaii, or Africa. Live on a remote beach and watch the waves all day. Maybe catch some fish. I've seen 'em do that, catch fish, standing in the waves with a long rod. I like the sound of the sea. This poxy river doesn't make any noise, it's boring. What would you do if you were rich kid?'

Oliver followed behind him, still anxious about being seen by someone.

'I'd fly to Bosnia and look for my Dad.'

Bullet swore. 'Shit, I wouldn't waste a fuckin' penny on mine. I hope he's dead. I hope he's dead twice over.'

Bullet put out a hand to halt Oliver. A security car was driving out of the building from the underground car park. An electronic gate rose and fell surprisingly quickly. Bullet pulled Oliver behind a bush and they waited until the Ford had gone by. They didn't notice Oliver and Bullet squatting down very close to the road. Anyone looking down from the windows of the apartments above could have seen them, but perhaps no one was. Looking for trouble was security's job.

'Come on, I can see a way in.' Bullet whispered, and then he was up and running for the bushes at the base of the tower.

Heart in mouth, Oliver followed. He'd been counting the floors. Sixteen of them.

Oliver joined Bullet as he pressed himself into some evergreens. They were situated below the balcony of a ground floor apartment.

'We wait here.' Bullet announced.

'Why? Why don't we go in by the underground car park?'

'Security cameras, can't you see 'em? This place is a fuckin' fortress. I bet this guy is really loaded.'

'I didn't come here to steal anything,' Oliver hissed. 'I just wanted to know if he was really dead.'

'You want to find out? You have to catch him by surprise. Of course, if he is dead, he might surprise us.' Bullet chuckled at that, but Oliver wasn't in the mood for jokes. 'Now shut up, wait. Can you hear the music? What is that racket? There's people up there. She's laying the table for lunch, the balcony door is open. We wait, OK? Wait and listen.'

Oliver waited. A rose thorn had caught on his jacket and he struggled to free himself. Now he was used to the background noise of Classic FM playing some piano piece, he could hear a voice coming from the apartment above him struggling to be heard. '...I said turn the music down, dear. Your lunch is on the table.'

Bullet grinned. Pointing up. Another voice answered her after a few seconds.

'Just a second, dear, I have to wash my hands.'

Bullet nodded, tapped Oliver on his arm and signalled that this was it. 'Now, follow me, say nothing and don't lose your nerve.'

Bullet jumped up and quickly checked to make sure it was all clear. No one was in the dining room. He scrambled up over the balcony with Oliver nervously following. Oliver was scared now. He knew that this was dumb, but equally he didn't have the nerve to quit on Bullet and run off.

Bullet was being very professional. Quick and silent. He signalled to Oliver to keep absolutely quiet. Fortunately the radio was so loud that it would mask any sound they made, but equally, Oliver was anxious that they couldn't hear the apartment owners either.

Bullet got the patio door to slide open further, and even though it made a grinding sound, he wasn't worried with the music playing. He finally had the door open for both of them to slide through...

A moment later an older man dressed in a sports jacket and immaculately pressed trousers entered the dining room. This was Harry Rosen and he stopped as he looked at the dining table. He frowned and looked over towards the kitchen door. 'I thought you said lunch was ready, dear?'

His wife Estelle was abrupt with her reply from the kitchen.

'It's on the table, Harold. Just as you like it. French loaf, paté, potato salad.'

Harry did a double take. He could see the table, he could see the plates, but he could not see any food. 'Estelle, have you been drinking again? There is no food on the table.'

Estelle came storming out of her kitchen, an intensely irritated expression upon her face. 'Is this one of your silly jokes, Harry?' She looked at the table in disbelief. 'What did you do with your lunch?'

Harry faced Estelle. Estelle faced Harry. Lunch was the issue here, but there were echoes of more fundamental and difficult issues present.

Harry tried to be conciliatory. 'Perhaps you'd like us to eat at the club dear?'

The elevator resonated with the sound of laughter. Oliver and Bullet were riding up to the sixth floor and stuffing their faces with french loaf sandwiches, filled with pate and potato salad. Oliver could barely eat he was laughing so much. 'Do you think they'll call the police?'

Bullet laughed and pulled a face as he pretended his sandwich was a phone. 'Hello, 999, police? Someone stole our lunch. We paid two million pounds to live here and someone stole our lunch.' Bullet laughed again. 'Call the cops? Listen, we need lunch more than they do.' Then he was suddenly more serious. 'You sure it was the sixth floor?'

'Yes. 602.'

'I bet there's cameras everywhere.'

'What will we do if we set off an alarm?'

'We probably will, but they always wait to see if its a false alarm first. Believe me.'

Oliver considered this as he took another bite of his sandwich. They were approaching the sixth floor now. The elevator stopped and the door opened. Oliver poked his head out into the corridor to see if it was all clear. He looked down and Bullet was on his back on the floor looking out from the bottom of the elevator, checking to see where the cameras were. 'One camera right, above the fire escape door, one pointing down the other corridor.'

'What do we do?'

'Do what we came to do. Go up to 602 and knock.'

'Now?'

'Yes, now, go.'

Oliver left the sanctuary of the elevator and walked along the plush green carpeted corridor until he reached the door marked 602. His hands were sweating. He'd never felt so nervous in his whole life, not even when they were going to operate on him. He looked at the white painted door and was impressed to see the name 'M.Michaels' was actually printed in gold leaf just above the bell. He pressed the bell, it seemed the right thing to do.

'Any answer? ' Bullet asked from the safety of the elevator.

'Not yet.'

The elevator doors began to close and Bullet rolled out , walking as naturally as he could towards Oliver. Oliver turned to say something to him, but immediately stopped, for Bullet had a Swiss army knife in his hands and a bunch of keys.

'Move over. You sure there's no sound inside? No one moving around?'

Oliver shook his head. 'It's quiet. What are you going to do.'

Bullet smiled at him as he tried a key in the door. 'Y'know, all that money he must have paid to live here and they fit a lock as cheap as this. If I was his insurance company I'd refuse to pay out.'

The lock clicked and in two seconds Bullet was inside, turning only to pull Oliver in after him. 'Come in stupid. You want to pose for the camera all day long?'

It was dark and quiet. All Oliver could hear was the sound of his heart thumping away.

He was still in shock about the keys Bullet carried with him. Almost as if he expected to break into homes. 'You've done this before.'

Bullet grinned and he closed the door behind them, sliding a little on the highly polished ash wood floor. 'Well, sometimes it's too cold to sleep outside. Vince, he was a neighbour of my mum's, he's doing time now, but he always told me that the reason amateurs

get caught is because they break things. If you've got keys, people don't question you if you look as if you live there.'

Oliver was about to say something sarcastic about Bullet's appearance, but thought better of it. Bullet switched some lights on. The whole ceiling lit up with powerful little spotlights recessed into the plasterwork. It was if they had been transported to an art gallery. The walls in the vast semi-circled lobby were lined with framed pictures of Mitch Michaels with his arms around celebrities, or playing golf with them. All of them the same; Mitch Michaels smiling, the person he was with looking awkward or grinning inanely, like you do when posing for a picture you didn't really want.

'Well, kid, here you are. Where's your TV star, eh? Where's your ghost?'

A light was blinking in the security office. The security man was on the phone, bored and with his back to the display board. He was struggling to be polite to one of the apartment owners.

'I'm sorry, Mrs Rosen, but I'm not authorised to call out the police about a missing sandwich. No...I'm sorry. Mrs Rosen, there's a security patrol outside now and they haven't reported anyone in the grounds. The alarms would have gone off. Has anything valuable gone missing? No jewels? Just your sandwich? Are you sure you actually made a sandwich, Mrs Rosen?'

The security man was smirking now. A stolen sandwich, it would have to go down in the daily log sheet. It would be classed as a major incident. An apology would have to the Rosens. They were paying enough for security. He stole a glance at the video screens and his eye caught sight of the silent alarm going off in 602. Now he really had something to do.

'I'm sorry, Mrs Rosen, we do have an intruder. Keep your windows secure. I'm calling Major Pierce now.'

His insolent smile had vanished. This was a real alarm. He picked up another phone. 'Intruder alert. 602? Michaels. Unauthorised entry.'

Bullet had already helped himself to the scotch, drinking it neat from the bottle as he ransacked drawers and cupboards. He didn't care what Oliver was in there for, he'd just known the kid would lead him to something where there would be stuff worth nicking. He was enjoying this.

Oliver was looking at the view. Although it was day, it was the same view as his 'dream'. An apartment right on the river with a balcony. There was a huge portrait of Mitch Michaels with a naked woman wrapped around him over the gas fireplace. Oliver could see that it had been done in the style of a James Bond poster. The woman, he realised with surprise, was an actress he'd seen on Eastenders. Oliver could see himself reflected in many mirrors and everywhere there were bright colours and weird objects, some of them quite phallic. There was no sign of Mitch Michaels. Oliver closed his eyes. He could remember his dream, entering a room, taking off his jacket, the woman approaching him, the hard slap.

He recalled a more detailed moment. Just before the slap, the woman approached from behind a mirror door.

Oliver went over to the wall of mirrors and began to try to open them. He could hear Bullet crashing around in the next room, when suddenly he let out a shout. 'Bing-fuckin'-go!'

Oliver went to the open doorway to the living room and was shocked to see the mess Bullet had already made. A beautiful Chinese lacquered bureau lay on its side and Bullet was holding up cash and many NatWest plastic self-sealing cash bags containing something that looked like pills.

'This is big time, Kid. Fuckin' thousands of pounds here. See these? Es. This bloke is a major dealer. Can you fuckin' believe it? He's got a hundred grand's worth of ecstasy here, at least. Who the fuck was this guy?'

'What are you doing?' Oliver complained. 'We have to go. Someone will come.'

'We got in, didn't we? We'll get out. Got to get me a bag. Find a bag. I'm not leaving all this behind.'

'Get it yourself. I'm not a thief.'

Bullet got up, grabbed a roll of money from the stash and went over to Oliver. He yanked him close and stuffed the roll of cash down Oliver's shirt. 'Now you are. If you take it out, I'll fuckin' throw you into the river. Now get me a bag. We're taking this stuff.'

Oliver broke free and Bullet angrily returned to his stash. He took another swig of the scotch and began to stuff some of the cash rolls down his own shirt. 'Stupid fuckin' kid.'

Oliver didn't look for a bag. He went back to the mirror wall. He wanted to leave, but he just wanted to see that room first, make sure absolutely that Mitch Michaels wasn't there, or asleep, or...

He found the mirror door and pushed it open.

He was in the bedroom. It was a plain room. Huge with a large, unmade bed centre stage. The walls were plain, save for a strange object on the wall that looked very much like a whip, only it had many strands coming from the stem and looked like you could hit numerous parts of a person with it all at once. All along the twenty foot window ledge there stood rows of old fashioned brightly coloured Japanese tin space toys. Oliver recognised one as Robbie the Robot. He was sure, too, that he'd read that these toys were immensely collectable.

There was, however, no sign of the owner. Oliver walked to a free-standing antique plain wooden cupboard and opened it. Suits. Many suits. Nothing like what Bullet had found. Oliver turned and as he did so snagged a cord. The bedside phone fell to the floor and somehow it triggered the answerphone. The tape could be heard rewinding and Oliver ignored it as he walked back to the door. Only the door had gone. He was faced by a wall of mirrors again and he didn't know which was the exit.

He opened the nearest mirror door and stepped into a small dark room. The door swung closed behind him with a click and his eyes couldn't adjust quickly enough, and he stumbled, bringing something heavy down with him. When he stood up again, he banged his head, which hurt like hell. Trying for the door again his hands found a hanging cord and he pulled on it. A blue light came on and Oliver just stood there and gawped. He was surrounded by pictures of naked women...all of them photographed on Mitch Michaels bed, some of them pictured with Mitch in weird and contorted positions. Somewhere in that bedroom there was a secret camera in the ceiling. It was disgusting, but guiltily fascinating. Oliver found himself staring in wonder at all the things they were doing to each other's bodies. He understood now what the whip thing was for that hung on the bedroom wall. What he couldn't comprehend was why people would want to hurt each other like that. In some pictures, girls and Mitch were bleeding. What was going on?

The answerphone was playing back the messages now and Oliver dimly became aware of what they were saying on the other side of the door.

'...Michaels, you can't hide forever. Call me. We have a deal to make, remember?'

Oliver certainly registered that one, but had no idea what it meant.

'Hey Mitch, the fucking Selma interview. Did you realise we have to shoot it in Mexico? Get back to me, soon.'

Oliver was wondering if Mitch Michaels had heard any of the messages. How long had he been dead exactly?

'Mitch, this is your mother. Remember me? What's this I hear about you with this Paula woman. Didn't I tell you about Catholic girls. Leave her alone, she'll kill you with lawyers and priests.'

Oliver was looking at some other photographs now. Something about one of the women on the bed with Mitch. He couldn't see her face properly. He looked at another and was astonished to discover that he was looking at Harriet! Harriet naked and having sex with Mitch. Suddenly he understood her angry reaction when he'd mentioned his name to her. Oliver tore the photo up and threw it on the ground.

Bullet arrived at the door, his eyes lit up when he saw the photographs plastered all over the walls. He looked drunk, or high on something. His eyes were mere slits in his head as he peered through them. He whistled.

'I thought you were keeping quiet. Jesus, will you look at this. He must have screwed hundreds of women.'

Another message came through on the answerphone.

'Mitch, how would you like to go fishing? I want those tapes, you bastard. Tomorrow, or else we're going fishing.'

Oliver looked up at Bullet. That was the message. That was what had happened to Mitch Michaels. They both knew it. That's where he'd ended up. With the fishes.

'Bastard was into everything. Takes pictures of chicks, got enough 'Es to supply a rave and he's got tapes, a real stud-muffin. Who the fuck was this guy, kid?'

Bullet picked up a photo, pulled a face and threw it down. 'He's got a belly on him too. What the fuck did the chicks see in him? Money I bet. They go for money everytime.'

'We have to go.' Oliver warned Bullet.

'No, I want to see where he put the camera.' Bullet said, staggering out into the bedroom and collapsing on the bed. He bounced back up again pretty quick, rubbing his head and pulling the pillow back. There was a gun lying there. Black and cold. Oliver's heart sank. Giving Bullet a gun when he was in this state was asking for trouble.

'Now what have we here?' Bullet picked it up and took aim at Oliver.

'Better hope it ain't loaded, kid. Guns go off just like that, all the time.'

'Put it down, Bullet. You don't need it. We're in enough trouble.'

'Wonder if it's loaded?' Bullet asked, placing it on his lap and looking for a way to open it up. 'Hey, it's a Baretta, 9mm. Real hard case this, Mitch guy. I'm beginning to like him. Seen his ghost yet?' He looked at the gun again with real pleasure. 'Shit, I always wanted one of these. You know how much these are worth since they were banned?'

Oliver was looking for the door Bullet had come in by and found it at last. He turned to say something to Bullet and found he was pointing the gun at him again.

'I could shoot you and no one would ever know. Bet you didn't tell anyone you were coming here, did you? Bet no one knows the name of this dead guy, 'cept you? Nothing to connect him to you or you to this place.'

'Bullet, we have to go. Put the gun back.'

'Wonder why he left without taking the gun? I would have taken the gun if I'd heard that message about the fishes. What do you think about your dead bloke now, Oliver? All the cash, the pills, the pussy pictures? He was so rich he could keep thousands of pounds in a drawer. He was so sure no one could get to him. Fuck, I bet this bed cost him ten grand.'

'Bullet, we have to go now.'

Both of them heard it then. Someone was trying keys in the lock to the front door.

They could hear the distinctive buzz of someone talking on a two way radio.

Bullet was instantly angry. He was up off the bed and running to the bedroom door behind Oliver in an instant. 'Shit, security. Come on, we have to keep them out.'

'What are you going to do?' Oliver asked, his heart thumping loudly now.

Outside the apartment four security men were puzzling over the keys. 'It says 602, but it's not budging. Someone's got in, broken the lock. I hate bloody locks.'

The men looked at each other. The senior man, the Major, sighed. 'Well someone is inside, and if they don't open it, we'll have to force it. Knock. Did you knock yet?'

The security man knocked. 'Mr Michaels? Is that you? Mr Michaels? Can you hear me? This is building security.'

There was no answer. They hadn't expected one.

'I bet it's another false alarm.' The Major asserted.

'Don't forget the stolen sandwich.'

The Major looked at the younger security man with pity. 'You forget it. We're going to have to force the door. We have to respond to an alarm, it's in the residents' charter.'

Inside Bullet had been busy. He'd gotten the sofa positioned across the entrance lobby directly in line with the front door. He hid himself behind it with the gun aimed and ready should anyone want to come in. He turned to look at Oliver who was standing there looking at him with his pale, vexed face.

'Get out, alright? Get out onto the balcony. You can drop to the floor below. Do it, Oliver. Do it now. No need to get caught.'

Oliver did as he was told. He didn't like it, but he desperately didn't want to be caught.

He rolled open the balcony sliding door and stepped out onto the balcony. He was immediately hit by a gust of wind and he saw that the weather had changed completely. It was cold and windy. He stood looking over the side for the balcony below, but he couldn't see it. All he could see was the river, at full tide and on the turn. He felt dizzy. He looked back and Bullet was still behind the sofa, busy stuffing the tubes of 'Es he'd found into his pockets, keeping one eye on the door. Bullet looked back at Oliver for a moment.

'Don't piss around. Get your fuckin' legs over and drop down. Now!'

Oliver did as he was told, although he was scared and he still couldn't see the balcony below. He swung his legs over and began to lower himself down, hoping he could swing a bit, get some motion so he could drop clean to the ledge below. He closed his eyes, his arms felt heavy and the wind was tugging at his thin body.

Bullet was aiming at the door again, trying to concentrate as his eyes were going in and out of focus all the time. The pills or the booze, he didn't know-or care-which, only that his 'buzz' was being interfered with and he resented that. 'They're going to get it' he kept saying.

Oliver thought his foot was connecting to something below him. He'd managed to get his hands down to the last rung of the railings...he called out to Bullet.

'I can't reach. What about you? What are you going to do?'

Bullet took another swig of the scotch, but the bottle slipped out of his hands and in anger he picked it up again and threw it against the front door.

There was an immediate response. The security men outside put the boot in and kicked the door open. Bullet fired twice, missing both times, but scaring himself and the security men so much they immediately pulled back. Glass flew everywhere as some pictures fell to the floor.

'Bastards,' Bullet shouted, looking back to where Oliver should have been dangling.

But Oliver had gone.

Bullet knew it was time to go himself. He could hear the security men calling up reserves and just to keep them out he emptied a couple more shots into the hallway. He knew he'd gotten some result because someone shouted in pain out there. Satisfied, he stashed the gun in his jeans and ran back to the balcony. He legged it over and with a clean swift motion, lowered himself down to the balcony below.

Oliver wasn't there.

'Shit!' Bullet looked over the balcony to the river below, but Oliver wasn't in the water. He'd just vanished. It was just typical, you try to help a kid and he just disappears.

No time to think. He had to get moving. The balcony door was locked, but a swift kick cracked it and another got the flimsy lock broken. He was in and on his way out in under a minute. No one was going to catch Bullet. Of that he was sure.

It was cold. That's what it was, cold. He wasn't aware of anything else, just the cold and the necessity of breathing. He knew he should be moving, but where was he? How to move? He couldn't feel anything. He was just cold. He felt something by his head, something hard. He tried to reach for it, but his arms seemed to move in slow motion. He felt water pouring into his mouth and he spluttered as it entered his nose as well. This helped. It was crap, but it helped. His hands found some wood, just driftwood, but it was floating. He clung to it, but he was so cold and it was so hard to grip. Now there was the matter of not being able to see anything. Why was it so dark? Dimly he began to grow aware that something was covering his face. He pulled at it, but it was soft and sticky and there was pain...mud, or oil, he was covered in mud and oil. He wiped at his eyes and slowly light began to flood in, but pain, incredible stinging. He momentarily went under the water again, came up coughing, eyes stinging. Think. Think. What has happened? Where are you? Why are you so cold? Is this a dream? Is this a dream?

The river was picking up speed. The tide was flowing out. And it was getting colder.

Bullet emerged from the apartment 502 wearing a smart leather jacket and a baseball cap to match. He didn't take the elevator. There were too many people using it, so much shouting and urgency. An alarm had gone off and people were coming out of their homes, taking the fire escape to safety. Bullet smiled to himself. He was going to get out of this. No one was going to touch him. They probably thought someone was still in 602. He had no worries. Pity about the kid. Probably drowned, but that's the luck of the draw. Kid would have probably died of cancer anyway. Looked sick. Wouldn't have lasted anyhow.

'The police are here.' he heard someone shouting. 'Someone's got a gun.'

Yes they have, still loaded. Things were going to be different now. No one was going to bullshit Bullet. He was going to run things his way now. Should have got some ammunition, but that was always available, if you knew where to look. Place in Clerkenwell. He'd go there.

'Can you help me?' An elderly lady asked him as she struggled down the stairs with her cat.

Bullet smiled and took her arm. Perfect. The old bint would get him out past the cops. He was home free. 'No problem, lady. Let's get you out of here. Probably a false alarm. You know how these things are.'

'You can never be too careful.' she replied, happy to have someone to lean on.

Aura left class early. Rehearsals weren't going well and she wasn't really into experimental theatre anyway. Too much metaphor, and not enough character for her. She meant to go home, but the visit to the library from Lena, had her worried. Where had Oliver gone? She knew she was being ridiculous to worry about a boy who was probably quite capable of looking after himself, but she did worry. She didn't know why really. There didn't seem to be any rational reason for it.

It was a quarter to three in the afternoon. The boy was probably back home, safe and sound, but nevertheless...she couldn't but help worry and think about Bullet. That boy was cursed and he'd taken an interest in Oliver. That always meant trouble. She remembered another boy who'd started coming who left after mysteriously breaking his arm. Bullet had denied everything, but if there was a problem...

She parked as near to the river as she could, then walked. She was glad she was well wrapped, there was a biting cold wind. She'd started her walk from Park Row by the new University grounds and she thought she'd work her way along the river towards Ballast Quay, nearby Oliver's home. If Oliver was around she guessed this would be the place.

The tide was going out and there was a strong smell of diesel (or whatever the river seemed to smell of). She'd never really liked the smell of the river. She preferred lakes, the rolling mists on lonely lakes.

The Trafalgar pub was quiet, although the street was jammed with cars. She thought of asking the people sat by the windows overlooking the river if they had seen anything, but she felt a bit stupid.

'Oh, it's you.'

Aura found herself face to face with Lena. She was looking pensive and pale.

'Have you seen him?' Lena asked.

'I was going to ask you the same. I was coming over to see if he was home yet.'

Lena shivered. 'Grandma Otis has sent me out. She's convinced he's in trouble. She keeps on saying.. 'The river, the river,' but where? How? The tide's been up, he wouldn't have been looking for anything when the tide's up.'

Aura was puzzled. 'What do you mean?'

Lena sighed. 'Oh, it's silly really. He found that head on the beach and he's become obsessed, or so Grandma Otis says.'

This was news to Aura. 'Oliver found the head? I heard about it on the news. That's horrible.'

'He found the feet, too. That's what started it.'

Aura looked at Lena with enough scepticism to unnerve her. 'It's true. I swear it. He's a magnet for trouble. A magnet. Grandma Otis thinks he's gone looking for Mr Michaels' ghost.'

Now Aura was amused. 'Looking for a ghost?'

Lena shrugged. 'Grandma Otis is...'

'She's a medium. I know. My father knows her. She's quite famous. She's worried about Oliver? She thinks he's come to harm?'

Lena nodded. 'She thinks it might be too late.'

Aura turned away from Lena a moment and abruptly felt a sharp pain in her head. It was curious. She turned back, looked across the river a moment. Something odd, something directed at her. Suddenly she had it. It was the thing that had been nagging at her for two hours now. She glanced at Lena but couldn't find the right words to explain what she felt.

'No. It's not too late. He's here. Your Grandma Otis is right. He's here. I can feel him. Come on, we can get to the beach along Crane Street. Come on. He's here.'

Lena watched Aura run and, although she thought it was all a waste of time, she did feel a slight rise in hope. Just having someone to search with, someone who cared, was something.

'I'm coming!' she called. But she ran slowly because she had no doubt that they'd find him, but not alive. Not the bright kid that had been there that morning.

Aura found the wooden floodgates next to the canoe club shut. No time to find someone who had keys. She was agile enough. She leapt up and grabbed the top bar, drawing her legs up and crawled over, dropping to the concrete below with practised ease.

She had absolutely no idea as to why she had said what she did, or why she believed it, but she had experienced the most intense feeling back on the street. Perhaps it was just a romantic thing? She wanted to find him, perhaps she just wanted to believe fantastic things were possible, or...

The tide had left an incredible amount of scum and deleterious material. Yet nothing so big it resembled a child, or even as much as a...she stumbled and discovered she was looking at a dead fish with a cancerous sore on its side. Gross. Lena was trapped the other side of the gate and had gone by way of 'The Yacht', a riverside pub adjoining the canoe club, to find a way onto the beach.

'Is there anything there?' Lena asked through an open window.

'No,' Aura answered, then added, 'Not yet. The tide's still going out.'

'If he's in the river, he's either dead of the cold or washed out to Gravesend and beyond.' Lena added unhelpfully, mentally worrying about who would have to look after his cat if he was really gone. Who would tell his cat? That cat seemed to understand things more than most people she knew.

Aura walked to the retreating water's edge and scoured the water, both ways. She sighed. Nothing. The momentary thrill of sureness had been quickly replaced by despair. How could she have even thought that she would have been able to find him?

'It's useless.' Lena was saying from behind her.

Aura was almost inclined to believe her when she spotted driftwood. It was not in the mainstream, but nosing around a buoy in the river. It was not so far from the water's edge, reachable. She didn't think twice. She wasn't a strong swimmer, but she could swim. Aura shook off her coat, ran into the water and struck out for the buoy. She immediately became aware of the incredibly strong current and the cold, but she thought she could cope with it.

Lena back in the pub had already run to the phone to call for help. Even if Aura was wrong, she'd need help after going into the river.

Aura began to struggle. It was colder than she thought it would be and the current made her so slow. She began to realise that if she made the buoy at all she'd be lucky, never mind make it back.

I'm here.

That's all she heard. I'm here. I'm here. A voice in her brain saying...I'm here, I'm here, I'm here. A beacon. It was him. The signal that she'd heard on the shore.

Aura swam with a renewed energy. The buoy was within her grasp. The driftwood was still there and as she looked up she could see a hand, blue, a blue hand holding onto the buoy.

I'm here. The voice almost shouted in her head.

Aura reached the buoy and the driftwood. Oliver was unconscious, or seemingly so. He was lying across a log in the water, his body half in and half out of the water, his head bloody and his face and hands so blue it was painful to see. Aura was breathless, but her fingers could detect a heartbeat, even though all she could feel of herself was her own heart beating wildly.

'What happened? What happened to you?' She heard herself ask, but Oliver was obviously not going to reply.

She looked back to the shore and knew that she didn't have the strength to make it back. Especially bringing Oliver with her. There was some activity there now. She felt confident that Lena would sort out something.

'You're going to be OK, Oliver. You're going to be OK.' It was something you said, but who knew what he'd swallowed, or what the injury to his head was? 'Just keep breathing.' Aura huddled him close to her as she scrabbled up on the log beside him. Even though she was cold, she was warmer than he was. Something of her body heat would help him. 'Just hang on. Hang on.'

Lena was on the shore now, waving. A boat was coming out. She'd organised a boat. Aura felt an immense sensation of relief. She looked down at Oliver's face and noticed his puffy eyes and his swollen lips. Suddenly she felt annoyed. 'Boy, you've survived a tumour. Don't you know how precious life is yet? You have to learn to look after yourself. It's all we've got, me and you. Life.'

I'm here. I can hear you.

His lips hadn't moved, but she heard him in her head. This time she knew she'd heard him.

'And I'm here too, Oliver. I'm here too.'

CHAPTER ELEVEN

Perhaps when you are young you are supposed to recover more quickly from any of life's disasters, but it was two days before Oliver was able to hold down food again and breathe normally. The Greenwich Hospital had put him on a life support system and kept a watch on him for the first twenty-four hours. He'd experienced a drip on one arm and an oxygen mask on his face. Furthermore, parts of his skin had been covered in some purple stain where it had come into contact with contaminants in the river. His head was bandaged and he looked more like a war victim than a kid who'd been foolish enough to dive into the River Thames from a sixth floor apartment.

The doctors and nurses had been very worried throughout the first two days because Oliver had not uttered a word. Lena had visited and not gotten even a smile of recognition out of him. He had been oblivious to everything. They had performed tests, but gotten nothing. Oliver was simply not there. Living, breathing, but deeply traumatised.

It was Old Joe, when he came over on the Sunday, who broke the spell. Oliver had managed breakfast and they'd removed the drip, although it had left red, raw scar on his arm.

Oliver, who still hadn't said a word, looked up and found Old Joe there, just looking at him from the foot of his bed. Some of the other kids in the ward were making jokes about him, but Old Joe just kept staring at Oliver and Oliver could feel something, could feel a thin shell breaking all around him. He had the sensation of the shell shattering into a thousand pieces all around him. The shell that had protected him, kept him alive from the moment he'd hit the cold, cold, water. All at once he could hear everything, feel everything.

'They told me you were here.'

Oliver blinked a moment. His mouth was dry. He commanded himself to speak.

'I'm sorry. I was supposed to meet you.'

'She's in the clinic.'

'Who?'

'Aura. She went into the river to save you. She's in the clinic. They say she's sick.'

'Aura saved me?' Oliver felt tears welling in his eyes. Suddenly, it was if the floodgates had opened in his mind. Aura had saved him. He'd called out for her. He remembered that. He'd called her name, over and over. Couldn't even say why. But in the water, all he could think of was the shell and Aura. He'd wanted Aura to come for him. Take him home. He'd not thought about anything right up until the moment Old Joe had appeared, and now, memories exploded in his head. Bullet with the gun, the jump into the water, the cold, the realisation that he was going to die if he didn't will himself warm, and Aura. How he'd just wanted Aura to hold him, make everything better.

Old Joe was holding Oliver's hand now as he sat there, in his hospital bed and let the tears flow down his face. The old gnarled hand was comforting, warm.

'It's alright.' Old Joe was telling him. 'It's alright. You are alive. God has spared you. She is alive, too. It is good to live through these things. You learn, you never forget. I never forget they killed my family. Sometimes I cry, sometimes I shout, but I never forget. I will always see those Serbian faces, laughing as they burn our homes. Sometimes I ask myself, why did I survive? What purpose was served by keeping me alive, and then I remember, it is for me to remember. To never forget, tell others, never forget.

'Now you. Now you have memories. Something happened, ya? Something bad. Remember why. Remember you survived. Perhaps one day you will speak to your father of these things?'

Oliver heard his father mentioned. 'Did you hear...'

'I have a message from an old friend. He will put your father's picture on TV. I need a picture. You have one?'

Oliver nodded. He had one picture at home. It was of his father holding him up high over his head when he was four years old. It was the only picture he had. 'Can I have it back?'

Old Joe smiled, releasing Oliver's hand. 'It can be scanned, sent attached to the e-mail. You can have it back almost immediately. When you are better, we will send it.'

'Where is Aura? I have to say thank you.'

'Somewhere. She knows you are grateful. You will see her when she is better.'

Oliver looked up at Old Joe through a cloud of hot tears. 'Joe?'

'Ya?'

'I was stupid.'

'Ya.'

'I let everyone down. My Grandma will hate me now. She'll send me away. I've done something stupid every day I have been here. She'll send me away, I know she will.'

Old Joe took Oliver's hand again. 'No, she won't. You are family. She loves you. You get better. You come and see me as soon as you can. You know where I will be.'

Old Joe released his hand again and left Oliver's bedside. Oliver was aware only of the impression of his large gnarly hand being no longer there. Time had ceased to function in its normal fashion. He had so many things to think about. His father, Aura, Grandma Otis, Bullet. On top of everything, he felt so guilty, so terribly guilty.

Old Joe was leaving the hospital just as Harriet was arriving. Late, hurried, carrying too much and harried. She had other things to do, but Oliver had to be visited. She didn't pay any attention to Old Joe. She marched over to reception to find out where she had to go, worried about the time, the awkward place where she'd left her car and a million other things. She wasn't annoyed to have to visit Oliver in hospital, it was just a bit inconvenient. But visit him she had to do, she had questions that needed to be asked.

Grandma Otis was in her dining room examining her silver collection as she talked to her visitor. She'd dreaded this moment and knew it would come the moment Oliver had been hospitalised. Social services had come to call. The pointy-faced woman wore an oversized man's blue jacket covered with shiny stains, she was probing, professional, but officious and patronising.

'I am old,' Grandma Otis conceded, 'but since when has that been a crime?'

'I am not saying it's a crime.'

'You are saying that someone my age can't manage the "burden of a difficult child". Well who says he's difficult? You? You've never met him. You've come here with a set of opinions about a child you've never met.'

'I'm merely suggesting that there are care solutions. He's young. He could go into one of our homes and he'd get some discipline.'

Grandma Otis looked the woman in the face. Stared really hard at her. 'I'm not having Oliver put into care. I know what happens to children in care and care isn't one of the things that happens. They're neglected, molested, taught to be criminals, spend half their time on the streets, end up in jail. You think I don't read the papers or talk to people? Your sort just like to crush them, beat them and hide them away. Oliver is a special child. He's intelligent. His father's missing, his mother is sick. This is his home now and this is where he will stay. He's loved here. I've got a housekeeper, who is here all the time. In September he'll start school. He'll make friends, start a new life.'

'It's his friends I'm worried about. I've made some enquiries. He was videoed inside private property grounds. Someone broke into a home there. The police report says two children were seen. We've got an injured security man from a bullet wound. One of the boys was using a gun. You understand, this is a criminal matter now. Your nephew is implicated.'

'I've spoken with the police. They haven't laid a charge and don't intend to and you know he's too young to go to prison.'

'But he's not too young to go into care.'

'Now you are saying Oliver was the one with the gun? I'd like to see you prove that.'

'He was seen there. A gun was used. He's out of control. By your own admission, you let him go out unsupervised.'

Grandma Otis swore. 'And you're out there persecuting every other mother for letting their child walk the streets? Are you saying that you want all the children locked up? You're one of the reasons there's problems in this town. I see enough women who come to me crying because their kids have been taken from them. Oliver is staying with me and he's likely to have learned a good lesson. When he's speaking again, I'm sure he'll have a perfectly good explanation.'

The woman's mouth turned down at the edges. 'He can explain all he wants, but I think this boy should be on the "Child In Danger" list.'

'Now you're saying I beat him? First you say I'm not fit to look after him, now you're saying I dragged him to the river, beat him and threw him in.'

'I am saying to you that he is mixing with people who might do that. The police tell us that he haunts the river and looks for body parts. This isn't a healthy hobby. It's morbid and sick. He needs counselling.'

Grandma Otis slammed her cane down on the table. The social worker flinched.

'He does not "haunt the river", he lives by the river. This is his home. A boy is entitled to walk by the river if he wants to and if he finds bodies, well it's probably one of your lot who cut them up and threw them there.'

'I don't think we are getting anywhere, if I think Oliver is a child in danger, then that's how he will be registered. The courts will enable us to take him from you if he gets into trouble again, or is beaten, or...'

Grandma Otis swore at her again. 'Get out of here, you horrible woman. He's staying here and I'll go to court if I have to, to protect him from the likes of you. You're unnatural and perverted, that's what you are. Unnatural. I'd hate to be a child of yours.'

The woman rose, closed her briefcase and gave Grandma Otis a professional icy smile.

'I think you will find we have more pull in the courts than you, Mrs. Otis. My job is to see that children grow up in a safe and healthy environment. In my judgment this is not such a place. Goodday.'

Grandma Otis watched her go. She was speechless. She couldn't move, her heart was beating hard in her breast and she was consumed with anger. Take Oliver? Not whilst she was living. She reached down for her bag and brought it up to the table where she slammed it down with a loud clatter. She withdrew her mobile phone and punched in a number. She swore again and muttered: 'We'll see who has the most pull in the courts... Hello? Judge Parker, please. Yes...it's Mrs. Florinda Otis speaking.'

Harriet was sat with Oliver huddled in her arms, all her hurry completely forgotten. She stared at nothing in particular as she hugged him hard and Oliver's silent, hot tears dampened her sleeve. Oliver had told her everything. His night in

London with Bullet. The adventure to find Mitch Michaels' place. How Bullet had made them break in and how Bullet had found a gun and Oliver the photographs. The photograph of Harriet in particular, that he'd torn up. He'd spared her nothing and she'd listened with stunned amazement. The kid arrives in London and he'd done more in a week than she had in a year. Seen more, done more. She hadn't known about the photographs. She'd wished that he'd stolen them and not the money that Bullet had made him take. Not that he'd really stolen anything, as Mitch Michaels was dead. Stealing from the dead wasn't nice, but it wasn't as bad as stealing from the living. Stealing from Mitch Michaels should be completely rewarded in her opinion. (She wondered what had happened to the money? No one had mentioned this to her on the phone.) She'd never met such a creep before, or since. She remembered her night with him, how strange he'd been, how he'd made her flesh crawl. He'd been doing pills, although she didn't know what. All she remembered was him slobbering over her and begging her to beat him. She wished now she had. She didn't know how he'd taken pictures, she just regretted the whole thing, the entire memory. She was glad he was dead.

'It's incredible how you washed up in almost the same place as him.'

Oliver raised his head. He'd thought the same once he'd discovered where he'd been found. 'At least I still had my head on.'

Harriet smiled. This was a good sign. A bit of humour.

'You think your head is alright now?'

'It was something in the river. Hit my head. Just cut it open. Do you think they'll get Bullet?'

'I don't know. You'd better tell someone. The police have a picture of you outside the building. They don't know who the other boy is. They only found out about you because it was you who were fished out of the river and the hospital reported it.' She sighed.

'I still can't believe I was actually with you when you found Mitch Michaels' shoes with his feet in them. I just can't believe the type of man I attract. You see? I just have to have my hands done. I have to change everything.'

'Are you really going to have your hands done?'

'Hey, if the only type of man you attracted was Mitch Michaels, you'd change your hands Oliver. I'm going to do it, soon as I chose the right hands.'

'Do you believe that people come back from the dead?'

'What, and pay income tax all over again? No way, sweetie. If you're worried that Mitch Michaels is going to come back as a ghost, don't be. That sort of thing is just bad TV. He can't touch you, or hurt you. Believe me.' She smiled, just to make him sure.

'I want to see Aura. I want to say thank you.'

'We should send her flowers. Can you imagine going into that cold water to save you? She was so brave. We will definitely send her flowers. I will find out which clinic she is in, alright? I'll send them from you.'

'I'm sorry I caused so much trouble. I only wanted to see if Mitch Michaels was really dead.'

'He is. You nearly were. You'll have to behave now. Lena tells me that social services are going to see Grandma Otis. They can take you away from her, you know? They can do what they like.'

Oliver looked at Harriet with astonishment. 'Where? Where would they take me?'

'A home. Don't worry. We won't let them. But you mustn't get into any more trouble. They'll think she can't handle you.'

Oliver had never thought of this. A home? A home for children? He'd be an orphan. He couldn't believe it. Just because he'd fallen into the river?

'The thing is to get better quickly. We'd better think of something to say to the police. You'll have to tell them about Bullet. What kind of kid would make you jump off a balcony into the river? He must of known you would drown. I can't believe anyone could be that cruel.'

'He scares me.'

Harriet nodded. She hugged him again. That was the trouble with life. It was full of scary people, absolutely full of them.

The boys on the roof were laughing. Someone had produced some beers and there was something of a party developing up above the hotel. Robbie had let them on the roof of the Kent Hotel off Tottenham Court Road. Bullet had met Robbie at McDonald's and Robbie had taken him back. People who worked night shift at big London hotels got bored easily and Robbie got bored more than most. He was working reception, but mostly he was having parties, when a spare room came up, or no one used the Penthouse suite. Bullet thought it was cool to be up there, having fun, sleeping in a big wide bed. Robbie was often busy, so Bullet brought a friend off the street with him, just for company.

'There's nearly a grand in the till and more than that in the bar. You've got a gun, what are you waiting for?'

Bullet looked at Smiley and shook his head. 'I got a gun, but I've got it good here. This Robbie's mad for me. I'll do it when he craps out on me.'

Smiley pulled a face. 'Just do it. Do 'im. It's boring. What's the point of having a gun if you don't use it?'

Bullet shook his head. 'Smiley, you're more stupid than you look. This is cool. We've got a hotel to ourselves and hot baths an' everything. Fuckin' grand won't get you much out there. Not this, anyway.'

Smiley wasn't listening. He was watching the TV inside. Mitch Michaels was talking.

'Hey, I thought you said he was dead. That's Mitch Michaels, ain't it?'

Bullet swung around in time to see Mitch Michaels's head on the TV be replaced by a newsreader. They didn't have the sound up, so Bullet ran inside to look for the remote. He found it on the sofa.

'...the police say that although they have had the remains of Mitch Michaels' body for almost a week now, they weren't able to identify the body as they had been unable to find a match for his teeth. The break in the murder investigation came when Mr Michaels' apartment, in the prestigious Heritage apartment building in Docklands, was broken into by burglars last week, where it is believed an unregistered gun was stolen. Details have been emerging of a very "exotic" lifestyle led by the TV investigative reporter, where his probing into the drug underworld may have been compromised by reports of his own drug-related problems. A police spokesman has stated that they suspect that the London underworld had executed Mitch Michaels as a warning to others who might want to probe into their illegal affairs. The police tonight have issued a photograph of the suspected burglar who broke into Mr Michaels' apartment and say that if anyone sees this young man or have information as to his whereabouts, that they should on no account approach him, but may call Greenwich CID on 0181 555 5555. The police have appealed to this young man to come forward as he may well have information about Mitch Michaels assailants.

'We repeat. Police tonight have conformed that television's favourite "gang buster" Mitch Michaels, has been found murdered, his head having been severed from his body. His surviving mother, the former Bluebell dancer, Hilda Michaels, has been rushed to hospital in shock. Our condolences go out to her from all of us and our viewers at Weekend Television. We return you now to tonight's movie "She's the One" starring Cameron Diaz and Edward Burns.'

Smiley looked at Bullet with some admiration. 'Shit man, you're famous. You were on TV.'

Bullet grinned. 'I was, wasn't I?'

'You'd better hope Robbie doesn't see it.'

'So what if he does? You think he'd call? If they knew he'd being hiding me up here, he'd lose his job. Easy. Shit, I think we'll call room service.'

Smiley laughed. 'He said you couldn't use room service.'

Bullet picked up the phone and smiled. 'That was before I was on TV. I'm famous. I can call room service.'

Oliver was alone in the hospital ward. The other kids had been taken to the baths. He sat there feeling guilty, stupid and angry with himself. He should never have led Bullet to Mitch Michael's place. It had been a huge mistake. And now he'd damaged his head, just when it was beginning to heal. He just couldn't believe how stupid he'd been. He felt angry that he'd made Aura ill too. He didn't know what was wrong with her, but if she felt as bad as he did, then she wasn't well at all. He coughed. His throat was sore now. Something to do with all the water he'd swallowed. The doctor said he could go home the next day, but although he was keen to get back to Flop, he was scared what Grandma Otis would say. She'd wanted to come to the hospital to see him, but Lena had stopped her. Hospitals were full of germs and she had no business going there and risking her own health.

No one had come to see him after Harriet and Lena. He'd tried reading, but he hadn't much fancied that. He'd tried thinking, but guilt kept swimming up before his eyes and made him feel uncomfortable. He had resolved to be good, read lots, catch up on all the school he'd missed, not give anyone any grief, but he just didn't know why things kept happening to him. Harriet was right, he had to tell the police about Bullet. But what if Bullet found out he'd told them? He'd come looking for him for sure, and now he had a gun. That was scary. He lay back in his bed and tried to think of nothing again. Life was just so confusing, so complicated.

Just how did you live a normal life? How did you avoid trouble if it came looking for you?

The nurse came back with one of the children and saw him lying on his bed, with a mournful expression on his face. She smiled at him. 'There was a message for you.'

Oliver looked at her with suspicion. Who would be sending him messages?

'What?'

'Phone call for you about half an hour ago. Someone called Aura. She said something about you've only got seven lives left. Oh, yes, she said "thank you for the flowers".'

Oliver smiled. Aura. She sent him a message. She'd gotten the flowers. Somehow just the thought of her phoning him made him feel happy and safe. She'd lived. She could use the phone. He just knew she was OK. It removed a huge weight of his heart and mind. She was safe.

'Are you ready for your bath, or have you had enough water for one lifetime?' The nurse asked him.

Oliver smiled. 'As long as it's hot.'

'Oh, it's hotter than the river, that I can guarantee.'

Oliver climbed out of bed, moving more slowly than normal. He liked this nurse. She was funny. He felt she cared about all the kids in the ward. He remembered how it had been in the Louth hospital. Some nurses had been great, others sour and impatient, always going on about how hard their job was, how much nuisance the kids were. He remembered too endlessly staring out of the cold windows across the town, wishing he could run on the hills in the distance. He'd promised himself that he'd never ever return to a hospital once he got out and, yet, here he was. This time he meant it, he was going to make sure he didn't return.

He shuffled down the ward in his borrowed slippers, actually looking forward to his bath. Tomorrow he'd be good, forever. For at least a month.

CHAPTER TWELVE

Oliver had been home for more than three hours before Grandma Otis could see him. He'd been brought back home by Lena and put to bed straight away, even though he didn't want to. He was sure there was something on TV he could watch rather than just lie in his bed. Flop was beside himself. At first he'd been angry that Oliver had been away, and had given him a lot of miaows that probably weren't very polite, but then he'd jumped upon the bed and curled up right under Oliver's chin, pressing his cold wet nose to Oliver's own nose from time to time, just to make sure Oliver was still there. If Flop's sheer weight could have kept Oliver pinned to the bed, Flop would have willed it. Flop knew Oliver had been sick, he just knew that he'd been in trouble, and quite rightly he objected to having been left behind to fend for himself with Lena and Grandma Otis.

Oliver calmly let Flop lie there, even though it wasn't at all comfortable. He had to cough from time to time as his throat was scratchy, but Flop just clung there. He accepted it as punishment for neglecting his cat. Cats had a right to punish owners. It was understood.

The moment he'd been dreading finally arrived. Grandma Otis's visitor departed. He knew, any minute now she was going to come into his room and give him hell.

Flop pricked his ears and sat up. He knew. Indeed, the moment the door began to open, Flop was off the bed and under it, just his tail visible, swishing from side to side.

Oliver came face to face with Grandma Otis. She was dressed in black with a large ruby necklace swinging about her chest, her hair was up and she was wearing make-up. This was not the Grandma Otis he'd come to know. This was an entirely new woman. She looked quite elegant, even if she did have to support herself by holding onto the door.

Outside there was a wind and it was cooler than it should have been for the time of year. Grandma Otis was looking out of his window at the trees that struggled to keep vertical in the breeze. She'd been waiting for this moment, but now it was here, she couldn't quite think of what exactly to say. Oliver looked a mess. Bruises on his face and his head bandaged. If social services saw him now they'd say he'd been beaten. That was the irony of the whole situation. The boy couldn't be more liked, and here he was causing himself all the trouble in the world and nearly getting himself killed into the bargain.

'I should have you chained up. I have a weak heart, Oliver. I want you to think about that next time you have a whim to do something.'

Oliver saw that she wasn't angry with him. It encouraged him a little.

'It was stupid, Grandma, I didn't see it coming.'

'I know what it was and why. Quon showed me. I saw your fall. I saw it happen before it happened. I even warned you. Didn't Quon warn you about heights? Didn't he tell you not to climb? God has spared you twice, Oliver. How many times can you expect him to be looking your way when you do something foolish? There might come a time when he assumes that you don't really want to live after all.'

'I just wanted proof, Grandma. I wanted to know what I saw was real.'

'You didn't need to get yourself nearly killed to find that out. Quon is never wrong, especially about the dead. He nearly called you dead. You would be if that girl hadn't got the guts to save you. She deserves a medal. A lot of people wouldn't have done what she did. Oliver, stay home, read some books. You leave the dead alone now. They can look after themselves.'

Oliver looked at her, reflecting that she was right, but there were still questions he wanted answering.

'Grandma?'

'Yes?'

'Are they going to take me away?'

Grandma Otis shook her head and smiled. 'They'd like to. But I spoke to a few people and they'll leave us alone. You're safe. You're safe as long as you don't do anything foolish. I can't protect you if you won't tell me what you're doing. That's got to be the rule now. Be curious Oliver, a boy must be curious about life and its mysteries, but tell me where you are going, tell me who your friends are, bring them home, let me and Quon take a look at them. I'm not going to tell you who you can be friend}s with and who you can't but I can tell you who is good and who is bad.'

'I didn't want Bullet to be my friend. He just followed me.'

Grandma Otis nodded. 'There'll be justice for that boy by and by. The Devil is his friend right now, but the Devil is fickle, and he just leads those who listen to the edge, then backs away. He'll fall. He'll fall. If you even as much as get a glimpse of him, you run. You understand? You run.'

Oliver nodded. He'd come to the same conclusion.

'Don't even think about getting revenge. He's bigger than you and he's got the Devil on his side. You run and hide. Do we agree?'

Oliver nodded again. 'Yes Grandma. Can I watch TV?'

'You have to stay in bed today. You can listen to music, you can read. TV isn't a good influence. You'll have to prove to me that you'll keep your word before you can watch TV.'

Grandma Otis left the room, adding as afterthought: 'You be good this afternoon. I'm having tea with the Standley's.'

Oliver looked at the gap where Grandma Otis had stood. He felt that he'd been lucky. If it had been his mother stood there, she would have screamed at him if he'd done something as bad as this. No TV was hard, but he could live with it. Besides he liked listening to the radio and reading wasn't so bad. His mother's collection of books was waiting for him to read. They looked a bit depressing and fat, but he remembered his father saying, 'It's books that connect minds and generations.' He'd no idea what it meant, but it was something to do with reading old books.

'You can come out now, Flop,' he called out, leaning over the bed. Flop didn't answer. He was playing it cautious. Grandma Otis hadn't gone out yet, she might come back.

Oliver kneeled on his bed and inspected the bookshelf. 'Catch-22' caught his eye. It looked a very fat paperback indeed, but at least it was about war. 'Catcher in the Rye' didn't look very interesting, leastways not the cover; farming had never interested him much really. The Famous Five books he was definitely going to give a miss too, and all the soppy Mills and Boon books with 'love' stories in them. Yuk. 'It's "Catch-22" Flop. If I'm going to be in bed all week, we're going to need a very fat book to get through it.'

He plumped up his pillows, sorted out Radio One on his radio, turned up the volume and opened the book. He was ready. He was going to be 'good' even if it killed him.

Lena was downstairs, helping in getting Grandma Otis's coat on her. There was a healthy smell of baking going on and Grandma Otis was quite calm.

'This coat's getting bigger, I swear.'

'You just don't get out much, that's all. The taxi will be here in a minute. Old Mr. Standley will have a nice warm room for you. You'd think she'd have had done with the future by now.'

'It's her daughter. She's contemplating divorce.'

'But isn't she married to the deputy Governor of the Bank of England?'

'She is. Divorce is a big thing in those rarefied circles. Maybe they're hoping Quon can see his way to the other side of it.'

There was a toot from the taxi outside. Grandma Otis took Lena's hand.

'Take care of the boy. He's strong. He is stronger than both his mother and father, but he's just too trusting. I just don't think it's all over yet. You know how my knees swell. I don't want him to set foot out of this house for a week.'

'That's fine by me. You'll be back by six?'

'Yes. I don't like to stay too long. I get so tired these days.'

Lena let her go, watched her walk with her stick towards the waiting taxi, reflecting that she hadn't seen the old woman leave the house on her own free will for months. It would do her good to get out and about.

She sniffed her baking scones. They'd be about ready.

Outside it began to rain.

Old Joe didn't get the photo until the next day. Lena didn't have time to get to the library until then. She'd had to bring it herself as she was sticking to their resolution that Oliver wasn't to set foot out of the house. Old Joe took it from her in person. Lena still didn't think it was a good idea. Even if they found his father, somehow she knew it was only going to lead to disappointment, or at worst, they'd discover he was dead. Nevertheless, she handed the photo over and waited whilst Old Joe scanned it. She reflected on how competent the old man was and how it was such a waste no one would take him on for a job. But then again, she knew all about waste. Here she was, housekeeper, no longer the actress she'd once been, no longer the person with hopes and dreams. Not that she didn't enjoy her role running Grandma Otis' life. She didn't resent young Oliver having arrived in it as much as she thought she would. At least he'd livened it up. Probably more than he'd intended to, but at least the home was noisy now, and Radio One wasn't as painful as she'd thought it would be.

'I will tell you if we get a reply.' Old Joe told her. 'Please, is the boy alright?'

'He's eating, despite his sore throat. He'll be fine. I'll tell him you asked.'

Old Joe smiled. 'He will find his father. I feel this. Tell him, I have found Greta. Now I must find money for her to come to me.'

Lenā thought he was going to ask for money from her, but he didn't. She didn't know who Greta was, but obviously she was important to him.

'I want to thank you for helping Oliver.' Lena began, but Old Joe just smiled and shuffled away. He wasn't interested in Lena, or her 'thank yous'. He had some work to do.

Lena left, clutching the all important photograph of Oliver and his father. She looked at it for the first time. His father was tall, handsome, he had a look of a man who knew what he was doing, what he wanted. Oliver looked happy, laughing, swung high over his father's head. All of eight years ago. So much could happen to a family. The happy little boy turns into Oliver with a tumour, the father has disappeared, the mother, conspicuous by her absence in the photograph, had disappeared into her own world. Photographs revealed so much, could one predict the future from this photo? Why was this the most important picture to Oliver? Why didn't he have any more recent photographs? Wasn't his father a photographer? Perhaps this was an indicator of his withdrawal from his family. The fact that he'd hardly taken any pictures of his son.

Lena looked at her watch. Time enough to visit Harriet's shop, have some coffee with her. She didn't see enough of Harriet. She needed to remedy that.

Oliver had managed three whole chapters of 'Catch-22' and he was really into it now. It was definitely the best war book he'd ever read (not that he'd read many). He wasn't sure that he was supposed to laugh, but it did make him laugh out loud and instinctively he understood that this was the real truth of war. This was what his father had always said to him: war is stupid; no one ever really wins anything, everyone loses.

He was sat by the living room radiator. The radio was playing and Flop was sprawled out across the sofa. All was right with the world. Oliver had even removed his bandage and was back to wearing his new hat (having lost the old one in the river), a strange, squashed baseball hat in Chelsea colours. Grandma was upstairs, sleeping and Lena was out shopping. Oliver had almost stopped coughing and although he did sneak a look outside from time to time, he was content to stay home, and indeed he felt safe there.

The front door bell rang. Oliver put his book down and raced to the door. He struggled with the ancient lock, but finally got it open.

Aura stood there, dressed in green overalls and tennis shoes, carrying shopping bags. She looked so beautiful and radiant that Oliver just stared.

'Well, don't just stand there!'

Oliver just wanted to hug her, he could hardly bare to give her the time to come in, set her bags down and close the door...

They hugged. It was like they'd known each other a lifetime. Oliver clung onto her and she kissed the top of his head as she rocked him side to side. Neither one of them said a word.

Aura held him like this for almost five minutes and Oliver could have hung on for thirty minutes more. He let go eventually and rather sheepishly backed away.

'I don't know how to thank you.'

Aura smiled and kicked off her shoes. 'That hug will do. Some nice bruises you've got there, Oliver. How's your head?' Oliver removed his hat to show the new scars. Aura inspected them.

'Nice, looks like the sort of cut they make when they remove your brain.'

Oliver laughed and this seemed to melt the distance between them.

'Are you better? I called your home and they said you had new...' Oliver wasn't exactly sure how to say it.

'No, I didn't have pneumonia. But I was sick. Something in the water. God knows what they pour into it. Your skin looks burned, so imagine what our insides are like now we've swallowed that stuff.'

Oliver acknowledged that well enough. 'I had a scratchy throat.'

'Tell me about it,' Aura agreed. 'Still, we're alive.'

Oliver smiled. 'Come on, come to the kitchen. I'm going to make you some tea. I can make tea and we've got cake and.'

Aura laughed and allowed herself to be led towards the kitchen. She was just glad to see Oliver in one piece and looking happy. She enjoyed seeing him so excited and anxious to make her feel at home.

'I've got some news about Bullet.' Aura told him as they walked into the kitchen.

Oliver was all ears as he poured water into the kettle and switched it on.

'What? Has he been back to the library? Did you know they showed his picture on TV? I didn't see it, but I heard.'

Aura sat down at the table and set her bags down.

'He robbed a hotel in town. Got himself on video again. I don't think Bullet is very smart. He used a gun and he left a man tied to a bed in the hotel. Took his keys and robbed a whole lot of rooms. The police were at the library because Audrey called them, told them she recognised his picture on the TV. Anyway, he's wanted everywhere and he's going to be locked away for a long time when they get him.'

'Do you think he'll come back here?'

'He'd be stupid to come back here, but you can't rely on him not to do anything stupid. He's banned from the library and Audrey will call the police the moment she spots him. He was with you when you fell into the river, wasn't he?'

'He stole Mitch Michaels' gun. He kept it under his pillow. Bullet didn't want me to get caught. He told me to jump down to the balcony below.'

Aura looked at him with a bewildered expression. 'Harriet told me why you were there. It all sounds so bizarre. I can't believe you survived the fall from the sixth floor. I've looked at the building. It was lucky the river was there.'

'I was floating in the river, I remember. I kept thinking that I needed to surround myself with something to keep me warm. I remember a big shell, it was right around me and I was thinking about you. About how cross you'd be with me and...'

The kettle boiled and Oliver busied himself with the business of making tea. Aura watched him with a little smile on her face. He looked so confident, so used to looking after himself. 'What have you been doing with yourself?'

Oliver poured the milk and pointed to the sugar. Aura declined.

'I've been reading a book. "Catch-22". It's about the war. About pilots who have to fly and all they want to do is go home,but they keep saying you have to fly more. The only way you can go home is if you are crazy.'

'And you have to be crazy to fly, that's "Catch-22".' Aura remembered. 'We studied that book at school. We had a choice between "Catch-22" and "Northern Exposure". That was full of crazy people too. Maybe it's only crazy people who are interesting to write about? Shakespeare wrote about people who were crazy about killing people, or insanely in love. We're doing "Othello" for our final production next year. I want to play Iago, but no doubt I will end up playing a girl.'

'But you are a girl.'

Aura narrowed her eyes at him and looked as mean as she could. 'Yes, but sometimes I'd like to play a man. Try to understand how a man thinks.' She frowned suddenly. 'Do you understand "Catch-22"?'

'I like the book. I can't pronounce the names, but I like the book.'

Aura grinned at his oh-so-serious expression. He slid the mug of tea over to her and she took it gratefully.

'Do you want any of Lena's cake?'

'Uh-uh. Cake is not what my tummy needs right now. I'm still getting cramps.'

'I'm sorry.'

'Hey, at least I'm not covered in new scars.'

Oliver was looking at her and realised what it was that was different. 'You've changed your wig. Why is it so short?"

'Wig? I'll have you know that this is my real hair. My wig went the same way as your hat. Someone will probably find it on the beach down in Gravesend and think someone else has lost their head, or been scalped.'

Oliver smiled, although he was sorry she had lost her wig.

'Here, I've got a present for you. It's in the Boots bag.'

Oliver leant right over the table and snatched the Boots bag from the pile. He dragged it over to him and pulled out the contents. He looked at it with some astonishment and then realised it was a joke. 'Shampoo?' He laughed and Aura grinned, pleased to see him laugh and not take offense.

'Now if that isn't an incentive for your hair to grow, I don't know what is.'

'It'll grow now, for sure.' Oliver agreed, laughing again.

'Is your Grandma in? I called first. She said to go up.'

'You want to meet Grandma Otis?'

'I've got something to discuss with her, actually. It's something they found whilst I was in hospital.'

Oliver immediately knew what she meant. 'You're sick again? Is it my fault? Did I make it come back?'

Aura clasped her hands around the hot tea mug and smiled at him. 'It's not the same. Actually, I suppose I should thank you. I don't think they would have found it if I hadn't gone into the clinic after being in the river.' She shrugged. 'It's just a lump on my leg. I'm scared, that's all. This stuff doesn't entirely go away, you know. It likes to turn up in other places. I just wanted to talk to your Grandma...I can't talk to my father.'

Oliver knew what she meant. She wanted to talk to Quon. He came around the table and gave her a hug again. 'Don't get sick. Please. I...' There was a lump in Oliver's throat. He realised that he loved Aura. She was the most beautiful person he'd ever known and he just wanted her to be his friend forever. Just looking at her made him feel better. He wished his hugs could do the same for her. Aura hugged him back. It was different this time. It was like they were both drowning again and neither one knew who was supposed to be the rescuer.

'I'd better go and see her,' Aura said after a few moments. 'I'll take my tea with me. We'll talk after.'

Oliver let her loose and Aura placed a finger upon his nose. 'Come on, show me to your Grandma. I hear she's quite a dragon-lady. She doesn't spare people the truth.'

Oliver shrugged. He didn't know about that. He went over to the kitchen door.

'Come on. Wait. We'd better take her some tea. She'll be cross if we don't take her some tea.'

'She's got you trained quickly then.' Aura commented with a smile.

Grandma Otis was indeed impressed with Oliver when he brought her tea and Aura.

'My goodness, I knew Oliver was smitten, but you are truly beautiful my dear. It's as if a summer's day has walked into my bedroom. Just look at you. And to think you hide that lovely figure under those awful men's overalls.'

Aura smiled. She didn't mind the insult about the overalls, but she was not used to people thinking she was beautiful, but it had happened more often since she she'd lost the black wig.

'Hello, Mrs Otis. I hope you didn't mind me wanting to talk to you. I know I came to see Oliver, but...'

Grandma Otis dismissed her remarks with a wave of her arm. 'My dear, I will speak to you for as long as it takes and as many times as you want. You saved Oliver's life and there's no price on that. It takes a lot of guts to dive into this river. I can remember when I was a girl going swimming in the river, and two other girls died a week later, the water was so poisonous. My father wanted to beat me for being so foolish, he would have, too, if I hadn't developed a fever. You are brave and foolish. I hope Oliver has thanked you.'

Aura pulled Oliver close to her and squeezed his shoulders. 'Oh, he's been a gentleman. Sent me flowers and hugged me. He's alive and that's what counts.'

She leaned towards Oliver's left ear and whispered. 'Leave me alone with your Grandma for a while. There's something else for you on the table. It's the blue bag.'

Oliver turned to her and smiled. Aura gave him a quick peck on his head and Oliver was out of there. Both Grandma Otis and Aura watched him go.

'He's taken to you,' Grandma Otis observed.

'I like him. He's quite different. He's like you, isn't he. I mean, psychic?'

Grandma Otis looked at Aura carefully and invited her to sit beside her. 'He's going to be very strong one day. A mind a clear as a bell. I think that's the problem. People pick up on it and he doesn't know how to shut it down.'

'He called me, y'know? When he was on the river. He was unconscious, but he was calling me.'

Grandma Otis looked at Aura, took her hand and squeezed it. 'I heard him talking to his cat the other night. He was talking about you. He's...' Grandma Otis searched for the right words. 'I think he loves you. He's never had any love, you understand? His mother, my daughter, was too wrapped up in herself, and his father has left him to grow up wild. I think he sees you as someone special.'

Aura felt a little uncomfortable. It was not everyday you had to cope with the concept of a boy of twelve being in love with you, but she understood it for what it was. More idolatry than lust. He just loved her because she existed and she noticed him, it wasn't just because she had saved his life. It was this love that had saved him, made him call out to her.

Grandma Otis sipped her tea and flipped Aura's hand over to take a look at it.

'I know your stepmother, you know?'

Aura didn't know.

'Kate came to me last autumn. Your stepfather. You fight with him a lot?'

Aura nodded, glad they were onto another subject now.

'You know Denis McTeal?'

'I know of him. He's a professional. He's studied and he doesn't exploit people the way others do. But...he doesn't treat his women well. Kate tells me that he didn't visit you in hospital when you were a child.'

Aura found herself surprised. It was something she had forgotten. All those months she'd lain in hospital wanting her stepfather to come and he hadn't. Something about 'bad vibes' in the hospital. How he hadn't wanted his work affected by the negative waves in the wards.

'My stepmother came.'

'So did your real mother. You don't like her though, do you?'

Aura shrugged. 'It's hard to like someone who abandoned you. She hated my father and my stepfather. I don't pretend I love Denis, either, or that he loves me, but he has never let me down since then. He always keeps his word. My mother treated us both very badly. We never talk about her.'

Grandma Otis nodded. That was the truth spoken there. She could work with Aura.

'Aura, I'm going to make contact with my guide Quon. I want you to relax and think of what it is you want to ask him. Be patient and consider your questions well. Quon will tell you the truth, but sometimes we don't want to hear it. I can't take responsibility for what he might say, dear, but he means well. Now relax, wait, be prepared.'

Aura watched as Grandma Otis began some deep breathing, settling back into her pillows. She let her eyes wander around the cluttered room. It was just as she had imagined it. A magical place filled with all kinds of strange and mundane objects. Grandma Otis filled her with hope and dread, fear, optimism, every manner of sensation. Just how bad was the lump on her leg? Was this it? Would her life end here? Would Quon really tell her the truth if that was so?

Grandma Otis was looking more calm and Aura began to detect a faint green glow emanating from her. She was entranced. How was this possible?

There was no need for fakery. There was just the two of them. What was going on here?

Next door, Mr Ng looked up from his kitchen window. He felt a twinge. He knew what it meant. That woman next door was talking to the dead ones again. He automatically moved to a switch on his wall and flipped it. Immediately, he was surrounded by a hundred illuminated owls, all of them concentrating their power on Grandma Otis's house. He went back to his work carving a small animal object. He was safe. The spirits couldn't get him. Not whilst the owls were alive.

Oliver was looking at the contents of the blue bag with a sense of guilt. It was money. A roll of cash. The roll of cash that Bullet had stuffed down his shirt in Mitch Michaels apartment. He didn't know how much it was, he didn't dare count. There was a note from Aura enclosed.

'Don't worry he won't miss it. You've earned it. Start a savings account. And think of all the hats you can buy! Love Aura xx'

Oliver didn't know what to do, but he knew that he couldn't just leave it around. He moved over to his coat and placed the roll in his inside pocket. A savings account made sense.

He'd always wanted to have some of his own money. He looked up when he heard a sound. Lena was back. She was fiddling with the key outside the back door.

He went to help her. She'd need help with the groceries.

Upstairs Aura was crying. Quon was still talking to her, but hot tears were flowing down her cheeks as he did so. She asked questions, Quon answered. It was much like seeing her doctor, only more honest. Quon told her the truth.

Aura wanted to stop, but Quon had something else to say and she didn't know how to stop him. She didn't want to upset Grandma Otis.

Downstairs, Lena was full of chatter. She seemed to have emptied Sainsburys of everything they had. Oliver counted over twenty plastic bags. They were heavy too.

'I do this once a month, it saves money and time.' Lena explained to him. 'The traffic is a nightmare. I was thirty minutes trying to get through Blackheath. I don't know why they don't sort the traffic out around here.'

'We should fly.' Oliver suggested, but not too seriously. 'Y'know, like in "Back To The Future"? Or was it "Bladerunner"? I forget. No, it was both. We should have flying cars.'

Lena was putting the cans away when she looked at him with a strange expression on her face.

'You know, you've just broken my dream. I dreamt I was a young girl again and I was flying all over the city. I flew right up to people's faces and they didn't even see me. I was so happy. I just loved flying.'

'I don't. You get bruises.'

Lena looked at him and shook her head. 'I said flying, not crashing. Not diving from tall buildings. You've never had a flying dream?'

Oliver thought about it. 'No.'

Lena shrugged. 'You will, one day. They are always beautiful dreams.'

Oliver made no comment. He just handed her the tins and packets and she methodically put them away.

'Grandma Otis will want a cup of tea.'

'I took her one. She's got a visitor.'

Lena looked surprised. 'Oh?'

'Aura McTeal.'

'Ah, your "knight in shining armour". That's sweet. I'm so glad she called. She must be feeling better. Did you give her some tea?'

Oliver nodded and Lena smiled.

'No wonder you look happy.'

Oliver wasn't aware that he looked 'happy'. 'She isn't better.'

Lena stopped with the food a moment. 'What do you mean?'

'She isn't better. She's speaking to Grandma now.'

Lena said nothing. She continued to put the things away. A little while later Oliver heard his name being called. He ran to the hall and Aura was waiting there, putting her shoes back on. He could see her red eyes and the tear stained cheeks, but he didn't say anything about them. Instead, he put on his own shoes and followed her out to her car.

Neither one of them spoke as they walked. Oliver took her hand and she squeezed back. Oliver shivered in the cold wind, but he wouldn't have gone back in for his jacket even if it had been snowing.

They sat in her car and Aura blew her nose, trying to get back to normal. She put on the radio, tuning in Classic FM. Somehow the choral chants they were playing just made things even sadder

Finally Oliver could stand it no more. 'What did Quon tell you?'

Aura smiled and brushed her hair back with both hands. 'It's going to be alright. Another operation, but not like before. He doesn't think they'll use chemo. He even thinks I'll marry and live a long life.' She was sounding too brave, too strong. She could hear the hollow ring in her voice, she saw Oliver's pale face looking up at her, registering what she was saying, hearing the hope in her voice. 'I'll be fine, really. These lumps come all the time. It's just a scare, y'know? It'll be benign, Quon says it will be benign.'

Oliver shook his head. He could hardly bear to look at her. 'You can't be sick. You just can't be sick. They won't shave your head again, will they? Quon said no chemo.' At the back of his mind he was thinking about himself. If someone as beautiful and healthy as Aura could get sick again, what would happen to him?

Aura put a hand out to his own head and gave him a squeeze.

'No chemo. Besides the lump is on my leg. I had one removed last year. See?'

She partially rolled up her right trouser leg and showed Oliver her pale white scar situated below the back of her knee. She placed his fingers on the new lump, only inches from the last. Oliver could feel something hard under the skin. 'Listen, if you can survive the river, I can survive this.' Aura added. 'I should be thanking you. This might have got a lot worse before they found it. We're always going to be scared, Oliver, you and me. We're always going to have to be watching out for lumps and scars and headaches and you are going to have to watch out for me and I'll watch out for you.'

Oliver withdrew his hand and looked at her. 'We will stay friends?'

Aura smiled. 'We will stay friends. I saved you, one day you might need to save me.'

Oliver liked that idea. 'I had a dream about you last night. You had a dog. A small sick dog and it ran to me, put it's head on my lap. I was scared Flop would see it, but he can't see my dreams.'

Oliver suddenly noticed that Aura was looking upset. He'd obviously said something wrong here. 'What? What did I say wrong?'

Aura shook her head, trying to stop another tear rolling down her face. 'I'm sorry. I'm just falling to pieces today. It's just that I had a little black dog once. Crapper. No, don't laugh, I called him Crapper because he was always messing up my father's carpet. Nowhere else, just that carpet. When my mother ran off with the tennis player, she missed Crapper and she came back one night and stole him. She claimed Crapper was hers. He always slept with me, but she said he was hers. God, I never missed my mother, but when she took my dog I think I wanted to die. A week later they discovered I had the brain tumour and...', she sighed and settled back in her driver's seat... 'I suppose it's stupid, but I've always thought that if my mother hadn't taken Crapper I wouldn't have been so sick.'

Oliver understood this completely. He took her hand and squeezed it.

'When I got sick and they took Ma away, they tried to take Flop, too. But he hid. No one fed him, he just fended for himself, until one night I had a dream about him. I made my nurse, Susan, go and look for him. She did and she brought him back to the hospital, although he wasn't supposed to be there. I kept him in an old shed. He hated it, he hated the hospital food just as much as me, even though he was really starving. But Flop told me that he knew I was going to get better and that's why he'd waited for me to send for him when I could.'

Aura just cried then. Two sad pet stories. You couldn't get worse than that. Oliver held her hand and she just cried, sat there and sobbed, unable to stop.

Grandma Otis was watching the car from her bedroom window, Lena at her side. They could both see that Aura and Oliver were sat still in her car and they both could guess what the conversation was about. Lena was the first to say something.

'It's always the most delicate blooms that die early. Damn weeds go on forever.'

'She'll make it. She's got guts. It's good Oliver has her as a friend.' Grandma Otis mused. 'I wish I'd had a daughter like her. There's not a mean streak in her.'

When Oliver came back into the house, he was subdued and didn't feel much like reading. He went up to his room and huddled with Flop. Perhaps he had always known that he was always going to have problems? No one who has ever had a tumour escapes problems, but from the moment he'd seen Aura, and then discovered she'd had the same sickness, he had been inspired. He'd seen in her hope for his future. She was lively, beautiful, strange, in a way he'd never see before. She had been ill and survived. Now she was sick again. He knew she was being brave, saying it was just another lump...but it was as if a door had opened when he met her and now slammed shut in his face. This was going to be his life. You'd get well, then – wham! – a lump, or headaches, or another tumour. It never completely goes away. He'd never actually realised this until Aura had shown him her lump, her scars on her legs and her head. It was as if 'Yes, you can be all you want to be, but enjoy it, it won't last long.'

And about Aura. He realised he was being foolish, but now he knew what it was he was feeling. He loved her. He loved her as much as Flop. Even more. He could look at her and feel stronger. He could look at her and feel as if he could fly. He knew she only saw him as a kid, but it didn't make the feelings go away. He'd had no one to hug for such a long time and Aura was the most huggable person he knew in the world. Well, that wasn't true. Harriet hugged him, but that was embarrassing mostly and she, well, she was Harriet. Aura was Aura. He didn't know exactly how to explain these things. He didn't know why you loved one person more than another, or why some people liked you and others didn't. He just knew that Aura was like, well, like a hot scone when it came out of the oven. You had to eat it right then, even if it was too hot, because that's when it tasted and smelled its best.

Flop stirred and yawned in Oliver's face. He gave Oliver a quick lick, then resettled in a different position, happy to have this unscheduled cuddle in the afternoon.

'I'm going to have to be careful, Flop. I don't want to get sick. I just want my hair to grow back and be normal. Do you think I'll ever be normal, Flop?'

Flop opened one eye and stared at him for a second. Oliver knew what he was thinking. Flop wasn't being polite. It wasn't right your own cat could be sarcastic, but that was the way it was between him and Flop. They both knew each other pretty well. Oliver knew that he was never going to be normal, not if he could see a dead person speak. Even if it was in a dream. He just knew that other people would have to be normal.

There was a knock on his door. Lena was there with a cup of tea and someone else.

'Detective Kray is here to see you, Oliver. Can she come in?'

Flop did his usual disappearing act and Oliver sat up, blinking. His heart began to race. The police, in his room. Were they going to arrest him? What about the money in his coat? He suddenly felt a wave of nausea and fell back on his bed, the room spinning.

Detective Kray swam into view, her slim body swaying above him. Lena left them to it. 'That's a nasty cut on your head Oliver. I don't suppose you'll go swimming in the river again in a hurry, eh?'

Oliver struggled to get up, but Detective Kray could see he was a bit distressed. 'It's alright. You can lie down. A knock like that on your head? I'm surprised they haven't kept you in hospital longer. I just want to show you a few photographs. You're not in trouble. But someone is and I think you can help us.'

Oliver tried deep breathing. It helped a little. The words 'You're not in trouble' helped too. 'I'll help,' he answered at last. 'I can't remember much...'

Detective Kray handed Oliver his mug of tea and sipped some of her own. Oliver noticed for the first time that she wasn't wearing a uniform, but an ordinary grey tracksuit. Did Detectives wear tracksuits?

'Well, we have pieced together some information. It doesn't matter if you can't remember everything. We know you were in the gardens outside Heritage Tower, but just one of you entered Mr. Michaels' apartment. Were you supposed to be the look-out?'

Oliver sipped his tea, frantically trying to remember the story he'd discussed with Harriet. 'I was just going to see if Mr Michaels was there. I had this dream that it was his head I found and...'

Detective Kray nodded, getting out her notebook. 'Yes, your Grandma told us about your dream. It's quite fantastic. In ordinary circumstances I wouldn't pay much attention to that kind of phenomenon, but since you did find the feet and his head, that makes you very special. Personally I'm surprised you didn't have nightmares.'

Oliver nodded. 'Grandma said they were nightmares. But they were so real.'

'And that's why you went to see where he lived?'

'Yes. I got his address and I was on my way when Bullet...'

Detective Kray showed Oliver a picture. It was of Bullet. It was poor quality, but it showed Bullet with a gun pointed at a man. 'That's Bullet. What's he doing?'

'Holding up the Kent Hotel, with the gun he stole from Mr. Michaels. How did he get into the building, Oliver?'

'There was a balcony open. I told him we had to go through the front door.'

Detective Kray noted this. 'We have an intruder reported at a ground-floor apartment. So what did you do?'

'He went in and I waited for him.'

'So how did you end up in the river?'

Oliver couldn't tell the truth now. He had already lied about not going into the apartment. He wondered if they would catch him out in the lie. Did they have a picture of him there? Were they holding it back? Just waiting to prove to him that he was a liar? Would this mean they would take him away? Put him into care? The feeling of nausea came back.

'That's what I don't remember. I was standing by the river. Then this...' He indicated his head. 'I'm sorry. I didn't take anything. I just wanted to know if Mr. Michaels was dead.'

Detective Kray sighed and looked up out of the window. 'Of course. Mr. Michaels had been dead for a week before you went to his apartment. I was just clutching at straws. Hoping you'd seen something.'

'Did you catch Bullet yet?'

Detective Kray shook his head. 'We will. He's monumentally stupid. Steals a gun, robs a hotel. He's been selling drugs. We've got informants on the street wanting us to get him before he kills someone. He just doesn't seem to live anywhere.'

'He doesn't live anywhere.' Oliver remembered something. 'He's got keys. Lots of keys.'

Detective Kray noted that down. 'Does he have any place he likes to go to?'

Oliver thought hard about this. Bullet had to be caught, but he didn't want to be the one Bullet blamed for it. What if he came looking for him? With a gun? Bullet would use it. For sure.

'Well, he goes to Waterloo Station a lot and there's man in the Festival Hall who buys the credit cards and cash he steals.'

Detective Kray looked at Oliver with astonishment. 'Waterloo? Festival Hall? That's a big help. Anywhere else?'

Oliver shrugged. 'He likes Covent Garden.'

Detective Kray smiled. 'That helps, too. Of course, so do half the pickpockets in London. You wouldn't be holding something back, would you? You know a lot about him. He isn't worth protecting, y'know? He is going to end up killing someone. Boy like that, out of control.'

'He doesn't have any real friends. That's why he talked to me. Hasn't he been back to the library?'

Detective Kray shook his head. 'He knows he won't be welcome. Besides we think he's got money now from Mr Michaels' apartment. We found a lot of cash there he hadn't had time to take.'

Oliver frowned, he had an odd thought. 'I want you to catch him. Before he kills someone. He needs help. He is intelligent. He can read. He has read all the books in the library you know. He wants to go to live in Africa. He loves Africa.'

Detective Kray looked at Oliver with surprise. She'd heard the sudden passion in Oliver's voice. She couldn't look at Bullet with the same eyes, but she could see that Bullet had made an impression upon Oliver. Easy enough for an older kid to do.

'We will catch him. I'll make sure he gets put somewhere he can do a lot more reading.'

Oliver looked at the Detective with a tired expression and she smiled back at him. 'Now you get some rest and look after your head. It's the only one you've got. If you remember who pushed you into the river, you let me know, alright? Just remember, whoever pushed you in didn't expect you to come out alive. You absolutely sure it wasn't Bullet?'

Oliver blinked. 'Bullet was up in the apartment. I heard shots. That's when I fell in. When there was shooting.'

Detective Kray nodded. 'You see, you do remember something. Someone pushed you in. You might not have seen them, but someone pushed you in.'

Oliver clammed up then. This is where the truth and lies separated.

'Take care, Oliver. Stay out of trouble and stay away from Bullet.'

He heard Detective Kray talking to Lena on the way out and he wondered if she'd known he was lying. He knew they could probably charge him with trespassing. Why hadn't they? Would he be punished for saying he hadn't gone into the apartment? His fingerprints would be there. He felt this terrible hot flush of guilt. He hated having to lie.

Grandma Otis was calling him.

'Coming, Grandma!'

What did she want? She was going to tell him off for lying to the police. He was going to get it now.

'Come on, there's a documentary on aliens you might like.'

Oliver was once again caught by surprise. She actually wanted him to watch TV.

'Coming now, Grandma.'

CHAPTER THIRTEEN

Oliver was a prisoner for another five days. Never once allowed out of the house. Sometimes he thought that they weren't going to let him out until he actually finished "Catch-22". He was deep into the characters of Yossarian and Major-Major now, but he wasn't sure he'd actually live long enough to finish the whole book. Yet, when Lena finally relented and told him that they were going up to town to buy him some new clothes, he had to tell her that they couldn't go straight away as he was finally on the last chapter and he wanted to see how it all turned out. Lena was impressed. It was a long time since she'd read a big fat book herself, and there was Oliver, tackling one of the fattest.

He had finished it at last and instantly found himself depressed. Not because of what he'd read, but because he wanted to read more. He hadn't realised war was so corrupt. He hadn't understood that there weren't many heroes, just people who got medals for surviving the stupid decisions that Generals made. He knew there'd be many catches waiting for him in his life. Lots of them.

Grandma Otis was busy seeing clients when they left. He walked to the station with Lena. She was dressed up for the occasion, looked pretty.elegant, too. She even smiled when they were sat on the train together in non-smoking.

'We'll have lunch at *Café des Amis* in Covent Garden, then we'll go to John Lewis on Oxford Street. You'll need a new jacket and some shirts and trousers. The uniform is optional at the school, Grandma Otis says you'll have to look at them, but you can choose.'

'You mean you don't have to wear it?' Oliver was puzzled.

'It's that kind of school. Not everyone can afford a uniform, I suppose.'

'So if I don't wear one they'll think I'm poor?'

Lena hadn't thought about it that way. 'Perhaps we'd better get you a uniform.'

Oliver nodded. He didn't want to stick out anymore than he had to. 'And lots of hats. They'll steal my hats, I know they will. They'll pick on me because I'm bald.'

Lena sighed. 'Yes, they will' she was thinking, and there wasn't a thing she or Grandma Otis could do about that. Bullying was still a problem in the schools.

'Perhaps your hair will grow by September?' she suggested.

Oliver prayed every night for his hair to grow, but there wasn't anything there yet. September wasn't so very far away. He knew he'd still be bald by the start of term.

The journey was faster than he remembered and in no time at all they were walking out of Charing Cross station and crossing the Strand. 'You've never been here before', Lena was telling him as they walked towards Covent Garden, 'so don't get lost. If you do, make your way back to Charing Cross and wait for me in the little station cafe. You understand? Don't let me down, Oliver.'

'I won't.' But he was conscious of having to pretend he'd never been up to London before, let alone Covent Garden. He just hoped that Bullet wasn't around. The police had to have arrested him by now, surely.

Café Des Amis was great. Oliver had never really sat in a French restaurant before, with real French waiters. He hadn't even known that Lena spoke French either. (Although she'd been pretty piqued to discover that their waiter was actually an English Geordie film student from the London International Film School.) Oliver was impressed anyway. Especially when 'jambon anglais avec frites' turned out to be ham and chips. French food wasn't so different to English after all. He sat staring at a huge poster that had been painted onto the wall entitled 'La Bohème'; an opera, Lena had informed him, although, the more he stared at the faded scary, misty picture of old rooftops and narrow streets, the more it looked like Greenwich. It seemed to have been signed by someone called G.Puccini. He drank in the atmosphere. Loved the way the tables were jammed together and there wasn't really room to get between them and the windows which were like patio doors, indeed, some people were drinking coffee outside on the tables. The menu was behind him, chalked up on a huge blackboard. Lena had spent a long time looking at it before ordering and checking her watch. Oliver thought that somehow she was disappointed about something. Then, he heard a voice booming over them as a stranger approached.

'Oh, hello Lena, how delightful to see you. Is this your little boy?'

Oliver looked up and saw someone he knew really well, even though he'd never actually met him before. This was the presenter of 'Wackadoo'. Oliver had watched every show, every day when he was in hospital. It was the stupidest kids show ever, but he loved it because everyone knew how stupid they were being.

Lena seemed flustered. 'Richard. So nice to see you. This is Oliver. I'm his ..' she searched for the right word. '...guardian.'

Oliver smiled. 'I like Wackadoo. I watch it all the time.'

Richard gave Oliver a smile that Oliver immediately knew meant 'shut up kid'.

Lena looked at Oliver and he immediately knew what was coming. 'Oliver, why don't you have a look around?' She fished out a fiver from her purse and gave it to him. 'Go on, and don't get into any trouble. Be back here in an hour, alright?'

Oliver smiled. It was just what he wanted. He'd already guessed that this meeting had been pre-arranged. School uniforms could wait. 'Thanks. I'll be back.'

Oliver scooted out of there as fast as he could, before they could change their minds. It was impressive to meet someone on TV, but he didn't actually have anything to say to the man and he hadn't looked very interested. At least the mystery of why Lena had dressed up and chosen that particular restaurant had been solved. Oliver was sure that this man had turned up, as if he was expecting to eat with her. Never mind, now he was free for an hour and he could explore what he wanted without being nagged.

It was only as he left the restaurant and dashed down narrow Hanover Place that he realised they were right beside the Opera House. He didn't know much about Opera, but he knew what he didn't like. He turned right and headed towards the crowds on James Street.

Half an hour later he'd completed a big circle, taking in the shops, craft stalls and the Transport Museum and now, a tad bored and wishing he hadn't wasted two pounds on a sickly ice-cream he hadn't really wanted, he found himself on Floral Street. He was staring in a small shop window at some Tin-Tin objects and wishing he could afford the giant red moon-rocket or at least a pocket-sized stuffed 'Snowy', when he felt a hand upon his shoulder.

'Not a fuckin' ghost after all. Well fuck me, it's that little snitch, Oliver the bald kid.'

Oliver turned to face Bullet and got quite a surprise. Bullet had changed completely. He was sporting a razor haircut, wearing a smart suit and Timberland leather boots. This was a completely different Bullet.

'This is my turf now. You need my permission to be here.'

Same old Bullet, just a new uniform.

'Leave me alone. I didn't say anything.'

'Cops looking for me. Had two walk right past me, just half an hour ago. Couldn't find me if I was to turn myself in and jump right into their arms. Where the fuck did you go, anyway? I checked the library. You haven't been there in weeks.'

'I was in hospital.'

Bullet sneered. 'Got a cold did you? I figured you fell in the river. Arsehole. I told you to get down to the next balcony, not dive into the river.'

'I didn't dive. I fell.'

'Yeah? Hurt yourself? Got any scars?' Bullet snatched Oliver's hat off and for a moment there he was actually shocked at the sight of the new scars, but the microsecond of pity wore off and he flung the hat across the road. Someone passed by, but looked away.

'You have to leave. I don't want you here. Beat it, or pay.'

'I haven't got any money.'

'Well I have. Stupid kid. I got a lot of money. I got a place to live and I'm going to make me rich. No more fuckin' begging. You'd be surprised what you can get with a gun. Don't have to do anything, just show it. People just cram money into your hand.'

'The police have pictures of you.'

Bullet smiled. 'I was on TV. I'm famous. People are real scared of me now. So fuck off, kid. Get off my patch. You come here again, you'll regret it.'

Oliver made to get his hat but Bullet shoved him on. 'Leave it. Always covering your head. Show it, scare people, show them what a freak you are. Go on, run. RUN!'

Oliver turned and ran. He didn't know where to run, but he ran. He'd been humiliated by Bullet, but if that was all, he was lucky, he was getting away.

Bullet was shouting after him. 'Run, freak, run. You fucking tell anyone about me you're dead. You hear me? Dead. I know where you live.'

Oliver ran down Floral Street until it turned onto Garrick Street. He daren't look back. He ran across the road and ducked into a Waterstones bookshop. He had to stop. His legs were shaking. He suddenly realised he was scared, truly scared. Bullet was quite capable of killing him. He'd never actually realised this before. He would kill him and laugh about it.

He had to sit, find some stairs, try to get back his breath. He slowly became aware of someone staring at him and he remembered with a burst of hot shame that he wasn't wearing his hat. He couldn't bear being outside without a hat. How could Bullet have been so mean? Why was he so mean? Why did he hate him so?

Oliver realised he could still be seen from the street and he certainly didn't want Bullet to accidentally catch sight of him. He walked up the stairs to the art section and he was still out of breath and shaky. He stopped in front of some prints, trying to make head or tail of them. There were pictures of naked women daubed with blue paint. He didn't understand them, but he'd look at anything to take his mind of what just happened.

Oliver had been standing there, looking at the paintings for a few minutes now, when he became aware that there was also someone else casually browsing the pictures. Oliver suddenly had this creepy, electric feeling. He knew exactly who this person was standing next to him. He'd know him anywhere, seen his pictures, his strange ears, seen him in the flesh. Never mind how impossible it all was, how unlikely. Mitch Michaels was standing right beside him, studying the paintings.

Oliver forgot Bullet, forgot everything. He retreated to the end of the room and watched him. No mistake. It was him. Suddenly, Mitch Michaels about turned and headed down the stairs. Oliver was aware that he had forgotten to breathe. He took a huge intake of breath and made the decision to follow him. How could everyone have made such a mistake? How could he have thought the man was dead? Here he was, alive, walking around town. What was going on?

Oliver followed him out onto the street. Mitch Michaels walked with the air of a man used to the area, yet, there was something strange about him. Oliver followed. He wasn't concerned about Bullet now. He did think he should stop by a telephone and call Detective Kray, tell her what he was seeing. But he didn't want to lose his quarry.

He didn't have far to go. Mitch Michaels crossed St Martin's Lane and entered 'Pret Manger'. Oliver hadn't seen one of these places before, but he recognised it for what it was, All that stainless steel could only mean fast food, the French way. French coffee and pastries. Mitch was going to have coffee. Perhaps there would be time now to call the police.

Oliver followed him into corner coffee bar and took up a position at a tiny table by the door. Mitch Michaels was waiting to get served. The people behind the counter were taking their time about it, too. If fact, they let someone barge right by him and they served him first.

'Excuse me, I believe I was here first. That's my cappuccino.'

The counter person completely ignored him and continued to serve the other customer. Mitch Michaels was getting upset now.

'Listen, I demand to be served. Do you know who I am? I want a cappuccino and ham croissant. Are you bloody listening to me? Where's the manager? I want the manager. God, I spend enough here. I want a coffee, dammit!'

Oliver looked around the coffee bar, no one was taking a blind bit of notice of Mitch Michaels, it was almost as if he wasn't there.

Abruptly, Mitch Michaels turned on his heels and began to leave. He saw Oliver looking at him. 'I don't know what you're looking at,' he snarled at him.

He left the coffee bar and went out into the street again. Oliver followed. He was beginning to think the impossible.

When Mitch Michaels started to hail a taxi and not even empty ones stopped, Oliver knew the truth. He steeled himself for this. He walked up to Mitch Michaels and spoke directly to him.

'They aren't going to stop.'

Mitch Michaels looked at him with annoyance. 'Are you following me, boy? Leave me alone. I don't give autographs.'

'Why did you take pictures of Harriet? Why did you hurt her?'

Mitch Michaels looked at Oliver without comprehension. 'Harriet? Who the fuck's Harriet? Are you hassling me boy? Don't you know there's laws against stalking?'

He turned and practically stepped out in front of a taxi, only pulling back at the last moment. 'Taxi! Goddamn it. Don't they even need a fare these days?'

Oliver had to tell him. He just had to.

'They can't see you. You're dead. You're dead. No one can see you. You washed up on the beach. They cut off your head. You've been dead for weeks.'

Mitch Michaels looked at Oliver with no sign of comprehension whatsoever.

'Will you go away? I don't know what you are babbling about, but I hate boys and I hate freaky boys most of all, so bug off. You hear me? Taxi!'

'The taxi won't stop. You won't get coffee. No one can see you or hear you.'

'You can see me. Stop talking rubbish and go.'

Oliver went. But he didn't go far. When Mitch Michaels set off again, he followed.

Mitch Michaels walked further down the street and eventually walked into the 'Cafe Pelican'. Oliver didn't go inside. He knew what would happen. The same thing all over. He paused outside the window and there was Mitch Michaels sat at a table, remonstrating with the waiters, trying to get served. No one could see him. No one could hear him. Oliver didn't question the fact that he could see him and hear him. He was the one who'd found his head. It made sense to him.

In the end, it was just too sad to watch anymore and Oliver realised that he had to get back to Lena. He didn't know what time it was, but he instinctively knew he was late. He did have a momentary fear that he would run into Bullet, but somehow he'd gotten over the shock of seeing him now. Bullet couldn't stop him walking down the street. He couldn't shoot him. He wasn't that stupid, was he?

Oliver cut through New Row towards Covent Garden once again, his head full of wonder. London had to be the most exotic place on earth. Dead men walking the streets, people like Bullet and Lena, not forgetting Grandma Otis. He wanted to stop and phone Aura, tell her what he'd seen, but he wasn't sure she would believe him. How could he prove it?

Oliver crossed Bedford Street and saw the familiar sight of old Covent Garden market ahead, surrounded by all the tourists. He'd be safe here. He could hear street music in the air.

'Hey you!' A voice shouted on King Street. Oliver's heart missed a beat. He turned, afraid that he was going to come face to face with Bullet again. A clown reached down from his stilts and gave him a balloon. 'Don't look so serious, kid. You're young, you should be happy. What happened to your head?'

'Hit a tree.'

'Is the tree in hospital? Do you visit it? Just what kind of tree was it?'

Oliver smiled. A clown, telling stupid jokes, giving out balloons. Yes, he liked

London. He took the balloon. 'Someone took the tree. I think they made stilts out of them.'

The clown pretended to cry. 'Oh, a comedian. I can't stand rivalry. I can't stand these stilts. Do you know how wet the weather is up here?'

Oliver laughed and walked on. The clown called after him. 'Go on, leave me with these bruised stilts. You leave the trees alone. Hard head like yours should carry a warning: 'Trees beware – hard head ahead.' Gee, try saying that with your teeth in. Don't leave me, kid. Come back, don't mistreat that balloon.'

Oliver walked on, happy, smiling. He could still hear the clown yelling at people. He crossed the cobbled stones of Covent Garden, unmolested and five minutes later, when he walked back into 'Cafe Des Amis', Lena, all alone again, but in a daze, didn't even notice he was two hours late.

CHAPTER FOURTEEN

Two whole weeks had passed since that mad day in London when Lena had met a man and Oliver had seen Mitch Michaels' ghost. Little had happened since. The weather seemed to have improved and people talked of summer finally arriving, which meant they'd soon start complaining about the heat, instead of the cold. Oliver had started going to the library again, and Old Joe was still helping him getting messages out to Bosnia and Serbia and Macedonia, too. Anywhere where his father might be. There had been no sign of Bullet and more importantly, Oliver hadn't had one bad dream, or seen one ghost. In fact, he seemed to be getting to be the most normal, boring person he could think of. Even Flop wasn't much interested in anything, preferring to lie out on the sun and luxuriate in the heat, catch the odd fly when he could be bothered.

Grandma Otis had announced that she was going to take them all to the sea. Not for her the mundane Torquay or Brighton, she had booked all three of them on the Eurostar. They would be travelling to Paris, then by train to Deauville, where they had been loaned a villa by the Standleys. She hated going by sea, even though one look at the map would indicate that it would be shorter. But, according to timetables, one could leave Waterloo and be in Deauville in little over seven hours, should one make the right connections, have God on your side, not lose any luggage, believe the timetable and providing no one was actually on strike on either side of the unlucky tunnel. Even if they did not achieve this, Oliver had already told her that he'd be happy to see Gare du Nord and with luck, Paris itself. He felt sure Paris would be just the most amazing place, although Lena wasn't sure. She had the idea that Paris smelled of sewage and she'd sooner get to Deauville, which at least smelled of sea or horses, whichever interested one the most.

It was because Oliver was about to depart that Aura had come to take him out to tea. They'd entered the park by Circus Gates and walked all the way up the hill, past the Royal Observatory and out through the far gates; then even further across the barren heath to Blackheath Village, where they'd had a massive tea of scones and cake and Coke with her Aunt Sara Simmons, who'd once been an actress and had pictures of herself all over her walls to prove it. Oliver had never heard of any of the actors, but he was sure they were all quite famous. She seemed very proud of a film poster framed in the hall which showed her name under someone called Sophia Loren, who Aura assured him was a huge film star. His query as to whether she was more famous that 'Wallace and Gromit' was met with stoney expressions.

She'd been starring in 'The Mousetrap' for ten years before her hips gave up the ghost. She wasn't complaining. She had a nice little house with a 'girl' to look after her, who was called Poppy, but Oliver didn't think that was her real name, as she was from Thailand. He'd thought her nice, but she was too shy to stay with them for tea.

It had been Aura's idea to walk. She'd had the new lump removed and it was just as Quon had said, benign. She didn't like the idea of her leg being so scarred, but at least she wasn't ill and to prove it, walked.

They'd left her Aunt's at six. The evening was warm and breezy. People were flying kites on the heath and it looked to Oliver that there was a funfair beginning to assemble outside the Royal Gardens wall. That would be something he'd miss, but Deauville sounded alright to him. He wasn't going to complain. He was surprised at how sparse the heath was. How dry the grass seemed. The ground was cracked everywhere, as if the previous months' rain hadn't made the slightest difference. He was distressed at the lack of trees. He couldn't understand why no one had ever planted any trees. If it was his heath, he would have planted huge avenues of trees along the roads, at least it would hide the cars.

Aura took his arm. 'I'm going to audition for a part in a film. It's about some girl who is a model by day and runs a gang at night and she writes songs which she thinks are going to change the world.'

Oliver smiled. 'You're sure to get that part. It's perfect for you.'

Aura looked down at her legs. 'Not if they see the scars.'

'A girl in a gang would be proud of her scars.'

'Oh yes? This is the boy who never takes his hat off, even in bed?'

'The doctor said I shouldn't get too much sun on it.'

'It might stop the hair growing, wearing a hat all the time, did you think of that?'

Oliver hadn't thought of that, actually. Now, there was a dilemma. To wear a hat and be normal, or let the sun help his hair grow.

Aura smiled and put an arm around him, gave him a quick squeeze. 'Try leaving it off for a couple of hours a day. Maybe get a tan on it whilst you're in France?'

Oliver nodded. He wasn't going to promise, but he was going to swim in the sea. He was really looking forward to that. Grandma had said there was a fine beach with clean sand. They were going to enjoy the villa she'd borrowed, right by the beach and eat fresh fish, every day.

'Aura?'

Aura looked at him with a sly expression. 'What? This sounds like one of those, two part questions coming.'

Oliver laughed. 'No. I just wanted to ask you something. I didn't discuss it with anyone else yet because they'll laugh at me.'

'I never laugh at you. You're the weirdest boy in the world but I never laugh at you.'

Oliver ignored that remark. 'Listen, if I can see ghosts, does that mean I'm going to end up like Grandma Otis? I mean, will I wake up one day and dead people will be speaking through me, like her?'

Aura looked at Oliver with some concern. She hadn't actually considered this. It was the weirdest question she'd ever been asked, if only because it was probably true. He was going to develop the same talents as his Grandma.

'I think you have to...' She didn't know what to say. 'If it happens, you'll know. At least you know it isn't bad. Your Grandma copes with it alright. Quon is a pretty nice guy. I mean...you might go years before it happens. Did you ask your Grandma when it first happened to her?'

'She said it happened to her when she was married and in Africa. That's when it first happened. But I'm already seeing things. Well, that's not true. I've only seen one thing. Mitch Michaels.'

'Oh yes, the famous ghost of St Martins's Lane. Actually, I thought it was kind of funny.'

'Funny?' Oliver stopped in his tracks and confronted her. 'Funny?'

'I mean, the way you told me he was sat in *Café Pelican* trying to get the waiters' attention. That's what my father used to say all the time when he used to take me there: "What do I have to do to get served here, die?"'

Oliver didn't quite get it. 'But that was the point, they didn't serve him because he's a ghost.'

'And I'm saying that you go in some places for lunch and you are lucky if you get served dinner. You sure they weren't just ignoring him? Waiters can do that you know. They go to a special school where they learn to look past people without ever seeing them. People come from all over Europe to this place just to learn how to do it. English waiters are famous for it.'

Now Oliver knew she was taking the piss.

'You're mocking me again.'

'I am not. I liked your story about Mitch Michaels. I like to think he's wandering all his old haunts and never actually getting served. It's probably karma.'

'Karma?'

'Karma's what you get for being who you are. It's a kind of spiritual booby prize. You're bad in this life, you get to be a toad in the next, or worse, a saint. That would be truly karmic.'

Aura had lost him again. There was so much to learn. They resumed walking again, enjoying the warm breeze. The road across the heath was blocked solid with traffic, but they were walking, it didn't affect them. They watched as someone cantered a horse across the heath. Oliver hadn't seen a horse since leaving Louth and even then, he hadn't seen many.

Aura looked at her watch as they entered the straight avenue to the Royal Observatory. Every parking spot was taken, and people in cars filled with hot, impatient kids and slavering dogs were loitering, waiting for spaces. But it didn't matter, it was summer and the park was an oasis in a stark landscape. Oliver loved the place and all the rustling chestnut trees, and just then, in the distance, he could hear the sound of a military band playing.

'I promised to get you down to Harriet's for six.' Aura remembered. 'We're going to be late.'

'I haven't seen her for ages. She said she was busy. Do you think she's met a man?'

'I don't think there are any left this side of the river she hasn't met.'

Oliver wasn't sure, but he thought that was a catty remark he'd just heard.

'I hope you get the part in the film. Do you think they'll need any bald kids in it?'

Aura laughed. 'If they do, I'll make sure they call you, OK, Come on, let's cut through the park, get away from these fumes.'

Aura ran off to the left through the open grassland. Oliver ran after her. Watching with amazement as she suddenly cartwheeled down a slope and ended with a forward roll. Oliver could only manage two forward rolls before getting into a muddle. Aura laughed at him and set off again. Oliver watched her run, then set off in pursuit once more. He laughed. He'd always wanted a friend like this, he hoped it would go on forever.

They'd arrived exhausted after running and fooling around. Somehow, it was nearly seven before they entered the market courtyard and approached 'Frock Lobster'. They could hear the sound of soul blaring out from the speakers and there appeared to be quite a party going on. Aura stopped a moment outside a shop window. 'God, I look a mess! She didn't say she was having a party.'

Oliver looked at the crowd of women and a few men crammed into the shop and saw how elegant they were, how loud. He heard the unmistakable 'pop' of a champagne bottle and the accompanying laughter. 'Do you think we're welcome?'

'Welcome or not, I need something to drink. I'm really thirsty.'

'Me too,' Oliver declared. 'Do you think she's got Coke?'

'She'll have everything, that's the kind of woman she is.'

They entered the shop, squeezed their way to the makeshift bar. Oliver saw Kit and Kelly serving there, although it looked to him that Kit had been serving quite a lot of whatever it was to herself. 'It's Oliver!' She squeaked. 'Have you seen her?'

'Who?' Oliver asked.

'Harriet. She's holding court in the next room.'

Oliver grabbed a can of Coke and squeezed his way through, leaving Aura to fend for herself.

'He's here. Oliver, take a look at this.'

Harriet swooped down on him and held up both of her hands. They were heavily bandaged with elaborate white crepe. She gave him a hug and indicated that he should sit close to her. The back room was filled with people and they were all studying the palm prints on the walls.

'I did it, Oliver. I went and did it. Demi Moore's hands. Someone faxed her palm-prints to me from the same clinic she uses and I had Aura's stepfather read them. She's a woman in control. I like her and men like her. If I don't find a man now, it will never happen.'

Oliver looked at her bandaged hands and all he could think was: 'Doesn't it hurt?'

Harriet nodded, smiling somewhat crazily. 'But I'm numbing it with the Krug dear. One more bottle and I'll feel nothing for a very long time, I think.'

'How long?'

'One month. Just one month from now I will have a new life. A completely new love life. Eat your hearts out, kids. Harriet's back in town. Did you get a drink? You look so hot? Are you well?'

'Aura and me have been running in the park.'

'Aura? She's here? I want to see her. Aura? Come in here. I hope you've got a drink.'

Aura appeared with a cold beer in her hands and a mouth full of crisps. She laughed when she saw Harriet's hands.

'My God, you did it. I don't believe it.' Harriet waved her hands at her and Aura just stared at the bandages. 'God, you are so brave. So totally crazy. I really hope it changes your life. I really do.'

Harriet smiled, accepting Aura's hopes with grace. Then she remembered. 'Oh, you have to meet Farina. She's here from Turkey and she is the best fortune teller in the world- ever.'

Aura held up her hand. 'No way. I never want to know.'

An old woman appeared dressed in what Oliver assumed to be traditional costume.

Harriet pointed to Oliver and Aura, but Farina had already spotted them both. She took Oliver's hand and then grabbed Aura's. She wasn't going to let go of either, even though Aura struggled.

Aura and Oliver looked at each other. Life was hard enough without being confronted with the 'best fortune teller in the world'.

'What can you see? Will I be a detective?'

Farina ignored him and closed his eyes.

'I hate having my fortune told,' Aura told Oliver. 'I'd rather not know anything. It's always the same anyway, tall dark strangers and red-haired twins, or something like that.'

Harriet sipped on her champagne, distracted by others who wanted to talk to her.

Aura didn't know how the old woman could concentrate with old Soul II Soul ballads being played on the stereo, let alone with being jostled by the crowd. Oliver just hated having his hand held so tightly, he could feel her long crimson nails biting into his flesh.

'I don't understand,' Farina said at last. 'Are you brother and sister?'

Oliver laughed. Aura smiled. They looked at each other as if to express the opinion that she knew nothing.

'I'm sorry, but we are not related. So, what terrible things are going to happen to us?'

Farina suddenly dropped their hands and looked Aura in the eye. 'It has already happened,' she said, 'both of you are supposed to be dead.'

The old Turkish woman turned away from them then. She was done.

Oliver looked up at Aura and she reached for him, pulled him close to her. She whispered in his ear. 'We've cheated death, Oliver. We don't need fortune-tellers. We're going to live a very long time. OK? '

Oliver nodded, suddenly overwhelmed by her sweet body scent and the heat of the room.

'I feel dizzy.'

'Come on, it's too hot in here.'

Aura quickly pulled him out. She could see his red face and she knew she was overheating too. It was all part of the treatment they had been having, you just couldn't take the heat anymore.

They made their way to the front door where the crowd had spilled out onto the pavement. They stood there, taking in the cooler air, when another fuss began, as new people arrived. Oliver saw them first. 'Lena! Grandma Otis?'

Indeed it was. Grandma Otis came into view, supported by her cane and dressed up for the party in her best autumn colours Jaeger suit. Lena had her by one arm and she too was impressive in her pink summer Country Casuals. Oliver had never seen Grandma Otis outside of the house and she looked fine, smiling and accepting a drink and a chair that was brought out to her.

'Oliver? Where's that boy?' Grandma Otis was calling.

Aura pulled him over and they stood before her. Grandma Otis looked at him and suddenly gave him a hug. 'They've found him, boy. You make me very proud Oliver. All your letters and dreams. The International Red Cross has found him. He's coming home.'

Oliver just stared. He could see Old Joe arriving now, wearing his usual faded brown suit with a pink flower in the buttonhole. He was waving, but Oliver could feel his legs buckling under him. He'd been hit by a tidal wave of emotion.

'It's your father, Oliver. He's alive. In Sarajevo. He's been found.' Grandma Otis explained.

Oliver spun around into Aura's arms and just sobbed. He couldn't explain why. He just couldn't explain what he was feeling. His father was alive. A million things raced through his head. He'd just learned to love all these people and now his father had been found, he'd take him away, he'd never see Aura again, or Harriet, or Grandma Otis, or anyone and it was all his own fault for trying to find his father...

He just sobbed and Aura wrapped her arms around him and held him tight.

Somewhere in the background, he became aware of Harriet shrieking and yelling about getting Old Joe some champagne, but Oliver just felt so overwhelmed, so suddenly lost.

Lena was talking to Aura as she held Oliver in her arms.

'He's been in hospital for two years. He's been temporarily blinded, but they say he'll be able to see if he gets an operation. There's something else. He appears to have lost his memory. It was the picture in the newspapers that found him. A German relief worker recognised him. Old Joe has been in touch with them. He speaks German.'

Oliver took a deep breath. He couldn't be like this forever. He had to surface for air.

He pulled his wet face away from Aura's T-shirt and wiped his eyes.

'I said he was alive. I knew it. He wouldn't have died without telling me.'

Aura made him drink some Coke and she found him a place to sit on a cushion as she went to talk to Old Joe.

Old Joe was enjoying his champagne and he smiled as Aura gave him a kiss. He could see her eyes were red and glazed with emotion. Old Joe shrugged.

'Ya, we find him, but I didn't say he would be in one piece.'

'You made a miracle happen, Joe. I hear you found your own niece.'

'She wants me to go home. She wants me to go to Hamburg. She's in Hamburg.'

Aura was surprised. 'Hamburg? Would you like to go and see her? I will get you a ticket. You can go tomorrow. God, I'd take you there myself if I could.'

'It's taken care of,' Grandma Otis declared, having overheard. 'He's coming to Paris with us and we'll send him to Hamburg from there.'

Oliver suddenly stood up and moved to the bar. 'Kit? I want some champagne. I want everyone to drink to my Dad and Old Joe.'

Harriet got it organised in no time. She had Kelly pick him up and plonk him onto the bar, and got Kit to push a mug of champagne into his hands.

'To Oliver's Dad and Old Joe!' everyone shouted. They didn't know who these people were, but a drink's a drink and a toast is a toast.

'To Harriet,' Kit and Kelly shouted. 'May she get her perfect man!'

'I'd better, or I want my money back.' Harriet declared to everyone.

Oliver was happier now. Perhaps these people would somehow remain his friends. Perhaps his father wouldn't take him away from them immediately. He sipped his champagne and laughed at Harriet attempting to dance with Kelly and making a fool of herself.

Aura and Grandma Otis were watching him closely from outside. Grandma Otis had taken Aura's hand and it seemed to her that Aura was altogether a happier person. She was glad that she had befriended Oliver. She knew it meant a lot to the boy.

'Of course, he'll break all our hearts.' Grandma Otis said, with a sigh.

'That does seem to be what men are for,' Aura agreed, starting on a new beer.

also available

from Citron Press

BOMBAY MIX *by* RICHARD BAUM

A politician stealing money to finance a sleazy TV station, a coconut seller who swaps the sidewalk for the catwalk, a crooked stockbroker trying to stop the destruction of his childhood home – it could be just the story to get people reading The Bombay Nose again. Unfortunately for plumbing journalist David Leadbeater, it could be just the story to land him in jail. Bombay Mix is a wild satire that lifts the lid on a city driven by money, politics and directionally challenged taxis.

ORDER NO Q0113

TOILET ELEPHANT *by* NICK JOHNSTON-JONES

There's a revolution waiting to happen in your lavatory, and it's elephant-shaped. Meet William Brodie, fresh into his first year at Short Sharp Advertising. Meet the various morons and megalomaniacs of the marketing community whose futures rest on a revolutionary new toilet cleaner that goes right under the rim. What happens when an unstoppable market force meets an immovable mammal with tusks? Why do public lavatories have those little gaps at the bottom of the doors? Can love be down-sized, and if so, what's the return? Just some of the questions that Nick Johnston-Jones' richly comic first novel fails to answer.

ORDER NO Z0128

THE HIGH HISTORY OF THE HOLY QUAIL *by* BRUCE DURIE

ALL THE WORLD'S A MAGE... There are only two rules in life – It's Not Fair and Don't Be Late, as Slouch finds when he is apprenticed to Vizagriz, wizard of Al Faq'Ahl. Is all Magick a consequence of a mysterious artefact known as The Holy Quail? What is the InterWeb? What exactly are heroes for? And why does there have to some drippy woman along on every Quest? Slouch finds out more than he wanted about the amatory proclivities of Faerie Folk, is arrested by the Enchanted Cops and discovers what happens when Deities fancy a bit of telly late of an Era. A comic fantasy masterpiece in the honoured footsteps of Fritz Leiber, Lord Dunsanay and whoever wrote The Revelation of St John the Divine.

ORDER NO C0107

GOING INDIGO *by* SAM NORTH

Exiled from his small country town by the tragic combination of a missing father and a mother committed to a mental institution, Oliver, a pale bald-headed twelve year old boy arrives at King's Cross Station accompanied by his cat, Flop. He is dreading his new life with a fortune-telling Grandma he has never known. If nothing had prepared Oliver for the stern manners of Grandma Otis's companion Lena, absolutely no one had prepared Lena for this wild neglected child and his scrawny cat. Oliver soon discovers that the new people he's living with are possibly crazier than the ones he left behind.

ORDER NO J0201

CITRON PRESS